A NEW DAWN

TED TAYLER

By Ted Tayler

The Phoenix

The Olympus Project
Gold, Silver and Bombs
Nothing Is Ever Forever
In the Lap of the Gods
The Price of Treachery
A New Dawn
Something Wicked Draws Near
Evil Always Finds A Way
Revenge Comes in Many Colours
Three Weeks in September
A Frequent Peal of Bells
Larcombe Manor

Vinci Books

vinci-books.com

Published by Vinci Books Ltd in 2026

1

Copyright © Ted Tayler 2017

The author has asserted their moral right to be identified as the author of this work in accordance with the Copyright, Designs and Patents Act 1988. This work is a work of fiction. Names, characters, places and incidents are the product of the author's imagination or are used fictitiously. Any resemblance to actual persons, living or dead, places and incidents is entirely coincidental.
All rights reserved. No part of this publication may be copied, reproduced, distributed, stored in any retrieval system, or transmitted in any form or by any means, including photocopying, recording, or other electronic or mechanical methods, nor used as a source for any form of machine learning including AI datasets, without the prior written permission of the publisher.
The publisher and the author have made every effort to obtain permissions for any third party material used in this book and to comply with copyright law. Any queries in this respect should be brought to the attention of the publisher and any omissions will be corrected in future editions.
A CIP catalogue record for this book is available from the British Library.
Paperback ISBN: 9781036700546

The EU GPSR authorised representative is Logos Europe, 9 rue Nicolas Poussion, 17000 La Rochelle, France
contact@logoseurope.eu

Chapter One

Monday, 3rd March 2014

"It's your turn to fetch her," said Athena.

Phoenix was swinging his feet out from under the duvet and heading for the next-door nursery. Half-asleep was the default mode so far this year. He had heard Hope's preliminary sniffles and whimpers as he lay beside his partner. Experience told that those whimpers would have increased in volume tenfold by the time he padded along the corridor and into her bedroom.

Hope screams eternal was a phrase adapted for use soon after their daughter arrived on New Year's Eve.

Sure enough, as he opened the nursery door, the first high-pitched yell greeted him. Hope's little red-cheeked face pressed up against the side of the cot. Phoenix scooped his daughter up into his arms and held her close.

"Hello, princess," he said, "I can tell why your mother didn't name you, Patience. You don't enjoy hanging around, do you?"

A few gurgles were all he got in reply. Hope squirmed left and right, trying to see into each corner of the room at once. Phoenix was thankful the winter had turned out to be the mildest he'd known. Just a few precious moments alone with his little girl and Phoenix would deliver Hope to her mother. He could afford to let that warm bed wait a while longer.

Phoenix recalled the early days spent in 36C Meadow Road on the Westbourne estate with his first wife Karen and their daughter Sharron. Then, the central heating was forever on the blink. He worked nights at Shaw Park Mines and hadn't been as involved with the night feeds as on this occasion.

Karen had been breastfeeding, at least for a while. But, because he slept during part of the day, Karen's Mum, Kath, dropped in to help. Both women lavished attention on Sharron, but it had been her father she idolised from the outset.

He did his growing when he was in the flat before going to work and at weekends. He and Karen had both been far too young to marry. His plan was more about taking people out of this world, not bringing them into it. Nevertheless, their daughter provided someone he could truly love for the first time, a natural response to an infant who loved him unreservedly.

Back in the present day, Hope was becoming restless. Phoenix walked back to the main bedroom. Athena sat up in bed, wide awake and prepared for battle. A clean, dry Baby-grow, a fresh nappy, a milk bottle, and an impressive array of ointments, powders, and wipes were laid out in readiness. Things had progressed in thirty years.

Phoenix laid Hope on the changing tray and removed her damp clothing. The room felt comfortably warm, and

Hope kicked out her legs, enjoying the freedom nakedness offered. She grabbed at her toes, missed and rolled over onto her side. Athena moved into action, wiping, dusting, and making unintelligible noises that Hope found amusing.

Phoenix then dressed the little mite and handed her to Athena, who had Hope's night feed poised and ready to go. As mother and daughter settled into their now familiar positions, Phoenix sat on the edge of the bed and watched.

"It took a while, but we have got her into a routine," said Phoenix, stifling a yawn.

Athena nodded. Hope was fast demolishing the bottle of milk. Athena set the feed to one side and cradled her daughter against her shoulder; she gently rubbed and patted Hope's back.

"I wonder what it was like caring for a newborn infant in this old barn of a place for Erebus and Elizabeth?"

"Helen, their only child, arrived the year after me," said Phoenix, "the Hunt family money would have protected them. They wouldn't have faced the problems many other young parents did then."

"It was forty-five years ago, though; it must have been primitive," said Athena, with a grin.

"Cheeky beggar," said Phoenix.

Hope gave a long burp. She was ready to return to the bottle.

"Someone else thinks that was below the belt, too, by the sound of it. Do you want me to carry on, darling?" he asked.

Athena handed Hope over to him and watched as he encouraged their daughter to finish the bottle. Athena checked the clock on the bedside table. If she settled to sleep straight away, she might get three hours' sleep before they were due to rise — the nine o'clock meeting was the first thing on the agenda, as usual. But, no matter how pleasurable, domestic duties took second place in Olympus' activities.

A few minutes later, Hope was snoozing in Phoenix's arms. He wiped a few milk bubbles from her lips.

"Say goodnight to your mother, Hope," he said. Athena kissed their daughter's forehead, and father and daughter headed for the door.

Athena watched them leave, her heart full of love. How lucky they were. There might be plenty of clouds on the horizon for the Olympus Project, but here at Larcombe, only one matter genuinely troubled her. Since the turn of the year, Phoenix had been the perfect father and partner. How could he return to the fray when the time came?

He arrived four years ago, a loner, prepared to risk life and limb to bring criminals to justice. Their relationship surprised her and yet fulfilled her in equal measure. Now, she couldn't imagine life without him.

Phoenix had expressed concern several times over the dangers faced when tackling missions the Project handled. Only a few short months ago, they both escaped death in the New Forest at the hands of Hermes. The menace of the Titans had since receded, but evil still lurked around every corner.

Hope's arrival was fantastic news for them both, but the Project's activities meant its agents were always at risk. A loner might accept the odds; a family man might understandably have second thoughts about the wisdom of putting himself in the firing line time and time again.

Athena knew she needed to tread carefully. No matter how much she wanted to protect Phoenix, in the end, any decision to step back into a non-combative role must be his alone. Yet, deep inside, she doubted whether he'd ever be content in that capacity.

As much as he enjoyed the planning and preparation of missions he, Rusty and other agents carried out, she knew he relished being in at the kill. How did the old saying go? It's not enough for justice to be done; it has to be *seen* to be done.

When Phoenix returned after checking that Hope settled herself for a brief respite, he found Athena asleep. He marvelled at her ability to focus one hundred per cent on the minutiae of the many tasks she tackled each day. Then switch off and snatch a few precious moments of rest.

His trusted friend Rusty Scott was just the same. When they first went on missions, he recognised it must be second nature for members of the armed services. They snatched forty-winks whenever an opportunity arose. In the field, they never knew when the next chance would come to relax. Although Phoenix never served in the forces, his skill set made him ideal for the Olympus objectives. He often wished to 'switch off' as quickly as his mate and Athena, his partner.

Phoenix never lost sleep over the people he killed. His conscience was clear in that regard. Only people who deserved to die suffered by his hand. Where was the problem?

Yet, he had faced death at Cropredy and Eton Wick in the past year while on Olympus operations. He and Athena took a day trip to the coast to visit Erebus's yacht, 'Elizabeth'. One of the Titans attacked them as they returned to Larcombe via the New Forest. Those had each been a close call. If he were a cat, he would be adding the number of used lives.

He had Athena and Hope to care for now, which was

why since the New Year, he often lay awake staring at the ceiling, wondering what the future held. Then, when sleep enveloped him in her arms, there were the dreams with which to contend. Not nightmares yet, but disturbing dreams, nonetheless.

A new dawn had broken over Larcombe Manor. A new day; a new week lay ahead. Phoenix stood at a crossroads. He was uncertain which way to turn for the first time in his forty-six years.

On the other side of the Georgian house, Rusty Scott and his partner were awake and preparing for the day ahead. Artemis had showered and dressed. Rusty was still thinking about it.

"Come on," Artemis urged her lover with a friendly poke at his back.

Rusty stayed under the covers for a few more seconds.

"I'm only just coming to terms with this, you know," he said as he swung his legs out of bed.

"What, being naked in front of a younger woman?" asked Artemis.

Rusty strolled unselfconsciously around the bed to where Artemis sat, brushing her hair.

"I've been comfortable with us from the first day we met, sweetheart," he said, taking the brush from her hand. He brushed her hair, and they looked at one another in the dressing-table mirror.

"No, it's this apartment. Since I arrived here, I've lived in the stable block quarters. They were male-orientated, but we rubbed along there, didn't we? When Athena elevated you to the hierarchy here, she naturally wanted us to distance ourselves from the other ranks. We needed to be close at hand if Olympus matters took an urgent turn for the worse. That had to be a plus for the Project, but I feel uncomfortable here, in Thanatos's old rooms."

Artemis touched his hand to indicate he could stop. She took the brush from him, laid it on the table and stood. She put her arms around his neck and looked up into the rugged face of the man she loved.

"He was a traitor, Rusty," she whispered, "and he paid the price. Athena had the place redecorated and fitted out with new furniture. Nothing of your former colleague remains. Just what's lying in the unmarked grave in the pet cemetery. We're together and among friends. Our work is interesting and rewarding. I've never been happier."

Rusty shrugged.

"You think you know someone," he said. "All those years I worked with him, day in, day out. Even though he could be a pain sometimes, I never suspected a thing. Phoenix dubbed the originals Erebus recruited at the project's outset as 'The Three Stooges.' It suited them. Erebus led the way, and they followed like sheep. Although Phoenix poked fun at them now and then, he never doubted their loyalty."

"Thanatos felt slighted when Erebus favoured Athena to assume responsibility here when he retired," said Artemis. "I wish I'd met the old man; he sounds like a special person. Nevertheless, Thanatos felt power was his right and sold out to a faction that offered him the possibility. But, unfortunately, he backed the wrong horse."

With that, Artemis gave Rusty a shove.

"Now, get in that shower. I'll get us something to eat before we go to the meeting."

Rusty did just that. As the hot water cascaded over his head and broad shoulders, he tried to push the dark thoughts out of his mind. He knew Thanatos wasn't the real cause of his unease; it was Phoenix.

A life of domestic bliss wasn't an attribute Rusty associated with the vigilante killer he'd known for four years. Instead, he had enjoyed training the new agent, refining the skills he already possessed and adding more. They formed an easy friendship that had grown so strong; they were like brothers.

Since little Hope had arrived, although they had attended meetings together and discussed, planned and put into operation Olympus direct actions; neither he nor Phoenix had left Larcombe Manor on active service. Rusty was itching to get back in the field. He wasn't sure if his brother-in-arms welcomed that prospect.

As nine o'clock ticked around and the first meeting of the new week was upon them, Artemis and Rusty left their apartment and crossed the landing. The sweeping staircase took them to the ground floor. As they passed the oil paintings of famous ships and portraits of the Hunt family ancestors, it was impossible not to remember Erebus. How would the old gentleman tackle this situation?

"A penny for them?" asked Artemis.

"I was thinking of the old man. You were right. Erebus *was* special. I don't think he would have sat on his hands for three months, waiting for Phoenix and Athena to sort things out. He would have anticipated the problem and more than likely met up with Phoenix in the orangery after a fortnight. That's where they always went — just the two of them. It was always interesting and productive if I was lucky enough to join them. He had a knack for cutting to the chase. If a decision was needed, he took it. There was no argument."

"Why not ask Phoenix to meet *you* there then?" Artemis suggested. "Get him away from the main building, tell him your concerns and sound him out on his future. I'm not daft. You've got itchy feet. Fighting is what you are trained to do and keeps you alive. Sat around the main table with Athena and the others isn't where you flourish."

They had reached the meeting room door. Rusty could hear voices; Phoenix and Athena had arrived ahead of them. The nanny, Maria Elena Urbano from Estepona on the Costa del Sol, was now looking after Hope.

The first arrival at Larcombe Manor at the dawn of 2014 had caused a stir; when the twenty-five-year-old beauty with long jet-black hair breezed onto the estate several days later to start work, the effect was even more noteworthy.

"Minos and Alastor are just behind us," whispered Artemis.

Rusty opened the door and ushered her through in front of him. He glanced back towards the staircase. The two senior Olympus servants appeared to stick closer together than ever; they followed him inside in perfect step.

"Good morning, everyone," said Athena. "I see we're waiting for Giles and Henry, as usual."

"It takes longer to get ready in the mornings than it used to, Athena," Rusty grinned.

"Yes, apart from the aftershave," added Artemis, wafting her hand in front of her nose in an exaggerated fashion. "They must decide what to wear and then check the mirror half a dozen times before they leave their quarters...."

"Then they drag their feet walking across from the ice-house so they can bump into Hope and her nanny, by accident, on their morning constitutional," said Rusty.

"She's attractive, that's for sure," said Athena. "I'll speak with Maria Elena; get her to change her routine. We need those two to be giving one hundred per cent concentration on Olympus matters. I shouldn't need to say that goes for everyone around the table. So far, the year has been quiet. The wet and windy weather was the major feature. We successfully completed the direct actions we sanctioned for our teams in London and Midlands. We took two 'crash for cash' entrepreneurs out of the game, making our roads safer and insurance costs cheaper. As for our schools, we uncovered attempts by Islamic extremists plotting to take over several schools. We passed the information to the Home Office; provided they act on that information, they can thwart those attempts."

The door opened and in rushed Giles Burke and Henry Case.

"Sorry, we're late," blustered Henry, "an unavoidable delay."

"Of course you were," muttered Phoenix, looking across to where Rusty sat.

Rusty grinned at his friend, but there was no reaction. Phoenix had 'zoned out' and was staring into space. Rusty wondered where his mind had wandered. Meanwhile, Athena was calmly getting the meeting back on the agenda and prefacing the first item.

"Our intervention is required to stop the menace of drugs sold to our children. Minos, this subject is close to your heart. Can you run through the background material, please?"

Almost nine years ago, Sir Julian Langford, QC, had lost his only son, Harry, to a cocktail of drugs. On the surface, nineteen-year-old Harry appeared to be a happy-go-lucky teenager with the world at his feet. However, in his darker moments, he suffered a crisis of confidence. Harry felt the weight of expectation on his young shoulders. While in a depressed state, he chose to take his own life.

While this was a tragedy for Sir Julian and his wife Claudia, it was even tougher to understand it happening in the relatively low crime area around Maidstone, in Kent, where the Langford family lived. That incident alone might have triggered a desire to join an organisation such as the Olympus Project. His time as a prosecutor and on the bench as a judge persuaded Sir Julian to join Erebus at Larcombe Manor.

He had noted a steady increase in the number of criminals before him, despite the establishment's constant preaching of the opposite message. They were kidding the public into believing we were winning the battle. He had seen first-hand the watering-down of justice that saw courts handing out shorter, softer sentences even for horrific crimes. Defence lawyers seemed to have the odds stacked in their favour in this modern age. Criminals often walked free from his court over a small slip by the police or the CPS, guilty or not.

After he had arrived at Larcombe Manor, he became known as Minos - the judge of the dead of the Underworld. Over the past eight years, he had been a vital cog in the wheel that drove the Project forward. His main wish was to tackle those responsible for manufacturing and peddling drugs and to ensure they received the appropriate level of justice.

For Minos, the suspended sentences so often handed out, partly due to overcrowded prisons but mainly due to a weak-willed establishment, held memories of different times. As a result, he was a strong advocate for the return of capital punishment.

"I'm afraid we face a long and difficult battle with this problem, Athena," Minos began. "The tentacles of this evil reach into all corners of the nation; into every level of society. Nowhere is safe anymore. I have details of a mother whose daughter became addicted to drugs while at an expensive public school in Surrey. She has started an online blog warning other parents that their loved ones could get groomed by dealers targeting independent schools. They select naïve pupils from wealthy homes because they know they have access to funds to feed their habit. Also, in the past, these same privileged children have been led to believe they are immune. They don't believe drugs can touch them. They spend many months away at school, far from the warmth of a loving family home. Their only compensation being they have too much money. This lady's daughter is recovering from her cocaine addiction; she told her mother her dealer charged her well over the normal price for her fix. He told her, 'You can afford it, darling. Why worry? Daddy will always cough up more if you run short.' What shocks me is that the education system pays little or no heed to the potential dangers. Pupils at this public school were ignorant of the sophisticated grooming techniques used by dealers. They choreograph every step carefully. From a bit of harmless fun when they take that first 'hit' to chronic dependence on recreational drugs. After that, a gradual decline into despair and death, as we are all too aware. Meanwhile, another case from the Midlands highlights how young these children can be. Two thirteen-year-old lads took their first drag on a cigarette on the way to school. Two years later, the boys' parents were alerted by school staff, informing them they caught the boys smoking cannabis on school premises. Aged sixteen, they left school with few qualifications and no ambition other than to get wasted as often as possible. Ecstasy, crack cocaine, and heroin were the next steps on their downward spiral. Their parents now had no clue as to their whereabouts. They had resigned themselves to waiting for the knock on the door that told them their son had taken his final fix."

Minos paused. He looked up to gauge the reaction. Not one pair of eyes met his. Everyone was staring at the shiny surface of the elegant Georgian table directly in front of them.

"It hits home hard, doesn't it?" he said, "it could affect any of you, as it did me. I thought things were bad in '05 when Harry died, but things have worsened, as these figures demonstrate."

Minos slid a pile of reports to his left, where Alastor sat. His colleague removed a copy and then passed the collection around the table so the others could study the figures. The room fell silent for a while.

Alastor spoke first. "The government's latest survey shows twenty per cent of secondary pupils have taken an illegal drug," he said. "Cocaine use has doubled in the past year. Thirty-five thousand eleven-year-olds around the country have tried Class A drugs. Up to half a million fifteen-year-olds have at least tried hard drugs, if not become addicted to them. Whatever policy this country is following. It isn't working. These numbers are scandalous."

"What the heck is 'Frank' doing these days?" said Phoenix, sitting up straighter in his chair. "That bloody multi-million-pound campaign was designed to reduce drug and alcohol misuse. A decade on, and it's dead in the water. Deaths from cocaine were in the low hundreds for teenagers a decade ago. This report suggests they've risen six-fold."

"At least there's one thing we're excelling at," muttered Rusty. "We might be well down the rankings in education and health care standards, but we hold the dubious distinction of having the highest level of cocaine use in Europe."

"You certainly don't overstate the problems of the task

facing us, Minos," said Athena. "However, we mustn't let that weaken our resolve. Where do we lay the blame for this escalation in the past decade?"

"The failure to control our borders has allowed hard drugs to flow into our leafy suburbs and schoolyards," said Henry Case. "By softening our stance on cannabis classification and dithering over whether we should go further or not, we led many to believe it's okay to use the drug. We can see the results of this in the pages of this survey. Young lives destroyed, a whole generation of children betrayed."

"What has been the government's response to these figures?" asked Giles Burke.

"This survey covered the use of drugs and alcohol among secondary school pupils," replied Minos. "Despite the alarming picture that the drug statistics paint, the government welcomed the report. The figures show a small fall in the numbers found drinking and using types of less addictive drugs."

"Unbelievable," said Phoenix.

"If I were a parent of a child attending school, I would be horrified," said Artemis. "We entrust our children to schools for large amounts of their lives until they're at least sixteen. Surely, we should expect the schools to safeguard them from the dangers of drugs? Not through education alone, but watching the school perimeters and checking who and what enters the premises?"

Minos flipped open another file on the table in front of him.

"In times of austerity, it becomes challenging to cover all the bases, Artemis. I have examples of brazen dealers preying on kids after they left school and walked home. Police increased their patrols around bus stations in North

Wales after reports of dealers targeting school transports. Dealers have no morals, no scruples, no conscience."

"Can we concentrate on two or three worst offenders?" asked Rusty.

"There are dealers who are more prolific than others," said Minos, "my dossier is here for analysis. Take your pick. You will find plenty from which to choose."

"We must start somewhere," said Phoenix, "to do nothing isn't an option. On the other hand, removing the problem from a few schools across the country might get the government's head out of the sand."

"Based on their reaction to this survey, it might take a lot of shifting," said Rusty.

"Phoenix and Rusty will assume responsibility for the direct action we take," said Athena. "I'm sure I can rely on the two of you to achieve the results we expect. Can you produce an action plan for next Monday's meeting?"

"No problem, Athena," said Phoenix, "it will be good to have something positive to contribute again."

"The drug menace won't disappear overnight," said Athena. "We will need to revisit it time and time again, even if the government wake up and make meaningful inroads. One thing is certain. I want the landscape to look very different from the one portrayed in this survey before our daughter starts school."

Henry Case and Giles Burke were next up as they delivered their security report updates. Artemis sat quietly, watching and listening, as her superiors ran through the list of threats facing the country from home and abroad. If the public ever became fully aware of the scale of problems the security services tackled daily, widespread panic would inevitably follow.

It was clear the official security organisations were struggling to cope. There was constant pressure from terrorist organisations and organised crime, increasingly from cyber-criminals, yet the highest pressure came from their government. Year after year, they were required to achieve more and more with fewer resources.

Artemis had experienced several years of this impossible task within the police force. But, in her short time with Olympus, she appreciated how valuable the secret organisation's input was, behind the scenes, in smoothing out the hot spots.

The meeting was ending. Athena closed by informing everyone that the next Olympus hierarchy meeting was in four weeks at Curzon Street, London. Zeus had postponed the initial meeting in early January following Hope's birth. Flowers, cards, and little gifts had arrived at Larcombe from the remaining Olympians. Zeus was keen to promote the new Olympus's image as one big happy family after last year's troubles.

One item on the agenda for the meeting was evident. There were new faces to introduce. Following the demise of Demeter, Poseidon, Hermes and Nemesis, there was an urgent need for fresh blood. So Zeus had searched high and low for people with the financial capacity to help bankroll Olympus' missions and ideology aligned with that epitomised by their founder, Erebus.

It appeared from the confirmed date of the meeting that quest had been successful.

Giles and Henry waited for Artemis to join them and headed towards the ice-house. They would soon disappear below ground to carry on the highly sophisticated surveillance and intelligence gathering in which the Olympus operations room excelled.

Minos and Alastor hovered. Athena could tell they

needed a quiet word with her. She knew it was unlikely necessary; they needed to be reassured that their perceived status in the organisation was still intact. Athena saw these few minutes massaging their frail egos as a small price. After all, they were more than happy to graft away on the analysis and interpretation of the data generated by Giles and his staff.

Rusty saw his opportunity. As Artemis scuttled over to join Giles and Henry, he collared Phoenix.

"So, when do we start on this drug problem?" he asked.

"Meet me in the orangery in fifteen minutes," replied Phoenix.

With that, Phoenix left the meeting room and headed for the stairs.

Rusty glanced over to Athena. She had just finished chatting with the Two Stooges.

"What did he say?" she asked Rusty.

"We're meeting in fifteen minutes in the orangery," he said.

"That's good," sighed Athena. "A few hours in his old surroundings might snap him out of this melancholy."

"Don't worry," said Rusty. "I'll keep him there until he breaks."

Athena smiled. She knew Rusty had the Project's best interests at heart. It was good to learn that at least one other person in the organisation had noticed her partner's darker mood since the New Year.

"Handle him with care, Rusty," she said as she swept through the doorway and practically ran up the stairs to find Phoenix. With luck, they could spend a few minutes together with Hope before Phoenix left for the orangery.

"I don't think kid gloves are what he responds to," whispered Rusty. "I reckon a sharp dig in the ribs is what he needs right now. Then we can both get back to doing what we do best."

Rusty closed the door behind him and headed out of the house. The late morning sun was bright but weak as he walked briskly towards the building Erebus had held so dear.

Everything at Larcombe Manor was coming alive after the winter. Despite the chill in the air, he could sense the changes occurring. Spring was just around the corner. It was time for the estate's grounds to come alive again. The time for Phoenix to rise again was long overdue.

Chapter Two

Little had altered in the magnificent orangery since Erebus had left Larcombe for his brief retirement on Ibiza. Although the sparse furniture was twentieth-century functional, rather than its original luxurious fittings, Phoenix imagined little had changed in general since the early nineteenth century.

Wealthy landowners had used orangeries to house orange and other citrus trees to protect them from Britain's harsh winters. By the time the Hunt family had this edifice built, glazed roofs were the order of the day to allow as much sunlight into the building as possible. The ability to afford such an adornment made their wealthy family appear even more noble and aristocratic.

The impressive structure featured external stone and brickwork, while the interior was decorative and plastered. South-facing windows encouraged the maximum light to flood through, and the walls facing north were thick to protect against the cold. Phoenix had counted the fifteen tall windows as he strolled past his first day at Larcombe when the old gentleman took him on the grand tour. As the months and years passed, the one hundred and eighty feet long orangery had found its way into his heart, just as it had his mentor's.

Phoenix understood how protective Sir William Hunt felt towards this place of sanctuary. It hadn't been somewhere to use for their meetings, a convenient spot perhaps halfway between the main house and the stable block where Phoenix had had his quarters. But it offered so much more.

As he sat waiting for Rusty to arrive, he sipped from a cup of coffee. The sun was streaming through the plate glass, warming him. It felt good to be alive.

Phoenix recalled a conversation when Erebus had described the fine dining that had gone on here back in his ancestor's time. The 'great and the good' were invited to the manor house for the Hunt family to flaunt their wealth.

Times change; his father had used the orangery for afternoon tea, particularly in the height of summer, although these occasions were exclusive to his family, not for visitors. Erebus had continued this tradition with Elizabeth and Helen.

After the tragic death of his only child, and Elizabeth's gradual mental decline, he returned here alone to reflect on carefree summer afternoons with loved ones. Those solitary periods of grieving had been the breeding ground for Olympus. A thirst for revenge, a desire to seek a reversal in the decline of justice. Above all, to ensure the punishment fits the crime.

Four years on, the legacy of the older man remained. Phoenix understood his place now in the grand scheme of things. His life with Athena and Hope was precious. He would protect them to the death, but it was he who must take up the fight against the evils Erebus had created Olympus to defeat.

Zeus, Athena, and the other Olympians managed the finance and the ethos and identified the organisation's most appropriate targets. He was the bringer of fire to cleanse the world of those who committed the most despicable crimes.

The door opened, and in walked Rusty Scott. A steward followed him, carrying a tray.

"Sorry, I was so long getting here," said Rusty. "I thought we might be here for a while, Phoenix. I got us this grub. Is that coffee in the jug hot?"

"It is," replied Phoenix, lifting the domed lid from the silver tray. His friend had to wait for the food to cook. The stack of food looked incredibly appetising. He licked his lips. Erebus was right; times change. The humble bacon roll had supplemented fine dining and afternoon tea.

The steward left them alone and returned to the main building. Rusty fetched himself a cup of coffee, then sat opposite his pal.

"Right," he began, "what's going on, Phoenix? You've been out of sorts for ages. You'll both be dog-tired with the new baby, that's only understandable, but it might go deeper than that. Are you thinking of withdrawing from active service?"

"It's been at the back of my mind, that's for sure," admitted Phoenix. "I keep asking myself whether I should place myself in danger with Athena and Hope to look after. I was sitting here, waiting for you to turn up, thinking what Erebus would want me to do. It didn't take long to conclude. I'm like the actor who lands a role and realises it was the one he was born to play. All his other performances are worthless compared to that role. Erebus identified me as the person he sought to wield his sword of vengeance. Who am I to go against his wishes, whether he's no longer with us or not?

"Hallelujah," cried Rusty. "Artemis and I were worried you might be ready for your pipe and slippers. Carrying out direct action missions is what we're best at, mate. Horses for courses, as they say. But I don't want to take it easy yet, either. We make a good team; I'd be hopeless on my own."

"When we were in the meeting this morning, I was thinking of those early days when you were getting me fit and training me," said Phoenix. He finished his coffee, got up, and walked across to get a fresh brew.

"You're almost the last of the handful of SAS trainers still stationed at Larcombe since the Project began, Rusty. It's been a while, too, since we've recruited new agents. So when Athena informed us of fresh blood at the top, I thought we needed fresh blood here, too. We've got agents who served in Kuwait, Kosovo, and Iraq, but we've held our agent numbers steady around the world in the past two years. I don't want you tied up with training any new intake; you're too valuable out in the field."

"Well, I haven't missed training the newbies, I'll admit," said Rusty, taken aback by the direction the meeting was taking. He'd assumed they would discuss possible changes for Phoenix, not for him. "But I'd like to keep a handle on it," he added.

"Naturally," said Phoenix, "my vote is for you to update the training manual and oversee your new master trainers. They do the work, and your role would be advisory."

"Where do we source these 'master' trainers?" asked Rusty.

"Athena heard a whisper a month ago that someone wanted to reconsider their role within Olympus. Kelly Dexter wants to start a family, and Hayden Vincent still has nightmares over Eton Wick. His leg wound wasn't that serious, but as we both know, it was a hairy mission, and we lost good men that day. I think he wants to take a step away from the front line."

"They could prove to be a good fit here," said Rusty, "we know them well already, and they're excellent agents. So, OK, they've got my vote. So, Kelly wants to start a family, then? It will be good for Athena and Artemis to have another female around the place."

"Maria Elena will be busy too; she'll be running a crèche before she knows it. So you'd better prepare for big changes in your life, Rusty. Artemis will become broody."

"Heck," said Rusty. "I'm older than you, don't forget. I'm not sure I'm right for fatherhood. Let's not think about that for now. Why don't we concentrate on the job that Athena sent us here for first? Shouldn't we be getting on with planning our response to this drug problem?"

Phoenix moved the files he had on the table to one side. He took the lid off the silver tray and picked up a bacon roll.

"Let's have lunch," he said, "there will be plenty of time for planning that later."

"This reminds me of the odd lunch we had together with the old man," said Rusty, munching on a roll. "God, that's good. Artemis is trying to wean me off fast food and fried stuff, but it's what I've always known."

"Me too," said Phoenix, "my first wife wasn't much of a cook. Her mother, Kath, was brilliant. Especially at Christmas, although there were only seven or eight for dinner, she cooked enough for twenty and hated seeing it go to waste."

When the rolls were gone and the jug of coffee emptied, the two friends sat quietly for a few minutes, wondering what they were doing to their waistlines. Phoenix stood up, stretched, and Rusty realised it was time to get back to work.

"Athena wanted to add another item to the agenda this morning," said Phoenix. "But we agreed to leave it until after the next Olympus meeting. There's a new threat emerging in the Middle East. It is an area that will continue to be ravaged by war, no doubt, just as it has been for twenty years. However, I believe this latest outfit, ISIS, poses a bigger threat than Al Qaeda ever did to our shores. This terrorist organisation emerged ten years ago from the remnants of Al Qaeda in Iraq. It laid low after U.S. troops went into Iraq in 2007 and began to re-emerge in 2011, taking advantage of the growing instability in Iraq and Syria to carry out attacks and bolster their ranks. Fallujah and Raqqa fell to them in January. They are poised to launch an offensive on Mosul this summer."

"What's their main objective?" asked Rusty. "Why do you believe they pose a credible threat to the UK?"

"They aim to form a caliphate stretching from Aleppo in Syria to Diyala in Iraq to create a so-called Islamic State. Evidence suggests young Muslims in mainland Europe and the UK are being radicalised and persuaded to join the fight. The freedom of movement the pro-Europeans are so keen on means ISIS members may already be in every major Western city, recruiting both men and women. The incidence of terror attacks as a part of their overall campaign is guaranteed; those attacks will target civilians and weaken European governments' resolve to get involved on Middle Eastern soil. The Americans withdrew from Iraq, as did the UK, and public opinion in the States is against going back in large numbers. I guess US special forces may be there in the low hundreds, but significant numbers of boots on the ground are something else."

"If they come here causing trouble, we'll help the authorities take them out, as we always do, Phoenix," said Rusty.

"That's why we need to recruit more agents," said Phoenix. "We have adequate numbers to tackle the threats that face us at present, but not an all-out terror campaign. When I say 'we', I mean both ourselves and the UK authorities. Since 2010 this government has imposed year-on-year budget cuts on the armed services. There have been reductions in the workforce across the board. Police and border control numbers slashed. As a result, we are less able to defend ourselves than in the darkest days of the early 1940s. It will take a massacre of unbelievable proportions to get the government to abandon this mania for austerity and wake up to a few harsh facts."

"There may not be so many of us these days, but quality counts," said Rusty.

"We might not get the chance to test ourselves, Rusty. In the old days, wars were started by politicians, who argued until they were blue in the face. Then when they failed to get their way, they declared war on one another. While they stood back and watched, the likes of you and I went to fight a few bloody battles to see who picked up the spoils. Today's conflicts wage on Twitter and Facebook; if someone sailed their fleet up the Thames and landed troops in Central London, it would be all over social media in minutes. The public would demand to know what the government would do. The armed forces would fill out forms; check budgets to see whether they could afford to put bullets in the too few guns available. If I were them, I'd invest in a few thousand white flags and hang the expense."

"Are you sure you're okay, mate?" asked Rusty. "Only

you're more negative than usual, and that's saying something."

"It's the lack of sleep. If I could sleep for eight hours, that would be fantastic. To make Athena's parents are coming to stay at Larcombe this weekend. They came to Bath to see their only grandchild early in the New Year. Giles needed me in the ice-house, and Athena took Hope to meet them at the Royal Crescent Hotel. Naturally, they wanted to know where I was. Athena had to cover for me."

"I thought her father knew the basics of what you were up to here?" asked Rusty.

"Geoffrey's no fool. Athena and I discussed the problem, and, well, you know how it goes, mate, discretion is the better part of valour. So Athena decided it would be possible to collect them from Bath Spa station and bring them to Larcombe this time. She plans to put them in rooms at the front of the house, overlooking the fields and the driveway. We'll keep them away from the business end of the operation as far as possible. The thing that's got me wound up is they mentioned the 'M' word on their last visit."

"Tricky," said Rusty with a smile. "Have you made any progress in deciding who you'll be when this marriage takes place? If it's such a hassle, why not proceed with the baptism, anyway? Nobody worries too much if couples marry these days, do they?"

"That's another thing contributing to my sleepless nights, Rusty. Athena's parents are old school and keen on seeing their daughter walk up the aisle so that Geoffrey can give her away. Grace Fox wants to invite loads of their friends to the wedding and reception. Athena and I would be happier, either staying as we are or just having a simple ceremony in front of witnesses such as yourself and Artemis. I might get away with using my real name if it was low-key. However, Athena is against me using any assumed identity Henry Case might produce. Can you imagine trying to persuade Grace Fox not to splash news of their daughter's wedding across the pages of The Tatler?"

"Hmm, I said it was tricky, mate," said Rusty. "Glossy, half-page photographs of a man who died four years ago, with his beautiful wife might bring unwanted attention to Olympus."

"Not to mention on me," said Phoenix. "This weekend could be a nightmare."

"Let's lighten the mood," said Rusty. "Why not take me through your files and bring me up to speed? Then we can plan where to target our direct action. Even the murky world of drug dealing has to be better than what you're facing."

Phoenix laughed and turned over the file cover at the top of the pile on the table.

"These figures prepared for the Mayor of London's office earlier this year showed over eighty London gangs operating outside the capital. Gangs from more than half the thirty-two boroughs are involved, with those from Hackney, Brent, Greenwich, and Newham known to be the most prolific. In addition, Metropolitan Police data monitored the rise of fourteen 'super gangs' now active in more than one police area outside the capital."

Phoenix turned over surveillance photos from the icehouse one by one. They showed transactions happening in dozens of locations across the east and south-eastern side of the country — Oxford and Cambridge; Guildford and Epsom in Surrey; Crawley and Harlow in Middlesex.

"Giles and his team found this evidence after only a few hours trawling through CCTV footage. It's blatant, Rusty. They don't give a toss whether anyone sees them or not. God knows how many deals they make inside pubs and clubs, in the local parks and open spaces. It's an epidemic. These dealers are now so prolific that they operate in every police area across Britain. They're active in towns and cities within easy reach of London. Gangs deal in many parts of Essex and as far afield as Wiltshire and Hertfordshire. They're everywhere. Three-quarters of drug-related arrests made by police in towns in Kent are for crimes perpetrated by London-based gangs."

Rusty pored over the photographs, scanned the figures and blew out his cheeks.

"Where the heck do we start?"

"What these reports continue to emphasise is the gangs have expanded their supply methods. Artemis told Giles they termed it 'cuckooing' in the police forces she worked with at Durham and Portishead. The phrase has been in use for five or six years. It describes where dealers arrive in a new town and identify a vulnerable local addict. Then they move in, taking over that person's home and sometimes, like a cuckoo, force them out. The house or flat becomes their regional base, often staffed by teenage gang members."

"This isn't random, is it," said Rusty. "It's based on a well-established technique to establish a fresh sales territory like those adopted by dozens of major businesses. That must take loads of organising; street kids can't handle this level of sophistication. The guys at the head of these gangs are intelligent. They're genuine entrepreneurs. It's a pity they don't use their skills in legitimate businesses; they would wipe out the national debt in the UK in short order."

"True, but I can't see them settling for a zero-hours contract and getting paid peanuts when they can rake in the profits this game offers. So their next step after finding their new nest is establishing a customer base. They pass out business cards to prospective clients. Buy or extract phone numbers of known drug users from local dealers," said Phoenix. "They can send text messages offering introductory deals to draw in new punters. More gang members move in from London if a town or city district promises real potential. Some stay in the crack house they've recruited. Others find a bed-and-breakfast place to stay in for a few weeks."

Rusty continued leafing through surveillance photos and facts and figures in the files on the table. The afternoon sun had disappeared behind the main building, but the underfloor heating had started working. He knew it would be possible for him and Phoenix to continue working in comfort for several hours. He glanced at his watch, trying to gauge when the next call to the kitchens might be necessary. He could send for more coffee and something to take the edge off their hunger.

"We'll give it another thirty minutes," said Phoenix, spotting what Rusty had done. "I'll work out a plan of action this evening. Perhaps we could get together again after tomorrow's meeting? Maybe even take a trip to the Home Counties to see this innovative sales programme in action?"

"No guns, just a recce?" asked Rusty.

"Yeah," Phoenix replied, "the people we want won't be anywhere near the point-of-sale. We need to play this as we have in the past. Strike at the head of the snake. Leave the body to wither and die. As you said, the street-level gang members don't have the nous to run the organisation. If we can identify the brains behind a few of the busiest gangs and eliminate them, then these campaigns by the sales forces will falter. We can give subtle hints to the local coppers, pointing out where the cuckoos are based. With luck, they'll tidy up the loose ends. No doubt, they'll apologise for not having done it sooner. They've done the spadework for us in these reports. A lack of officers on the ground explains why they only seem to pick the lowest fruit on the branch. They can see the juicy prizes at the top of the gang structure, but they're out of reach."

"Out of touch, more like," grunted Rusty. "They spend thousands of hours trying to dig up dirt on politicians and personalities who've been dead for a decade. Meanwhile, our kids get poisoned under their noses, and they appear to do little to tackle the problem. Except for gathering data and writing reports."

Rusty started reading from a report by the National Crime Agency. It revealed the seven police forces closest to London had identified over eight hundred London-based criminals selling drugs in their areas. The gangs had been drawn to the middle-class, more affluent regions by what they saw as lucrative and easy pickings.

"Think about what we know from that first report," he said. "If eighty separate gangs are involved, maybe with more than one main guy at the helm, you're talking one hundred bodies the police will still need to catch and imprison. We can cast adrift foot soldiers by taking out the leaders. Make it easier to sweep up your loose ends. This NCA report also found criminal rivals in these satellite towns are easily subdued by the London gangs, who routinely use much greater levels of violence. However, some gangs have access to machine guns, and experts worry clashes between such groups will soon break out in provincial towns."

"I didn't say it was going to be easy," said Phoenix, "but remember what I said in the meeting. We must do something. The threat of increased violence is always there, but the gangs' best weapon is the mobile phone. These days they can buy pay-as-you-go phones virtually anonymously. That allows them to run a criminal business and cause enormous human misery. Minos underlined the result of their actions in the facts he presented this morning. We have seen an increase in the misery of drug addiction and the exploitation of vulnerable kids forced into helping these gangs."

Phoenix collected the photos and files together. He had had enough for the day. He wanted to get back to Athena and Hope. A shower might help him to feel clean again. Rusty accompanied him as they walked back towards the main building.

"Our first targets should come from those gangs that concentrate on school-age children," said Phoenix.

"I agree," said Rusty. "Then we can look at the colleges and universities later when we have the opportunity to revisit the problem."

"See you in the morning," said Phoenix.

Rusty bounded up the stairs towards his apartments, then slowed as he remembered that Artemis was below ground in the ice-house. His partner had another three hours until her shift finished.

Phoenix strolled more leisurely to the rooms once occupied by Sir William Hunt and eased open the door as noiselessly as he could. Athena was asleep on the settee. Hope nestled in the crook of her mother's left arm, wide-awake but totally at peace with the world.

Hope spotted movement and gazed towards the door. When she recognised a familiar face, she gave Phoenix one of her million-watt beams and gurgled a welcome.

"Ah, the innocence of youth," said Phoenix. "How soon it dies."

Chapter Three

Later that same night, in Cheltenham, Phil Hounsell sat in his car, steeling himself to walk the short distance to the detached house in Redgrove Park. As a young police constable, he had felt much the same. Phil went to tell the parents of an eighteen-year-old boy their son had died in a road accident. His superior officer told him to find the courage and get used to the idea that he'd regularly inform families of bad news.

"The sooner you get the first one out of the way, the better, lad," the older man muttered, "stick to the bare facts, don't go into details. There's no cause to divulge they found his head on the back seat. Along with the steel truss catapulted into his car after the lorry he was following shed its load. So keep calm, tell them what they need to know and above all, make them think you care."

Phil never enjoyed that part of the job, nor did he ever get used to it. It always felt like a part of him died, too, whenever he had to deliver the devastating news a beloved family member was never coming home again. As Phil rose through the ranks, he had issued his advice to young constables, both male and female, on approaching that first time. Whatever they did, he told them to avoid using the phrase we're sorry for your loss. Over the years, it had become so clichéd on TV shows that it lost any sense of being genuine.

Phil thought back over the past few months and wondered how he had found himself back in the old routine. His company Hounsell Security Services was coping. After leaving the police force, Wayne Sangster, Dusty Miller, and Jake Legg still comprised the small team he assembled. He shuddered as he recalled the heady heights he had imagined HSS might reach when they secured the security contract for Honey B, the pop star who provided them with their first lucrative assignment.

A few weeks later, towards the end of October, he had been driving home to his wife Erica and the kids in a cold sweat. A visit to Larcombe Manor that promised so much ended in the stuff of nightmares. He had been met by a man-mountain, who identified himself as Henry Case, Head of Security. He had then met Annabelle Fox, the charity's CEO.

His employer had given him the mission to persuade certain personnel at the Manor to attend a spurious meeting at Force HQ at Portishead, a force he had left only a few months earlier. Everything went pear-shaped. Annabelle Fox knew far more about him than he did about her. Not only that, she knew far more about Honey B than he did. He had been so gullible.

Phil had left the room where he met Annabelle Fox, and Henry Case blindfolded him. They had walked several hundred yards, then descended in a lift. When they emerged, Henry removed the blindfold. They stood in a long, dark corridor. He had been pushed inside the first room and left alone for several hours. There was no hope of escape.

Phil had had plenty of time to sit and think. He had seen the faces of two senior personnel at Larcombe Manor, but that wasn't an issue, surely? Ms Fox was the public face of the Olympus charity. He had visited a building on the estate with underground facilities of which the public was unaware. Could that knowledge alone be enough to sign his death warrant? What else went on here? What went on at Larcombe Manor? Did the fact Henry Case removed the blindfold suggest his life was in danger?

When his tormentor returned, Phil Hounsell had decided to tell him everything he knew. He could see no benefit in holding onto any crumb of information he had gathered over the past couple of months.

The interrogation had been gruelling, but at no time did Henry Case lay a finger on him. At last, it was over, and they gave him food and drink. The following morning, Henry Case returned to visit him. Henry told Phil to forget that he ever visited Larcombe Manor and should keep his nose out of Olympus Project affairs.

It had been a simple choice to make. The return journey to the surface involved the blindfold again. Phil guessed Case's boss didn't want him to see where the building lay on the estate. Or how many levels it contained.

From early November, his HSS staff had been travelling around the country. HSS provided security for a 'glam rock' outfit whose fan base contained few trouble-makers. The fans had aged with the remaining band members, and Wayne and his helpers enjoyed a smooth ride. The money arriving in the HSS coffers was OK, but Phil felt the need to find something to keep himself occupied. He thought it was time to stick closer to home for a while; it was less dangerous.

Wayne always had an answer.

"Why not advertise that we're in the business of finding 'Missing Persons', boss? You could cherry-pick jobs for locals that have disappeared without leaving a note. That would keep you close to home and bring in a steady income."

It didn't appeal to Phil. The job was always a pain when he'd been a detective. The police aren't interested in applying resources to look for mispers unless they're kids. As soon as they reached sixteen, it was often more trouble than it was worth.

Most persons reported missing return soon after their disappearance without suffering any harm. A small percentage, however, will have come to harm or have been the victim of crime. That initial missing person report could kick off a crime enquiry. In case the worst scenario developed, they took great care over the investigation from the outset. They had to preserve any evidence present and strictly observe the rules of disclosure. It could be a nightmare when the investigation carried on for a while. The pressure on the family increased, and the police were required to give support. If the media got involved, as they inevitably did, those pressures increased. Stretched police resources got pushed closer to the breaking point.

Against his better judgment, Phil posted advertisements in the local press in the Roman city of Bath, where HSS was based, and in the surrounding counties. He was only too aware of the potential number of cases that desperate families might contact him to pursue.

The annual number of missing reports around the UK exceeded a quarter million. Twenty thousand of those lost souls stayed missing for more than a year. The public was probably unaware that over a thousand bodies in mortuaries across the country stubbornly remained unidentified.

Phil often marvelled at how so many people slipped away and remained unnoticed in a country where CCTV cameras proliferated in their millions. These people appeared on many databases, possessed cards and licences, held social media accounts and were continually scrutinised by ham-fisted government authorities. Yet, somehow, they disappeared, often without a trace. The daily recurring question wasn't 'How?' in the home they left behind, but 'Why?'

The enquiries arrived soon after the first posting of the adverts. Phil discovered he had plenty of choices. A high proportion were teenagers. Teenage runaways were overwhelmingly female, with three-quarters of missing thirteen-to-seventeen-year-olds being girls. With adults, men dominated, with three-quarters of disappeared people over their mid-twenties being male.

Phil selected the cases that offered a reasonable chance of success. That, too, was at Wayne's suggestion.

"If you can genuinely show you have a high success rate, then clients will keep coming, boss. You might be their last hope of finding their loved ones again. They will have more faith that their money will be well spent and not poured down the drain."

In those first few cases, Phil traced eighty per cent of the family members that went 'walkabout'. Occasionally, the missing person returned home to the bosom of the family they abandoned. Mostly, Phil had to relay the message they were alive and well but didn't want to return.

"Be thankful for small mercies," Wayne told him. "Even the families of the ones you couldn't trace still have hope. It might be remote, but you haven't needed to tell them they're dead."

At the end of January, the 'glam-rock tour ended. Wayne and the lads returned to Bath, awaiting their next assignment. One morning in early February, a call came through to the office. It was from the couple who owned the house that Phil now sat outside.

Growing up in a happy middle-class home in Cheltenham, Carrie Ditchburn had every advantage. Her parents provided a loving family home, ensuring that Carrie and her younger brother, Nathan, never wanted for anything. Yet by thirteen, Carrie became a regular cannabis user and swiftly descended into drug addiction. She first attended rehab at seventeen.

Phil had driven to Cheltenham with Wayne to talk with her family. Carrie's parents filled in her early background.

"Life at home was fine. She knew she was loved and cared for," her mother told them tearfully.

"School was a different matter," her father had continued. "Carrie got bullied at junior school and somehow never felt she belonged. She struggled to make friends.".

"That went on until she moved to the local academy," continued her mother. "Carrie played truant, messed around in class, and was forever being kept in detention. In the end, they asked her to leave. We found her a place in a girls' school. The fees were expensive, but you always want the best for your children, don't you? We wanted to give her every chance to turn her life around."

While they chatted, the son, Nathan, now seventeen, had returned home from college. He sat quietly and listened to his mother.

"That should have helped, but it didn't," he said. "Carrie latched on to a group of girls that seemed to like her, and she mixed with them more and more out of school. Later we found out they smoked cannabis and socialised with older teenagers into drugs. Instead of helping her, that crowd started her on the slippery slope. She was only thirteen for crying out loud."

"It sounds a familiar tale," Phil told them. "What starts as a way of fitting in rapidly becomes an addiction."

"We could see she was troubled," said her father. "Carrie was self-harming. Her behaviour in school deteriorated even further, and when she was nearing her seventeenth birthday, she tried to kill herself."

"My sister got into a fight with a girl at school," said Nathan, "she thought everyone would be better off without her. So after a week in the hospital, she went to a rehab clinic, and when she came out eight weeks later, she was free of drugs for a while."

"Then, a month later, she ran away," her father said. "Carrie phoned her brother from London a week after she left to say she was safe. There was nothing about where she was, who she was with, or what she was doing. That was over two years ago, and we've not heard from her since."

"Neither of us," stressed Nathan, "she must have called from a payphone. Her mobile phone was still in her room. Mum found it after she left. It was as if she wanted to make a clean break. Dad went looking for her at weekends, to begin with, but it was hopeless. Searching for a needle in a haystack. We didn't have a clue where to start."

"The police were helpful when you reported her missing?" asked Wayne.

"As soon as we told them Carrie had called to say she was safe, they switched off," said her father.

"They pretended they hadn't," said Nathan. "They

went through the motions when Dad pestered them, but you could tell, you know?"

Phil and Wayne knew only too well. Phil had asked a few more questions. Wayne took details of Carrie's friends her parents were aware of still living locally if she'd contacted them. Mrs Ditchburn provided a photograph of her daughter, but the last physical one the family possessed was Carrie at sixteen. Nathan showed Wayne a couple of selfies on her phone. The image they saw was a young girl whose eyes looked sad, even when clowning around and pulling faces.

They said their goodbyes and promised to keep in touch with regular reports on any progress. Phil told them not to worry. They'd do their utmost to trace their daughter and get her to at least make contact if they couldn't persuade her to come home. As they walked to the car, Wayne sighed.

"What a bummer."

"You wanted us to take on 'mispers' to keep our heads above water financially," Phil muttered.

When they returned to the office, they began the time-consuming task of going through the contact numbers they had collected. Her so-called friends from the girl's school seemed reticent to get involved. Former boyfriends were on the list, and they swore blind they hadn't heard from her, nor did they realise she was heavily into drugs.

"Yeah, right," said Wayne, "lying scrotes. One or all of them were probably her supplier. That's not uncommon. We need to dig deeper."

"How do you mean?" Phil had asked.

"Let's look at their social media accounts. Those will give us a clearer picture; we can also check out their friend lists. If we're lucky, Carrie Ditchburn might be in there somewhere."

"Surely, they would tell her parents if they knew something?" Phil had asked.

He had thought about how Erica would react if Shaun or Tracey ran away. If kids who had been to their house, played in the garden, or always received an invitation to a birthday party had held back information, she would have laid into them and their parents something chronic.

"They can be a close-knit bunch, teenagers," said Wayne. "Someone around Redgrove Park knows at least a former address or a contact number for Miss Ditchburn; I'll bet."

"A lot of time has passed, Wayne," Phil said. "I lost touch with nearly everyone I was at school with by the time I finished my probationary period."

"Yeah, well, you joined the police, boss; what did you expect?"

"Fair point."

It took them a while to find a clue to Carrie's whereabouts. Phil resorted to sending the Ditchburn family vague but positive reports. He imagined them reading what he had written and believed he, too, had switched off.

Wayne found a girl who had been friends with Carrie at junior school. They met at the local Pony Club. Josie Dymond now worked at a busy livery yard. Horses were her life, judging by the photographs on her Facebook and Instagram accounts. Josie had well over a thousand friends across her social media accounts. Her posts suggested a well-adjusted, gregarious young woman who worked hard at a job she loved and partied hard at weekends.

"Here we are, boss," Wayne cried. "I've found her."

Phil had scooted his chair across to where Wayne sat. He looked at the screen.

"What a beautiful-looking animal," he said.

"Fifteen hands and eleven years old, it tells me in the comments underneath," said Wayne. "Here are a few of Josie Dymond, out with friends and family. She's got a friend called Carrie Redgrove. Her Facebook account only shows the female avatar, with no personal photos. There's no indication of age or relationships. She presents as being from London and working at being unemployed."

"So, young Carrie changed her name to throw her family off the scent. I wonder why Josie Dymond didn't appear on the list the family gave us?"

"Everything about this young lady suggests a well-to-do upbringing; there won't be a string of detentions, rehab sessions, and drug-dealing boyfriends in Josie's background. Her parents probably distanced her from Carrie once the trouble started, but you know what kids are. Josie and Carrie undoubtedly bonded at the Pony Club, and that bond never broke, no matter how different the path their lives took in the following years."

"You're a sentimental old bugger, aren't you, Wayne?" said Phil. "But like nearly every copper I've worked with over the years, a good judge of character."

"Stop it, boss," said Wayne, still scrolling through the history he discovered on Josie Dymond's Facebook page, "you'll make me blush. Right, here we go. The first contact I could find was ten months ago; Josie had a wild weekend after the Cheltenham Festival. A photo showed Josie with a group of jockeys and grooms at a club. Carrie sent a 'like', posted a few emojis, and then this comment."

"What are you like? Good to see you're still riding, lol." Phil read Carrie's comment aloud.

"Look at what Josie said in her reply, boss," said Wayne, "she asked Carrie to direct message her so they could catch up. It was clear Josie hadn't heard from Carrie for ages.

Unfortunately, we can't access that side of things, so we'll need to speak with Josie Dymond."

"When was the latest contact out in the open, Wayne?"

"I can't find anything in the past five weeks, boss. That might not mean much. They could chat regularly, either online or by phone. Just because Carrie ditched her mobile when she left doesn't mean she doesn't own one now."

The following morning, the two men had driven up through the Gloucestershire countryside. They found Josie Dymond hard at work, grooming one of the dozen horses in her charge.

At first, the attractive, well-spoken young woman was wary of their questions, but Phil used his experience to persuade her that Carrie's parents deserved to know the truth. He promised to keep Carrie's whereabouts secret if that was what she wished. In the end, Josie agreed to meet them in the local inn at lunchtime.

Josie began her story with a soft drink and a baguette on the table in front of her. Wayne sat with his pint of lager and tucked into a steak and ale pie with chips and gravy. Phil sat opposite her. The slimline tonic with ice, and mushroom risotto, grew less appealing with each sentence the young woman uttered.

Within months of relocating to London, Carrie smoked up to eight joints daily. She lost her job in a fast-food outlet because of her frequent no-shows. Most of her friends used cocaine and heroin, but Carrie resisted until a bitter break-up with a boyfriend left her depressed. Josie asked if Phil knew Carrie had tried to kill herself a couple of years ago; he nodded.

"Carrie started taking cocaine," Josie continued, "she convinced herself it would be okay, but it wasn't. So she bought more and got into a three-day weekend coke binge and then four days off during the week to recover. Carrie wasn't working. She had several boyfriends she mentioned, but I always got the impression they were doing her more harm than good."

"Did she mention any names?" Phil asked.

"There was a Dwight she talked of until recently; he had an unusual surname. She only mentioned it once. I think he had just hit her, so when she messaged me, she referred to him by his surname alone."

"If you could remember it, it would be a great help," Wayne told Josie.

Josie picked at her food for a while. Wayne ordered another pint. Phil was driving back to Bath, so he sipped slowly from the slimline tonic. The ice had long gone.

"Carrie was always trying to get me to lend her money," Josie continued. She stared at a beer mat on the table in front of her. "Carrie pretended it was for clothes for an interview. I felt guilty not giving in, but I knew she would use my money to buy drugs. We were close for a while until my parents kept us apart because she started being disruptive at school and always in trouble. I don't have money to throw around, even though I work hard at a job I love. I manage from month to month. Try to keep some money back for a holiday abroad; you know how things are. I'm like other kids in their teens and early twenties these days. I live for today."

"Did she get another job? Where did she work?" Phil asked.

"Carrie never hung on to any work she got. She lost lots of different jobs. Carrie was mostly waitressing. She was high all the time and wouldn't show up for work. It was after another place fired her that Dwight hit her. I don't think it was the first time or the last."

Wayne told Josie that it was inevitable that Dwight was her dealer. It was only too familiar. A drug dealer finds a vulnerable girl needing a regular fix, and that's the basis of their relationship. If she kept delivering the goods, everything would stay sweet. But, if her habit became so powerful that she became clingy or demanding, it wasn't long before the poor girl got a slap to keep her in line.

Josie was almost out of time. She kept looking at her watch.

"Even the domestic violence wasn't enough to persuade her to kick the habit, but at least she tried to escape the clutches of this cruel Dwight character. Within days of leaving him, things got worse. Carrie found a new group of friends, who introduced her to mephedrone."

Phil had encountered this Class B drug while in the police force. He knew it was cheaper than coke and gave users a better high.

"So, what happened then, Josie?" he asked.

"Carrie called me one weekend. She had been out of it for days, hardly sleeping or eating. She was in a nightclub with her new friends, and Dwight arrived. He dragged her to his car, and they drove back to his flat in Kilburn. Dwight beat her and told her not to run away again. She said he threatened to kill her. She started using heroin again, more often. I begged her to come home; I was frightened for her."

"How did she respond to that?" Phil asked.

"She laughed. Said there was nothing for her in Cheltenham anymore. The last time she messaged me, she reckoned she'd got a job in Forest Gate. She moved out of Kilburn and was in a flat with several students, desperately trying to get help for her addiction. It sounded as if, at least, she was serious about turning her life around. I haven't heard from her since. Look, I need to get moving. My lunch break is practically over. If I remember Dwight's surname, can I call you?"

Wayne had produced an HSS business card and handed it over. Josie had run for the pub door and left the car park in her Ford Ka before Phil and Wayne left the bar.

"Kilburn and Forest Gate, then boss," Wayne said as they sat in the car for a while before heading back to Bath. "Twenty miles isn't much distance between you and someone who threatened to kill you, though."

"At least we have names and places we can follow up on now," Phil said. "We'll take a trip up to London tomorrow and see what we can find."

Chapter Four

The next day proved to be the first of several trips. Nathan Ditchburn hit the nail on the head; finding a missing person in the capital was like looking for a needle in a haystack. Hundreds of flats containing students in Forest Gate might have housed her, and hundreds of food outlets might have employed Carrie as a waitress.

As they returned from their first visit, Phil pointed out to Wayne that the photograph they picked up from the girl's mother was worse than useless. It was four years out of date, and her appearance would have altered dramatically, even if the effects of constant drug use hadn't ravaged it.

Wayne questioned whether they could even guarantee she was still calling herself Carrie. However, if Dwight were serious about following up on his threat, then a name change and putting distance between them would be a sensible precaution.

"We'll keep trying, Wayne," Phil has said, "at least we're in the right district. We'll find a student, or a café owner, who recognises her description in the end. I'll check up on the local support services, charities and drop-in centres. Maybe Carrie was serious about getting clean. She could be in rehab, and that's why we can't find her. We'll come back tomorrow, and after we've looked in those places, I reckon we should drive across the city to Kilburn. Find Dwight, and you can lean on him and get him to spill the beans on what he knows. Even if he hasn't seen Carrie since she ran away from him, it will cheer me up to see him take a dose of his own medicine."

"It will be my pleasure, boss," Wayne said.

The next day followed a familiar routine. They knocked on doors; visited cafes and fast-food establishments. Nobody professed to be living with or employing a twenty-year-old girl from the West Country. None of the drug support services had ever heard of Carrie Anything. By mid-afternoon, Phil and Wayne transferred to Kilburn.

Wayne went for a wander alone. He visited a few cafes and bars, looking for likely customers of a toe rag like Dwight. It took him thirty minutes. When he returned to the car, he told Phil he had a conversation with an ex-copper in a pub. Wayne told him Dwight Thacker would be in a bar on the High Road in the afternoons.

"Thacker? That's the unusual surname Josie couldn't recall. It has to be our guy," Phil said.

"I got the background on our man, Dwight, too," Wayne continued, "this guy was at the front desk over in Harlesden for years. He's known Dwight since he was a teenager. He's a former gang member. We're looking for a pale-skinned black man of twenty-eight, with a goatee beard, dressed in designer clothes. By fifteen, he had been arrested several times for street muggings. By sixteen, he earned up to two hundred pounds daily as a drug runner. He travelled across London by tube and taxi, and at eighteen, he was firmly established as a street dealer. He moved away from the capital in his early twenties to avoid having his collar felt when the police closed in. This bloke heard reports of Dwight earning up to two grand a day selling crack cocaine and heroin in small towns across Essex for the next few years. Somehow, he always evaded the police. They could never pin anything on him. Finally, around eighteen months ago, he slunk back to Kilburn and was dealing again on his old patch."

"So, he moved back to Kilburn. One of his newer customers was Carrie Ditchburn," said Phil. "This could be where we discover where she lived and worked before trying to escape Dwight's clutches. I wonder why he returned to Kilburn? It sounds as if he made better money in the provinces."

"He wasted the money he earned on the classic gangster lifestyle; lots of bling, fast cars, and expensive clothes. He visited several nightclubs weekly, spending a small fortune on champagne. Dwight never took the highly addictive drugs he sold. He smoked weed but nothing else. I guess the money ran out, and he returned to where he started. Scraping a living on losers like Carrie, dying for a fix, who slept with him, to keep getting supplied with the buzz they craved."

Phil and Wayne found the bar. But there was no Dwight.

"We can come back tomorrow, boss?"

"Yeah, let's find a place to have a coffee, maybe grab a bite to eat. Then we'll get off home."

The Irish café owner had kissed the Blarney Stone. Bridie Carragher never stopped talking from the moment when Wayne opened the door to 'The Wishing Well' and stepped across the threshold. Phil had a sneaking suspicion she fancied Wayne. The toasted tea-cake his colleague got with his mug of coffee was half as big again as the measly offering he received. She couldn't walk past their table without placing an arm around Wayne's broad shoulders and asking if he needed anything else. When she collected their empty plates, Wayne was wiping the butter off his chin with a serviette. Bridie leant over, her top falling open, offering Wayne a close-up of her ample bosom.

"Ooh, you've made a mess," she gushed, "what will we do with you?"

Phil decided Wayne was unlikely to answer for a while. His eyes fixated on the Mountains of Mourne. Phil pulled Carrie's photo out of his jacket pocket and nudged the lady proprietor.

"Have you ever seen this young girl around here, by any chance?" he asked.

"What's it to you?" Bridie replied and turned back to check Wayne's chin.

"You would be doing me a big favour if you had seen her," Wayne said, recovering his composure.

"That's young Carrie if I'm not mistaken, but she's thinner these days. She worked here for a while. Well, 'worked' is a generous description of what she did for me. I started her on, against my better judgement, after they fired her from the pizza place next door. She messed me around, borrowed money against her wages, and then, one day, she left me without a word. She mixed with some dodgy people; they were into everything. I hope she's not your daughter, darling. A nice girl turned rotten, I'm afraid."

"No, she's not family," Wayne said, "we're tracing her for her parents. They're desperate to find her. You don't know where she is these days, by any chance?"

"I might still have a mobile number for her, my love, but

I can't hunt for it now; it's coming to my busy time. Drop by tomorrow. I'll have something tasty to offer you. What do you say?"

Phil decided it was time to drag Wayne away towards the relative safety of their car. As the cafe owner hovered by the door with her arm stretched out towards Wayne's shoulder, Phil promised her they would both be back tomorrow.

"Just wait until you taste my Guinness cake, darling," she had cried as Phil whisked Wayne away from her clutches.

"Bloody hell, boss," Wayne complained, "she was full-on, wasn't she?"

"You weren't evening wearing the uniform, Wayne. Maybe, it's your body that's been attracting the women?"

"I'm comfortably covered; that's true, boss. Some women prefer that. If we can forget about her for the moment, be thankful we found someone who knew Carrie and might even put us in touch with her."

"It was a result, that's for sure," Phil said. They drove home to Bath in a far better mood than on previous evenings.

The good mood didn't last.

After she closed 'The Wishing Well' for the night, Bridie climbed the stairs to her flat over the café. A strong coffee, with a shot of Jameson's, was required. As she waited for the kettle to boil, she sorted out food for the cats. Then she wandered into her living room and turned on the TV. She wouldn't watch much of it. When faced with several hours alone before falling into bed dog-tired after yet another fourteen-hour day, it's good to hear another human voice. The TV was a comforting background to her lonely drinking.

Bridie nursed the mug of coffee and Irish whiskey as she

made her way over to her sofa. Her thoughts returned to that customer she had served this afternoon. He was something to get her excited. Bridie sat and let the drink warm her. The fantasies she allowed would have gotten her into terrible trouble with the nuns at the convent school back home. But, there was something she promised to do for them; what had it been? Ah, yes, a phone number for Miss Carrie Redgrove.

Bridie wasn't a fan of housekeeping or office administration. At least, not upstairs in her domain; enough of that was needed downstairs in the café, with the red tape and health and safety legislation. How a simple girl from Galway was supposed to keep her head above water was a mystery. She searched through the piles of paper on the table by the sofa. As was her routine, she finished her strong coffee and topped up the mug with more Jameson's and a dash of water for appearance's sake. Finally, she found what she wanted.

Bridie fished her mobile phone out of her apron pocket, entered Carrie's contact number, and rang. It went straight to voicemail. As she waited for the message prompt to finish, Bridie thought she should change her clothes when she came upstairs from the café. How long ago had it been when she decided she couldn't be bothered? The beep sounded.

"Hello, Carrie? It's Bridie here, from the café. Someone came in today looking for you, sweetheart. Your family are after getting in touch with you. Give me a ring back when you're free."

Bridie Carragher felt she had done her duty. The adverts were finishing; a programme she could stand watching was starting. One of Bridie's cats jumped onto the sofa to sit on her lap while she relayed her message. Another hour and she could get off to bed and dream of a man with shoulders as broad as the Shannon.

The message Bridie left was read at the same time she laid her head on her pillow. Unfortunately, it got deleted while her head still came to terms with her final Jameson nightcap. Dwight Thacker had confiscated the phone two weeks earlier when he tracked down his lady, Carrie.

The stupid bitch thought she could walk away. Dwight had too many contacts on the streets of London for that to happen. She'd told anyone who listened; she lived in a flat with students in Forest Gate. That was crap; Carrie'd gone to a woman's refuge to hide away and get clean. Finally, someone rang him with information on where she was in a day or two. He let her think Carrie was free of him. Then after he learned she was working in the kitchens of a hotel, he waited for her to finish work one night and grabbed her.

Once they returned to his flat, he reminded her how much she owed him. He listed all the free fixes she'd had. She cried and begged just as she always did. This time, she begged Dwight to let her go; instead of asking for another 'hit'. Dwight gave her a few slaps to bring her in line.

Dwight told Carrie to forget the hotel and the refuge. That was never going to happen. He needed her to work for him, to pay off what she owed. He'd taken her to bed then and reminded her that the only thing she was useful for was opening her legs and giving him what he wanted. He turned her out on the streets the following day. In addition to being her dealer, Dwight Thacker was now her pimp.

Just after midnight, Carrie returned to the flat. Dwight took the money she had earned and handed over a wrap.

"Sweet dreams," he said with a lecherous grin.

With hopes of an end to their missing person hunt on the horizon, Phil and Wayne drove up the M4 the following day, full of optimism. Wayne wore a clean shirt, Phil remembered. Although he was sure his colleague was nervous, he stood more chance with the Irish colleen than with the singers and dancers on the Honey B UK tour. They had been way out of Wayne's league.

Phil decided it would be best to visit 'The Wishing Well' before the lunchtime rush. Although that meant Wayne would miss out on the large slice of alcoholic cake Bridie served in the afternoons, this gave them a few more hours in Forest Gate, where they could search for Carrie Ditchburn.

It took as long to find a parking space as it did to negotiate the M25. Bridie looked up from the till as the café door opened.

"My word, the boys are back in town," she sang.

"Any luck finding that number?" asked Wayne.

"I did," said Bridie, omitting to tell him she had called her former employee last night. "I've got it right here for you. Are you not staying? Are you sure I can't tempt you?"

Wayne slipped the piece of paper Bridie handed him into his pocket.

"We need to get our business done first; then, we'll drop back in on our way home."

Phil turned away to return to the car; Wayne strolled towards the café door. Bridie ignored a table of three customers who looked keen on ordering an all-day breakfast. She was closing in on Wayne and grabbed his arm.

"Look, I may have done the wrong thing last night," she said. "I rang her, but she never answered. I left a message to say her family was searching for her. Who knows? She might have changed her phone since she was here. I might make her realise there was something good to look forward to, mentioning her family. London can be a dreadful, lonely place. If she went home, it might help sort her out. If it's not too late."

"Okay, thanks for telling us," Wayne replied. He and Phil returned to their car and drove across to Forest Gate. Bridie had told them what she knew. Josie Dymond had told them where Carrie said she was living. The following five hours were a complete waste of time. Wayne called the number Bridie supplied, but there was no reply. There was no sign of Carrie anywhere on the streets of Forest Gate.

They had driven back to Kilburn late in the afternoon. They dropped into the bar where Dwight Thacker was said to be a regular. This time they were in luck. Sure enough, there he was, suited and booted. On the surface, he looked every inch a successful businessman. Underneath lay the scum of the earth.

"How do you want to play this, boss?" asked Wayne.

"A watching brief, for now. Get our drinks and bring them to that table over there. We can keep an eye on him and the door."

Dwight sat alone. Rum and coke in a high glass on the bar in front of him. He was reading a copy of the Metro.

Wayne took a sip out of his pint of lager.

"I'll take it steady, boss, don't worry. At these prices, you'd think it was champagne."

"Let's try that mobile number again," Phil said, more in hope than expectation.

Wayne had entered Carrie's number into his mobile earlier. He dialled. On the other side of the bar, a ringtone sounded immediately. It was Marley's 'Don't Worry, Be Happy'. Dwight Thacker grabbed his mobile from the bar, cancelled the call, and slammed the phone next to his drink.

"Those PPI people. Never leave me alone these days, man. Keep getting calls from unknown numbers."

Phil looked at Wayne. That outburst explained a lot. Bridie Carragher left a message on that phone last night. It almost certainly never reached Carrie Ditchburn. Also, things had altered yet again in Carrie's circumstances. Josie Dymond's notion that her school friend escaped from Dwight and was on the long road to recovery in Forest Gate was misplaced.

"When this waste of space leaves here, we'll follow him," said Phil. "Wherever his flat is in Kilburn, that's where we'll find Carrie,"

Wayne cracked his knuckles, wishing he could walk across the room and give the arrogant thug payback for the beatings Carrie suffered. But they didn't have long to wait. Dwight soon finished reading. He drained his glass, collected his phone and headed for the door.

Phil followed him out. Wayne left the pub thirty seconds later and followed. Dwight strolled along without a care. He wasn't aware of anyone following him. Too many people on the High Road were walking in the same direction. They hadn't gone a hundred yards before Dwight walked up the steps to the front door of a Victorian terraced property. Phil passed on by and gazed in a shop window. Wayne crossed the busy street and popped into a small general store to buy an evening newspaper. He stood outside under the awning, glancing up towards the door that Dwight entered.

Dwight had been inside no more than five minutes. The door suddenly swung open. Dwight came out with a sports bag over his shoulder. He ran down the High Road as if training for the next Olympics. Wayne had to wait for a gap in the traffic to cross. Phil was at the bottom of the steps. He looked concerned.

"Something spooked him," Phil said, "that bag was heavy. I was sure he never clocked us. Let's go and have a look. According to the card by the door, it's the top-floor flat."

They climbed the stairs and found the door to the flat partly open. Phil pushed the door with his shoulder and entered; the apartment was tidier than most he visited. He walked through to the bedroom. He only saw one thing that looked out of place. Drawers lay open, and a wardrobe stood half-empty. The bathroom next door also showed little sign of a male occupant. Dwight Thacker had done a runner.

Wayne walked into the bedroom behind him, sighed and donned a pair of blue gloves.

"Carrie Ditchburn, I presume," he said, checking for a pulse. The young girl was no longer in pain. The needle that delivered her final hit was still dangling from her arm. Bruises on her naked body told their own story. Her face was unmarked. Even in death, Wayne could see she had been a pretty girl.

"OD, or an accident?" Phil asked.

"No idea. Carrie's been dead for several hours, though. We need to start phoning. Get an ambulance here and the police. Then let the authorities take over.

"Thacker will be long gone. We might as well get back to Bath after we finish here."

"I would love to taste a slice of Bridie's Guinness cake. But I don't fancy telling her Carrie died within twelve hours of her leaving that phone message. Even if Carrie never heard it. Dwight controlled her mobile like he controlled the rest of her life."

The drive back to Bath had been a miserable one. The late evening traffic, the weather, roadworks and idiot drivers conspired to make things as bleak as possible. Phil explained to the officers who arrived on the scene they had been searching for the young woman. He gave them the details, and the mobile number, of 'a person of interest', one Dwight Thacker. The officers knew him only too well.

Phil asked permission to inform the Ditchburn family of their daughter's death.

"It might be unusual, but we're both ex-coppers. We've done it a hundred times before, and we're working on their behalf. It will be better coming from us rather than you having to ring someone at Cheltenham police station who doesn't know the family from Adam."

The two officers looked at one another — anything for a quiet life.

Phil dropped Wayne off at his home and then drove to Cheltenham. Why was it that bad news always had to be delivered at such unsociable hours? He got out of the car and walked towards the front door.

He was still five paces from his destination when the door opened. Mrs Ditchburn stood in the doorway; her husband stood behind her, resting an arm on her shoulder.

"Thanks for coming," she sobbed, "we've been dreading this moment. As soon as we heard the car stop on the road ten minutes ago, we knew why you were here."

An hour later, Phil left the Ditchburn family alone to grieve. He drove home with one thing left to do tonight. Despite the lateness of the hour, he wrote up a report of the case. Not just for the HSS files but to pass a copy to Larcombe Manor.

Someone had to make sure Dwight Thacker faced up to the damage he had done over the years to vulnerable men and women he'd supplied with drugs. But, unfortunately, the law never seemed to pin anything on him; perhaps the Olympus Project would bring closure to Carrie Ditchburn's family.

Chapter Five

Tuesday, 4th March 2014

Phoenix was ready to face the day. Working through his ideas for targets last night had rekindled his enthusiasm. He couldn't wait to get back in the field after deciding on a course of action when carrying out the missions against those villains he'd selected. As he emerged from the shower, Athena stood in the bathroom doorway, holding Hope.

"I hope you slept well?" she asked.

"Sorry; I worked late on the direct actions for these drug dealers," he replied, "I hope I didn't wake you when I came to bed."

"I barely slept," said Athena, "Hope kept stirring and was irritable. I think she's developing a cough. You slept through everything."

"Ah."

"Exactly," she said, "you can take her for an hour. I can catch up on a few things. Maria Elena will collect her at nine o'clock."

"I'll see you at the meeting?"

"If I don't fall asleep and miss it altogether? Yes, you will."

Phoenix took his daughter from her mother's arms and beat a hasty retreat. It was a frosty morning at Larcombe Manor, despite Spring being imminent. Hope didn't appear to mind. Whatever had upset her overnight was forgotten. She was happy to be with her father for quality time.

Cradling Hope on his shoulder, Phoenix rang Rusty. As he talked through the options with his best friend, he continually pirouetted around the room, trying to keep the phone away from Hope's chubby little hands. She had a penchant for shiny things. Maria Elena had soon learned not to wear a necklace; Hope would grab at the chain and almost strangle the poor girl or break it.

"Okay, Phoenix," said Rusty. "It sounds as if you've got your hands full, mate. I'll see you at nine."

Phoenix passed responsibility for the precious bundle over to the nanny just before leaving the apartments for the morning meeting. Hope was drifting off to sleep after a feed. A lullaby had accompanied her first meal of the day. Phoenix had always enjoyed 'Enter The Sandman', and there weren't many traditional songs for which he knew the lyrics. When Athena wasn't around, he couldn't see the harm in his daughter learning the magic of metal.

When he reached the meeting room, he discovered everyone else waiting. Athena looked up, gave him a smile that told him she forgave him, and then threw his best-laid plans into turmoil.

"I'm sure we remember Orion, the former policeman who paid us a visit last year?" she began.

Phoenix remembered Phil Hounsell only too well; they had gone swimming together.

Artemis recalled a steamy night in Bristol before she met Rusty Scott.

Henry Case was the first to speak.

"Thought my warning would have been enough. What has Hounsell poked his nose into this time?"

"Quite the opposite," said Athena. "He has been searching for missing persons of late. Something less dangerous than working hand-in-glove with a menace like the Titans. There was a tragic ending to their latest search. A twenty-year-old girl from Gloucestershire died from an overdose in London last night. Her dealer boyfriend discovered the body but fled the scene and is still at large. Orion passed the details of the case onto us. He thought it was something we might enjoy. Her death is a typical outcome for the teenagers we discussed yesterday morning; an early introduction to soft drugs, followed by a descent into a hell that too often ends in early death. This girl made several attempts to break free of this so-called boyfriend, but he kept dragging her back into the cess-pit in which he operates. I propose we promote this Dwight Thacker to the top of your list, Phoenix."

Athena handed a copy of the case notes to her partner.

"If you're comfortable carrying out this ex- copper's wishes, so be it," said Phoenix. "I'm not saying this guy doesn't deserve punishment. He does, but it sets a potentially dangerous precedent. Unless we dispose of this Thacker character, without anyone ever discovering the body, there will be at least one person outside Olympus who knows what we have done. He will have proof we operate outside of the law. That could bring the authorities down on us."

"My interpretation of this report is that former DCI Phil Hounsell has 'old-school' views on justice," said

Athena. "Perhaps those opinions hurried his departure from the force?"

"We debated this when we worked together, Athena," said Artemis, blushing. "Phil Hounsell believed the world a better place without the criminals killed by vigilante killers. With the failings of the police and the legal system growing annually, he felt they were doing society a big favour. I argued we had to work with the system we had. I couldn't accept having vigilantes dispensing their form of rough justice."

"Are you sure you're in the right job?" asked Rusty with a wry smile.

"Events following those debates made me change my mind," said Artemis.

Phoenix kept quiet; he didn't want to add fuel to the flame.

Giles Burke offered a solution.

"To allay the fears expressed by Phoenix, maybe Hounsell might be affiliated with Olympus somehow? He holds the title of Orion, the hunter. Although that came from Demeter, it does describe his potential worth to the Project."

"Who would be his handler?" asked Henry Case.

"Allowing Orion free access to Larcombe Manor would cause problems for several of us who live here," Athena said. "My vote would be for Hayden Vincent to be his point of contact. That can be established immediately, on the outside, and can then continue after Hayden and Kelly Dexter arrive on-site to reinforce our training team."

Even Phoenix had to admit it was the perfect option. Artemis also breathed a sigh of relief. The risks of her coming face to face with her former boss had drastically diminished.

"I'll brief Hayden on what we need from Orion going

forward," Athena continued. "We will accept genuine intelligence on criminals he identifies during operations his company HSS carries out. We will act where appropriate. Olympus will reimburse any expenses incurred by HSS in such cases. I think that covers things adequately. Phoenix, I apologise for the need to readjust your timetable to accommodate Dwight Thacker. Will you still be ready to present your report by next Monday's meeting?"

"I'm ready to take Rusty through everything now. We're getting together after the meeting to put the finishing touches to my plans. If this villain has gone to ground, then the police might be hard-pressed to find him. They haven't been that successful in the past. Thacker may have left London and headed for the provinces. According to this report, that was where he did his business for several years. We'll need Giles and his crew in the ice-house to start a search for him."

"Artemis and I will get on it as soon as we return there after the meeting," said Giles. "The case notes say the flat was on Kilburn High Road, so we can soon find him on CCTV. A man in a smart suit, running with a sports bag across his shoulder, should stand out from the crowds."

"After that, we need to narrow down where he might have run to," added Artemis, "we welcome any help to find him. London's a big place; plenty of places to hide."

"Not from you and Giles," said Rusty.

Athena switched back to the next item on the agenda. Time was of the essence. An hour later, the meeting had ended. Rusty and Phoenix left for the orangery to analyse and update the plans Phoenix had worked late into the night to prepare. Henry, Giles, and Artemis returned underground to resume their intelligence-gathering duties.

Athena went upstairs to the apartment and phoned her

parents. The weekend and their trip west to see their granddaughter were just around the corner. Athena was as anxious as Phoenix about the arrangements and what lay ahead. Geoffrey and Grace Fox arrived at Bath Spa station at lunchtime on Saturday. An Olympus driver from the transport section would then ferry them here to Larcombe Manor.

In the orangery, Phoenix and Rusty evaluated their plans.

"We'll start with these two," said Phoenix, laying an array of images on the table for Rusty to inspect. "Then, when Giles and his team deliver the goods on this rat Thacker, we'll work out how to fit him into our schedule."

"So, in Tower Hamlets," said Rusty, selecting a photograph from the gallery, "we have a dial-a-drug gang. They appear to take more than a thousand orders daily from desperate customers. This operation is slicker than most; it delivers Class A drugs to hundreds of people across east London daily?"

"Yes," replied Phoenix. "Orders for crack cocaine and heroin are advertised on a twenty-four-hour number across the borough. Customers can either phone or text to pay to have drugs delivered to their door. Waqar Ali, twenty-six, the ringleader, set up the phone line, and it's he who takes the orders. He has half a dozen runners who distribute the drugs for him. Ali has been in trouble with the law. Six years ago, he was found guilty of possessing firearms and ammunition to endanger lives. He's a nasty piece of work."

"What about this evil-looking thug?" asked Rusty looking at the next target. "I hope he's good to his mother?"

"Well, he never goes home, so that's in his favour, I guess," said Phoenix.

"Where does he operate?" asked Rusty.

"In Hackney," Phoenix replied. "Not too far away from Waqar Ali. It makes life easier for us if we don't have to travel too far between jobs. Remember the landlord's mission last year? This one might let us use the Chiswick safe-house again as our base. Gavin McTierney, whose photograph you're admiring, is thirty-four. He runs a gang that has terrorised the borough for several years. Last June, McTierney went to a flat armed with a knife. A row ensued over money owed for drugs he had supplied to the occupants. McTierney found Isaac Bartholomew, thirty-one, in the flat alone. He stabbed him in the chest three times; Bartholomew bled to death. His flatmate, Steven Blake, twenty-eight, returned to the flat to discover the body. As Blake walked home from the local pub two weeks later, after the wake that followed his friend's funeral, he died in a traffic incident. Rumour has it that McTierney drove a Transit van onto the pavement and deliberately ran over Blake. This thug strikes fear across the borough; nobody will give evidence against him. The police recorded the incident as a tragic accident."

"Did you have any more thoughts of taking a trip up to East London?" asked Rusty. "Just to scout out the area beforehand."

"These two will be easy to find on their respective turf. Thacker may be less visible, given the events of the last twenty-four hours," Phoenix sat back in his chair and thought for a moment.

"I suppose we could stay in Chiswick," offered Rusty. "Pay a visit to Ali and McTierney, and then rest up before bringing Thacker back to Larcombe from wherever he's hiding."

"I can't see an issue with that, mate," nodded Phoenix, "we can't risk leaving a body on that part of the job. As for the other two gang leaders, the more public their deaths, the better. That works on several levels. It removes the heads of two prolific gangs and shows crime doesn't pay. It sows seeds of doubt in the minds of their crew that a rival gang is muscling in on their patch. That could cause them to take their eye off the ball. It should allow the authorities to mop up the soldiers once the generals have gone."

"In an ideal world, it would mean fewer drugs on the streets," grumbled Rusty, "but another outfit will move in to fill the gap soon enough."

"That's life, mate," said Phoenix, "let's think how we'll do this when we get down to business. Then I suggest we call Giles to see what progress they're making. If they've got anything, I'd prefer to get up to Chiswick as soon as possible."

"You're a crafty sod," laughed Rusty. "You're looking for an excuse to be away on the weekend when your future in-laws are staying here."

Phoenix shrugged his shoulders and passed no comment. He outlined his plan of action. In the ice-house, Artemis checked more CCTV footage. Giles and Henry had soon found Dwight Thacker running for his life on the pavements of Kilburn High Road. He had darted into the tube station, so they had lost him for the moment.

"I think I've found him at Marble Arch," said Artemis.

"He's heading towards Stratford and moving further east," said Henry. He looked at the image Artemis had isolated on the screen in front of her.

"That's our man. Well done."

"My bet is he's going to ground in his old patch," said Giles, "we'll look for him at Stratford. The surface rail link will take him towards Ilford; perhaps he's going back to

Romford or Brentwood. According to Minos's data, those were towns he had dealt in over the years."

Step by step, they hunted their prey. Dwight Thacker arrived in Brentwood a few minutes after half-past six on Monday evening. Despite its historical pedigree and a population of seventy thousand spread across the borough, Brentwood does not have a station in its town centre because it's on a hill. The train station lies to the south of the town; that was where Artemis had picked him out, among a stream of commuters walking towards the town.

The last place he showed up on camera was in the town centre, near the ancient monument of the St Thomas a Becket Chapel. Brentwood, or "Burnt wood", was a resting place for pilgrims on their way to Canterbury, travelling the Roman road from Colchester to London. So far, she could find no evidence of him having left the town. The search for Dwight Thacker would continue with the CCTV history from this morning.

"I'm in for a late finish again," she groaned.

"Don't worry, I'll stay and help you out," offered Giles.

"Thought you might be off to the pool later?" asked Artemis.

Her immediate superior blushed. Artemis knew Giles was swimming more frequently these days. It had nothing to do with wanting to keep fit or rebuilding muscle weakened by his emergency appendix operation last year. The nanny from Estepona was the main attraction in the pool these days. Giles was a keen swimmer. Henry didn't swim. That was an advantage Giles Burke wasn't going to miss.

"If you're sure you can manage?" Giles said. "I might go for a swim, thank you."

Artemis watched him as he cleared away folders he'd been working on and tidied his desk before finishing work for the day. He tried to appear calm but was all fingers and thumbs.

"More haste, less speed, Giles," said Artemis, with a smile, still looking at her computer screen, "someone has got it bad. Good hunting."

"You too, Artemis," Giles called out as he hurried through the doors to the lift. "I'll see you in the morning."

Alone in the control section, Artemis paused to consider her options. She leafed through her copy of the HSS report Phil Hounsell had provided. Dwight Thacker had lived and worked in Essex until eighteen months ago and used the budget bed-and-breakfast places in dozens of the county's towns. His runners might have been 'cuckooing' in the local crack den, but Dwight was the head man, not slumming it with the lowlifes.

The last confirmed sight of her target had been in the town centre. CCTV coverage in Brentwood was more than adequate, which was a bonus. Artemis flicked from one captured feed to another, moving further out from the centre, as far as the cameras covered. It was a painstaking, time-consuming task. After a long shift underground, she knew she was prone to miss something if she didn't take a break soon.

The time on the screen showed 11:15 pm. A tall figure passed under a street lamp, looked right, and crossed the street. Artemis checked her detailed street map. Someone had just left the Swan pub heading up Kings Road towards Rose Valley. That was where one of the B&Bs had been on Thacker's list of frequent stops.

The grainy image was typical of many she'd studied over the years. Of course, the street lamp didn't do her any favours either, but the clothes, the gait, everything pointed to it being their man.

"Gotcha," she exclaimed.

Artemis looked at the clock on the wall of the control room. That read 11:15 pm, too — time to call it a night. Rusty would be asleep by the time she got back to their apartment. This news would have to wait until the morning meeting. As she walked back towards the main building, she wondered how Giles had fared. There were no lights on in the stable block. The agents and crew members were sleeping. There was still a chill in the air, and she hurried her steps to get inside into the warm.

In a guest house in Rose Valley, Brentwood, Dwight Thacker was dozing. The gun under his pillow reassured him. His conscience didn't trouble him; it never had. Carrie had been a stupid cow. The women he supplied with drugs were foolish and weak. Same as the blokes. Carrie had been one of many women Dwight had used over the years; none of them meant anything to him. Tonight, in the pub, he had seen a few fresh-looking girls. They had clocked him, too; his sharp suit, jewellery and Rolex watch made him stand out from the other muppets in town. It was only a matter of time before he found a new girl. In minutes, Dwight was fast asleep. He had always been an arrogant young man. He believed nothing or no one could touch him.

Wednesday, 5th March 2014

In Brentwood, Dwight Thacker sat at the breakfast table, scanning the morning newspaper headlines. He was searching for news from Kilburn. Were the police writing off Carrie's death as another drug statistic, or did they want to talk to him to discover what had happened? Page after page turned, but there was nothing on her demise.

Dwight breathed a sigh of relief. The law wasn't interested then; the media wasn't desperate for a news story either. Give it a few weeks, and he might return to the flat and carry on working in the capital.

In the mad panic to flee the scene on Monday evening, he'd crammed a few clothes and toiletries into a bag. He threw them in on top of the gun, ammunition, and the spare cash and drugs he had hidden under the floorboards.

If the police had been keen to talk to him, the flat would have been a write-off; he could never have returned. But, if luck stayed with him, he could get access to the rest of his clothes, his CD collection, and his sound system. His neighbours might be pleased not to hear his reggae music thumping through their walls every night, but he was missing it.

Dwight finished his meal, drank the last of his coffee, and passed the newspaper to a middle-aged sales rep at the next table. He headed upstairs. It was time to make a few deals. When he reached his room, he checked his various phones. He had several pay-as-you-go mobiles; one needed a charge. Dwight realised he still had Carrie's old phone in his jacket pocket. He removed the SIM card and hammered it several times with the butt of his revolver, then bent it in half and eventually broke it. He decided to ditch the card and the phone in separate waste bins while he was out in town later.

Dwight checked his watch. It was a quarter to nine. He needed to find somewhere quiet to wait up, away from prying eyes. Dwight had dozens of local contact numbers on his phone. Those young professionals with plenty of cash to spend would be commuting or at work. He could ring them in the evenings when they were in the market for buying drugs. His lower-end clientele tended not to be early risers. If they were heavily addicted, unemployed, grafting or stealing to feed their habit, they wouldn't surface until closer to lunchtime.

He should make a brisk trade; they would be desperate for a fix. He was in a good mood. He was going to make a few special offers. If his luck did take a turn for the worse, ready cash was what he needed. The sooner he converted the gear he held into folding money, the better. Dwight headed for the library. That was always good for a few hours.

At Larcombe Manor, Athena and Phoenix had left their rooms for the meeting.

"I imagine you and Rusty will be back in the orangery later?" she asked.

"That depends on news from the ice-house," replied Phoenix. "If they've identified Thacker's whereabouts, then Rusty and I should get off to London as soon as possible. Our targets in Hackney and Tower Hamlets must be studied at close quarters before we strike. If Thacker is nearby, we can kill three birds with one stone. We intend to use the Chiswick safe-house as our base, as we did last year."

"How much time do you need to carry out the 'recce' on the two gang leaders you've selected?" asked Athena. "Will you have completed the missions by the weekend?"

"Difficult to say," said Phoenix as they reached the meeting room. He opened the door and stood back to let Athena pass.

Athena looked at him closely, trying to gauge whether he was teasing her. Phoenix knew damn well her parents were arriving on Saturday. It would be typical of him to avoid being available.

Athena reminded herself that Olympus' business had to come first. The others were present and ready to get things underway.

"Good morning, everyone. What do we have to report from the ice-house?"

Artemis had briefed Giles and Henry when their duties had begun underground at eight o'clock. She was happy to deliver the good news.

"We traced Dwight Thacker to a bed-and-breakfast in Rose Valley, Brentwood. It was one of his more popular haunts when he spent time away from the capital. We are closely monitoring the CCTV activity in the vicinity. He was sighted on New Road five minutes ago, heading for the library."

"Didn't have him pegged as a literary buff," said Rusty.

"It will be somewhere warm to pass the time," said Phoenix, "keep tabs on him, Artemis; follow him as much as you can via the cameras. Report back to me immediately if he's off to somewhere new."

"How does that affect your plans for later?" asked Athena, dreading the answer.

"Rusty and I will drive up to London this afternoon. We'll start tracking Waqar Ali and Gavin McTierney first thing tomorrow morning."

"These are the two gang leaders you cherry-picked from the ones I reported on, I presume?" asked Minos.

"Just two of many rotten apples, Minos, but it's a start," Phoenix replied. "We plan to find them, follow them to establish their routines, and decide on the exit strategy. If we are confident Dwight Thacker is settling in for a lengthy stay in Essex, we can leave him alone for a while. We can then tackle our targets in London and collect Thacker later, deliver him here so that Henry can accommodate him temporarily in Hotel California. We cannot afford to leave his body lying around in Brentwood or anywhere else, so we need a solution where his disappearance leaves no trace."

"My pleasure, Phoenix," said Henry Case. "I'll think of something apt."

They dealt with the other agenda items in good time. The meeting closed, and Phoenix was ready to leave for the orangery with Rusty.

Athena grabbed his arm.

"Not so fast," she said, "don't you dare leave for London without coming to see me first."

"I haven't booked the transport yet," replied Phoenix, "so no need to panic. We need to visit Bazza and Thommo for supplies too. I want to leave by three o'clock at the latest. It will be dark by the time we get settled in the safe-house; that will help us cruise around our targets' familiar haunts without raising suspicion this evening. The serious stuff starts tomorrow. If Brentwood can stay on the back-burner, we can strike on Thursday or Friday."

"What about Dwight Thacker? What if he was only staying overnight in Brentwood?" asked Athena.

"I guess he'll stay for a while, but if he shows signs of moving, we'll have to rely on the ice-house to trail him. Rusty and I will stop what we're doing at a convenient point, shoot off to Essex, and bring him here before he disappears. The other two have no cause to change their plans. They are too involved in their murky business, and we're too good at our jobs for them to notice anyone is watching them. Dwight altering our schedule will only delay the timing of the strike until Friday or Saturday."

"Mummy and Daddy will be here at lunchtime on Saturday; I need you here with Hope and me."

"I know, Athena," said Phoenix, "but as you keep telling us, Olympus matters take priority. We'll get back as soon as we can. Why risk our chances of a successful mission by cutting corners to get back to meet Geoffrey and Grace? I'm sure they'll understand. You'll have to be imaginative with your cover story."

"You're a swine, Phoenix," grumbled Athena.

"I know," he replied, giving her a squeeze and a kiss, "but that's what attracted you to me in the first place. Right, I'm off to the orangery to catch up with Rusty. After we've finished, we'll head underground to pick up the things we need. I'll see you in a few hours. With luck, I can spend time with you and Hope before we leave for Chiswick."

With that, Phoenix left. Athena carried on with her Olympus duties. Maria Elena tended to Hope. In the ice-house, the surveillance of Dwight Thacker, Waqar Ali, Gavin McTierney and hundreds of other known criminals continued. In Tower Hamlets, Hackney and Brentwood, the prime targets, went about their business without a care in the world.

Phoenix and Rusty were putting the finishing touches to their plans in the orangery, schemes that would disrupt those carefree lives for good.

"I reckon we're ready, Rusty, don't you?" said Phoenix.

"I agree," replied Rusty. "Let's get below to see the lads in the armoury."

"Our transport will be available at half-past two," said Phoenix. "They needed an hour to make the necessary adjustments we specified. OK, let's visit Bazza and Thommo."

The two agents left the orangery and headed to the ice-house. After a swift descent in the lift, they were in the corridor outside the armoury. There was the usual sound of laughter. The two ex-SAS men loved their work. Phoenix knew they would have to stand a few minutes' banter before getting the kit they requested and returning to the surface.

Phoenix and Rusty entered.

"Here they are then," cried Thommo, "the glory boys. Off to the big city to strike another blow for justice."

"You put us through our paces here, Phoenix," said Bazza. "You keep coming up with strange requests for equipment that nobody else requisitions. When will you run out of ideas?"

"If I keep leaving hints, it's the same hand carrying out these direct actions. Sooner or later, an intelligent copper will put two and two together. Variety is the spice of life."

"Of death, you mean," said Thommo, which set both he and Bazza into peals of laughter.

"Do you watch much TV, Rusty?" asked Bazza. "We were watching a talk show last night, weren't we, Thommo?"

"Yes, mate, they had that former snooker professional Bob Smee last night," said Thommo.

"Excuse me?" Bazza asked, looking at the two agents, with a grin.

"That's the chap," Thommo had tears running down his cheeks.

Phoenix and Rusty were unmoved on the other side of the armoury counter. Then the light dawned. Rusty groaned.

"Very funny," he growled, "can we concentrate on business, lads? We need to be in Chiswick before it gets dark."

"Two big boys like you, afraid of the dark? Do you need us to come and hold your hand?" asked Bazza.

"I do think you need to get out more," said Phoenix, "spending so long below ground without any action is taking its toll."

Minutes later, the kit they needed was in the lift, and they were on the way to the surface. Bazza and Thommo had got their serious heads back. As usual, they hadn't uttered those last few words in jest. They wished them a successful mission and to come home safe.

On the surface, Rusty noticed a car leaving the transport section garage. He whistled.

"Top of the range, a luxury item for this trip then, Phoenix?"

"We're taking two vehicles, Rusty. You can drive the Mercedes; I'll follow you in the more nondescript family saloon."

True enough, a second car soon parked alongside the Merc. It was a bog-standard model which wouldn't attract much attention when they were cruising the streets of the London boroughs tracking their targets. The Merc was for use on one of the direct actions.

"Let's get the cars loaded; then I'll get back to the main building. I promised Athena I would spend time with her before we left. Sorry, mate, I guess Artemis will be on shift until later?"

Rusty nodded. "Yeah, I'll call her tonight from Chiswick. I'll meet you back here at three o'clock, okay?"

Phoenix walked back to the apartments he shared with Athena and Hope. Mother and daughter were playing on the floor of the lounge. Maria Elena was in the kitchen, washing up a few items.

"Hola, Senor Phoenix," she called, "you want something to eat, yes?"

"No thanks, Maria Elena," said Phoenix, "I ate earlier."

Athena tutted.

"Something that's not good for you, no doubt."

Phoenix ignored the comment and sat on the floor beside Hope.

"Mummy's getting on at Daddy again, Hope," he said quietly. His daughter beamed at him.

"It's ten to three," said Athena, "we don't have much time together."

"Sorry," replied Phoenix, "I can't help that, I'm afraid. But if we get these missions over and done by the end of the weekend, you can have a word with the criminal underworld. See if they'll take a break for a month or two; to give us a breather."

Athena could tell he was gently chiding her; they both knew the pressures Olympus was under daily. The time to rest would be when their job finally finished. Sadly, the chances of that happening were slim to none. The fight continued; it was never-ending.

"I love you," said Athena, "don't forget that. Good luck and take care."

The three family members shared a hug for the last few minutes they had together. Whether Hope realised its significance was doubtful. Phoenix and Athena did, and that was what mattered.

Rusty was in the driver's seat of the Mercedes when Phoenix returned at three. The small convoy made its way along the winding driveway, through the gates to the estate, and headed towards Bath. After threading through the afternoon traffic, they arrived at the safe house just over two hours later.

"Let's unload the kit first," said Phoenix. "It's dusk, so we shouldn't get any nosy neighbours getting a shock at seeing what's going indoors. Once we've checked out how the previous occupants left the place, we'll use my car to fetch supplies. Enough to cover us for the next forty-eight to seventy-two hours."

Rusty nodded. They emptied the cars in quick order, and inside they found that whichever agents had been in residence until recently had left several essential items.

"That's an improvement," said Rusty, "we don't need that much. We're good to go with a few odds and ends and a takeaway."

"The shops will be open for a while yet," said Phoenix, "let's have a coffee and a slice of toast for now. Those bacon rolls you ordered again today will keep me going for a few hours. Then, we can pick up a takeaway on the way back from our first recce."

Twenty minutes later, the family saloon was in traffic on the road to Hackney.

"Ah, the joys of driving in London in the early evening," moaned Phoenix.

"Top speed of ten miles an hour, mate," said Rusty, "it's quicker to walk."

They crawled past Shepherd's Bush, thankful that neither Bazza nor Thommo was in the back of the car. They slid quietly past Mayfair, with its sense of classic England; Old Victorian houses on tree-lined streets. Thirty minutes later, they were in a different world.

Hackney is a desolate sprawl of miserable council estates and tower blocks. On this Wednesday evening, the two Olympus agents spotted gangs of youths in hoodies roaming the streets; they disappeared into the narrow alleyways that criss-cross the borough. The average age of the gangs was around thirteen. Older, hooded drug dealers hung around the street corners, openly selling crack and heroin.

"That shit tip to our left is the Trelawney, isn't it?" asked Rusty. "I don't think that overstates its reputation."

They continued to cruise around the borough, following a designated pattern. It might have appeared aimless, but Phoenix had factored in a drive-by of every known hangout that Gavin McTierney might visit. As the night turned darker, sirens wailed in the nearby streets, and the signature throbbing sound of a police helicopter could just be heard somewhere above them.

"There's our man," said Phoenix.

A brand-new people carrier with blacked-out windows had pulled out into the line of traffic ahead of them. Its occupants had just left a popular nightclub. The club wouldn't be opening its doors for a few hours. This visit was a regular one. Gavin McTierney liked to put in a personal appearance when his thugs collected protection money from one of his best-paying customers. He never handled the cash himself, of course, but it was necessary to remind people with whom they were dealing.

"Where are we off to next?" asked Rusty.

"A couple of pubs and restaurants on his agenda tonight," said Phoenix, slowing at a pedestrian crossing to allow a line of teenage girls to totter across the street. "McTierney will eat at the last one on the list. Then, once we've confirmed his routine, we'll head to Tower Hamlets. That won't take long. Fifteen minutes, at a guess."

They continued their recce, unnoticed and unchallenged. Everything followed the steps the intelligence section itemised in background checks on McTierney and his gang.

Phoenix left the gang leader in the steak house to enjoy his free meal and drinks. He drove on towards their next target. It was time to find Waqar Ali.

"We're dealing with a gregarious young man," said Phoenix. "Who doesn't touch the drugs he peddles, even if he occasionally drinks alcohol? Yet we're more likely to find him in one of the sixty-odd pubs and bars in the borough than anywhere else. Waqar likes to get out at night and meet people. He spends so much time indoors, or in his BMW, taking phone orders from clients, that he needs to have time in the real world."

"Does he favour anywhere in particular?" asked Rusty, worried they could be in for a long night. He was eager to get back to Chiswick and that takeaway.

"We'll cruise along Brick Lane for now, then wrap it up for tonight if we don't find him. The data we have on McTierney suggests he's a creature of habit. We can find him later in the day tomorrow while we locate Waqar Ali first thing in the morning. He'll not move far from his home for a few hours. This twenty-four-hour dial-up drug service needs him to be hands-on most of the day."

"I could always ring him. Place an order," said Rusty, tongue in cheek.

"I want to pick him up away from his home. The details Minos provided indicate he's got the family around him. There was an arranged marriage at nineteen, just before he got into trouble with the law. So, now he's got a young wife and two kids. It is not a happy marriage. They live with her parents and grandparents. Minos thought there might be more of the wife's family members living in the house. Young Waqar doesn't get on with any of them."

"Fair enough," said Rusty. "I thought we could pick him up from home."

"He could just as easily be somewhere in the borough, parked in his brand-new BMW, jotting down the orders. Ali never touches the merchandise, not even to pass it to his runners. No, I'll add this to the list of things we need the ice-house to do. If Ali leaves home tomorrow, we need to track his car and interrupt his note-taking."

Twenty minutes on Brick Lane's winding street, moving from north to south, then back again, revealed no sightings of Waqar Ali. There was nothing to be gained by hanging around attracting attention. Phoenix drove towards Chiswick.

It was half-past ten before they could tuck into their curry. Two cans of lager each were the maximum Phoenix allowed them.

"Up bright and early tomorrow," he said, "you need to call Artemis. To apologise for forgetting to ring her tonight."

"Shit," said Rusty. "I'm still not used to this relationship, malarkey. I'll set the alarm on my phone to catch her before she goes to the ice-house at eight."

"I'll talk to Giles to catch up on the latest intelligence. He may be able to pinpoint where and when Waqar is on the move. We need to get a better handle on his routine than we managed tonight. I don't want to deal with the problem on his front doorstep. It would be safer if it were out in the open, somewhere with fewer witnesses."

"Have you decided which option we're going for in Hackney?" asked Rusty.

"Unless something extraordinary turns up tomorrow; yes, we'll stick to Plan A. If Thacker's plans have changed, we may need to revise *all* our plans. Let's sleep on it. Things will become clearer in the morning."

"Sweet dreams, mate," said Rusty. "No night feeds to interrupt you tonight. You should get eight hours."

"Not with your bloody snoring, I won't, even with a wall between us," muttered Phoenix.

Chapter Six

Thursday, 6th March 2014

Rusty's alarm woke him at seven; he rolled out of bed, showered and dressed, and then headed downstairs. He found Phoenix hard at work in the lounge.

"I've checked the kit we'll use today," his colleague said, "everything's ready. Get your breakfast. I've eaten but won't say no to a fresh cup of coffee."

Rusty went to the kitchen, slipped two slices of bread into the toaster and switched on the kettle. There was plenty of coffee and long-life milk on offer. As he fetched the carton of milk from the fridge, he picked out complementary portions of margarine and jam to make his toast more palatable.

"Looks as if someone raided the basket contents in the last budget hotel room they stayed in," said Rusty.

"Don't complain if people use their initiative, Rusty," said Phoenix. "The cupboard was bare the last time we used this place."

Rusty finished his breakfast and wandered back to the kitchen. He got his phone out of his trouser pocket and called Artemis. If he had to apologise for forgetting to ring last evening, he wanted to be out of earshot of Phoenix.

In the lounge, Phoenix looked at his watch. Half-past seven. Athena was bound to be up with Hope. He called Larcombe Manor and updated her on how things were progressing. She reminded him yet again about the weekend. Phoenix promised to do his best. That was one argument he could never win, so he kept their conversation brief. He asked her to cuddle Hope from her father and ended the call.

The next call was to Giles Burke.

"Giles, I wanted to catch you before you left the stable block and headed underground. I need a favour. Can you track Waqar Ali's BMW for me today, please? I know it might be a pain, hunting him from camera to camera, but it should save us time in the long run."

"Will do, Phoenix," said Giles, "but I'll go one better if I can. I'll get a local agent to conduct discreet surveillance on the guy's in-laws' property. As soon as Ali's out of his garage and on the road, we can follow him. He stops at various points around his patch, selecting those with the best mobile phone reception. Most days, he stays in the car; occasionally, he visits a café or goes to get a manicure. As soon as the BMW is stationary and unattended, our agent will stick a GPS tracker on it. We'll know where our target is twenty-four seven."

"That's a great idea, Giles, thanks," said Phoenix. "When you reach the ice-house, can you get Artemis to call me with the latest intel on our three targets?"

"No worries, Phoenix," said Giles, "good hunting today."

A chastened Rusty had returned from the kitchen. He had collected the breakfast things and taken them through to do the washing-up. Artemis rightly bent his ear about not calling.

"I was awake half the night," she had told him, "worrying something had gone wrong."

"Uncomfortable call?" asked Phoenix.

"Well, I need to come to terms with the fact I have someone at Larcombe who cares for me. I've only needed to look out for myself for the past thirty years."

"You don't need to tell me, mate. I've got two people at home relying on me to care for them and to come home safe from every mission."

"We're back on the same old subject, Phoenix. I reckon the pressures are worse when you're in our position, don't you?"

"Different, maybe, but I wouldn't want to go back to being alone, would you?"

Rusty shook his head.

"You don't realise it until you find the right person, but there's nothing worse than being alone."

"Christ, I wish Artemis would get a move on and call. You'll have me in tears here if this conversation carries on much longer."

The call came at two minutes past eight.

"She doesn't hang around once she starts her shift, does she?" said Phoenix. "Good morning, Artemis. What news do you have?"

Artemis updated him on both Waqar Ali and Gavin McTierney's schedules. Artemis told him she had emailed him a list of times and places each gang leader might be on Thursday.

"Everything should be as you anticipated. There's

nothing to suggest you need to alter your plans. As for Dwight Thacker, he's still in the same B&B in Brentwood. He paid another visit to the pub up the road last night. Thacker had company when he left; he is no longer mourning the death of the young girl he described as his 'lady'. The sooner you get these new girls away from him, the better."

"Thanks, Artemis," said Phoenix. "I'll expect to hear from Giles later if his man successfully gets a tracker on Waqar Ali's car. After that, we'll start positioning ourselves ready to carry out our first strike."

Phoenix printed off the contents of the email Artemis had forwarded.

"Good to go?" asked Rusty.

"Yes. We'll take the Mercedes. It's adapted for this job. The blacked-out windows give it the appearance of being a motor a gangster might own. You're driving today. We'll need your advanced driving skills afterwards to get us back here without incident. I'll make a call for transport to collect the car."

Phoenix collected the kit they required this morning and followed Rusty out of the safe-house to the car. The Skorpion SA361 sub-machine gun was a familiar sight on Britain's streets. Hundreds of these weapons from the Czech Republic featured among the arsenals of UK gangs in the past decade. It was light, even with its magazine fitted, accurate up to twenty-five metres, and capable of delivering up to eight hundred and fifty rounds per minute; it was an efficient killing machine.

Phoenix joined Rusty in the Mercedes.

"First things first," he said, pointing to an addition to the usual display, "flick that switch."

Rusty did as instructed. Nothing happened, as far as he

could tell. Phoenix didn't shed any light on matters either, so Rusty started the Merc's engine and drove through the gateway. After a minute, there was a break in the vehicles passing, and he merged into the nearside lane. They had a minimum of an hour ahead of them, inching their way across the London rush hour traffic to reach Hackney and their first job.

"When we finally get there, we'll locate McTierney, follow him, and pick our spot. His schedule has him stopping at places between the Empire and The Dolphin before ten. First, he has an appointment with his barber, one of the old-fashioned sort, where they give you a proper shave with a cut-throat razor. After that, he's due at ten at one of his dodgy places for a massage. He leaves Healing Hands at around half-past eleven. From there, he goes for lunch at one of his restaurants on Richmond Road. Five minutes up the road. If I can't make the hit at one of those three spots, I might as well retire."

"It's manic around here though, Phoenix," said Rusty, "with this traffic, I mean. When I floor it after you've done the business, we'll be snarled up in a jam until the law arrives, won't we?"

Phoenix produced a detailed set of notes on several sheets of paper.

"I've always admired those rally drivers, Rusty, haven't you? Unfortunately, I can't do the Swedish accent to give it true authenticity. It depends on which of his ports of call proves to be McTierney's last. The correct set of instructions from these sheets via your co-driver will get you through side streets and shortcuts to a place of safety. We've got another ace up our sleeve, don't worry."

"I can always rely on you to have done your homework,

Phoenix," said Rusty. "Why couldn't you have run me through this when we were back in the orangery?"

"Where's the fun in that, Rusty?" his colleague replied without a hint of embarrassment.

What seemed a long time later, they passed The Dolphin; it was just after twenty-five past nine. They drove on towards the Empire.

"Keep your eyes peeled," said Phoenix. "His driver will be as frustrated with the traffic volume as the rest of us. But every week since our surveillance started, he's dropped his boss at the barber's shop between nine twenty-eight and nine-thirty."

"It's coming up on our left about now," said Rusty. "Is that them?"

"Yes," snapped Phoenix. "Head for that gap in front of the Ocado delivery van."

Rusty heard a squeal of brakes behind them and fanfare of protesting horns, but he squeezed the Mercedes through the gap without hitting anything. McTierney's driver had stopped his vehicle half on, half off the pavement. He had got out and walked to the nearside rear passenger door, and opened it. The gang leader was now out of the car and walking a short distance to the shop door. McTierney turned to see what caused the noise behind him. What he saw concerned him, but it was too late to change the outcome.

A Mercedes with blacked-out windows had mounted the pavement. Its front passenger window lowered. McTierney saw the muzzle emerging from the dark interior; he spun around and ran for the plate-glass shop door as Phoenix opened fire. Gavin McTierney was dead before he was propelled through the shattered glass and onto the freshly swept tiles of the barbershop floor.

The driver had drawn his weapon and ran towards his boss to protect him. As he saw McTierney sprayed with bullets, he turned back to fire at the Mercedes. Another short burst from the Skorpion hit him in the upper chest and throat. He crumpled to the ground. His gun slid off the pavement and into the gutter.

"Let's get out of here," shouted Phoenix.

He grabbed the notes and reeled off instructions. Rusty reacted immediately; nobody wanted to be a hero. The traffic had come to a standstill. It was as if Hackney's residents witnessed a drive-by gang hit every day of the week. They moved their cars out of the way so the Merc could have free passage off Mare Street.

Five minutes of skilful driving from Rusty, with Phoenix in the passenger seat, barking directions, and they were on their way.

"Right, Rusty, flick that switch once more and take it slow. We can return to the safe-house now."

"Will you please explain?" asked Rusty.

"A modification to this Mercedes was needed to shift the blame for McTierney's death. Remember the Bond film? The revolving number plate wheeze. Any number of rival gangs exist within the borough of Hackney. Inter-gang rivalry is endemic. Henry Case informed me that the leader of one such gang drives a Mercedes of the exact vintage and model. We travelled from Chiswick until a few seconds ago with his number plates on our vehicle. Gangs are territorial, so we would have been unfortunate to run into the other car while on our travels. Eye-witnesses and CCTV will confirm who was responsible. The police will arrest the poor guy. A good brief will undoubtedly find evidence of him being in two places simultaneously. Sadly, on this occasion, he will avoid a prison term."

"And the transport waiting for us?" asked Rusty.

"That delivered a van for us to use for the rest of the week. You will drive this Merc up the ramp into the waiting lorry. Olympus engineers will replace the windows, remove the number plate gadget, and store the car in our transport section until it's required again."

"Onwards and upwards, then? Will we have time for a bite to eat before we start hunting Waqar Ali?" Rusty enquired.

"I don't see why not. We need to chase up Artemis for the latest information. If the GPS tracker is in place on his BMW, we might tidy matters up earlier than planned."

Rusty drove steadily back to Chiswick. When they arrived at the safe-house, a large lorry was waiting with the ramp in place. A transit van stood in the driveway next to the saloon car. Rusty carefully positioned the Mercedes, and the vehicle climbed gracefully into the back. The two agents sat inside the car for a moment.

"What are you thinking, Phoenix?" asked Rusty.

"I might have been a tad hasty, making the hit at the first place McTierney visited."

"Why so?"

"If they have an open coffin for his funeral, it would have been better if he had had his haircut and a proper wet shave," replied Phoenix.

The two agents got out of the car and descended the ramp. The driver of the lorry and his mate cleared away the ramp and closed the back doors. They said their goodbyes and headed to the London garage, where several other Olympus transport vehicles were maintained and stored.

As they watched the lorry move carefully through the gateway, Rusty patted his colleague on the shoulder.

"No, I reckon you did the McTierney family a big

favour. They would have moaned if you had taken him out after he emerged from his massage parlour session. It would be far more disconcerting to have an open coffin where the departed has a satisfied smile on his face than one with a few stray hairs and a five o'clock shadow."

Once inside the house, it was back to business. Phoenix wanted to find the exact whereabouts of Waqar Ali. He called the ice-house. Artemis picked up the phone.

"Hi there, Phoenix," she said, "have you had a good day?"

"Everything went as planned," Phoenix replied, "did you and Giles make any progress with locating Waqar Ali?"

"Our man attached the tracker to his Beemer earlier this morning. Ali's been on the move since he left home. He was on Commercial Street at around ten; then, he drove along Brick Lane and made several brief stops. At noon, Ali parked in the NCP car park on Whitechapel High Street. He's probably having lunch somewhere close. Our man is on the ground in the area now. Giles learned five minutes ago that Ali's sat in the Altab Ali Park, two or three minutes' walk from the car park. Naturally, he's on his phone."

"Get a message to Giles's agent," said Phoenix. "Rusty and I will head off to Tower Hamlets. It will take an hour and a half at best. I want Ali followed. Wherever he goes after his rest in the Park, digesting his lunch, I want to know about it. Give the agent my number, and he can talk us into position. Is that clear?"

"Crystal," said Artemis, "good luck. Tell Rusty....well, you know."

"No worries," said Phoenix and ended the call.

"Where are we off to now?" asked Rusty.

"Tower Hamlets, for a walk in the park. Your lady friend wanted to be remembered to you, by the way."

"Cheers. Do you want me to make us sandwiches? Unfortunately, it doesn't sound like we'll have time for a leisurely lunch."

"We can grab a take-out and two coffees from that place near the roundabout," said Phoenix, loading the kit into a bag for their afternoon mission. "We need to get moving straight away."

Ninety minutes later, they were driving into the Tower Hamlets borough. When they were still five minutes away, Giles's agent had phoned. Waqar Ali had left the park and retrieved his car. He then drove to Spitalfields Market, where he met his fellow compatriots. Their conversation was animated and in their native tongue. He had kept watch from a safe distance, so he could not indicate whether or not the conversation had been friendly. Ali had then left the Market area and was heading towards Blackwall.

As soon as they reached the borough, Phoenix called the agent back.

"Which way do we go from here? We're passing the Queen Mary University."

"Cross the Mile End Road and follow Harford Street. It would be best if you took the A1205 and A1261, which get you near the East India Docks. I'm near Poplar Business Park; Waqar's BMW is two cars in front of me. You're twenty minutes away. You might make it quicker if you get a few green lights."

"Call me as soon as he stops," ordered Phoenix. "Tell me exactly where and what he's doing. Thanks,"

Rusty got the message. He needed to get them there as fast as possible without getting pulled over by the law.

"Have you got a sheet of instructions the same as we had earlier, mate," he asked.

"Afraid not, Rusty," replied Phoenix. "Just be thankful we're in the saloon, not the transit van."

The agent rang back.

"Ali's on the move. He sat in the Park for ten minutes after I spoke to you last; then, a guy approached him. He was white, thirty-five to forty, and medium height. The guy might have been Greek or Turkish. He was well-dressed, cultured looking, a businessman rather than a working man. A bag was placed on the park bench between them as they sat talking. The other guy left it behind when he got up and walked away."

"Which way is Ali headed now?" asked Phoenix.

"My best guess is he's off home," replied the agent.

"Guess again," grunted Phoenix. "Waqar doesn't normally handle the merchandise. He certainly wouldn't stash it at his house. Something must have forced them to change their routine. The meeting at Spitalfields must be connected. No idea why, but the delivery had to be made in the Park, direct to Waqar. I'll check with Larcombe to see if they have any intel. You keep tailing Ali and direct us to him as soon as you find out where he's dropping off the stash. He'll go somewhere before he goes home; that's a given."

"OK, Phoenix," said the agent and hung up.

The minutes ticked past. The distance between the Olympus agents and their prey was narrowing.

"Giles? Do you have news on Waqar Ali and his crew?" asked Phoenix.

"Just a second, Phoenix. News of a gangland execution in Hackney made the lunchtime news. You didn't get a mention; you'll be pleased to hear. The police call it the result of inter-gang rivalry and signs of a power struggle within the borough. That culminated in one gang trying to take over a nearby patch. The Met stress that this doesn't mean the growth of the so-called super gangs is any more likely. It was an isolated incident, and they are pursuing a suspect with extreme diligence. Across the capital, there have been indications that gang members have changed their daily routines. Everything will get back to normal in a day or two. They're probably nervous about the extra police presence on the streets; because of what happened to McTierney and his bodyguard. Also, the word will be out that one of their own flexed his muscles, aiming to elbow in on a neighbour's manor. So they're looking over their shoulder to see if they're next."

"We might be able to help the police," said Phoenix, thinking on his feet. "They've announced publicly; they have a suspect. We know their suspect will be home free within an hour of them taking him into custody. They won't be able to make a charge stick. The police will have egg on their face yet again. So let's change our plans. Get your agent in Tower Hamlets to make an anonymous call to the Met, informing them of the whereabouts of a large stash of drugs. Please give them the number of Waqar Ali's BMW. We'll stay close by to ensure he doesn't make the drop and escape. We need to allow the police to find the drugs in his car or catch him passing the bag to his usual handler. The next guy in the chain, between Waqar and his runners."

"Artemis believes she has identified her, Phoenix," said Giles, "yes, it's a woman, not a man. Aisha Naru is a thirty-eight-year-old married mother of three children. On the surface, she is a model wife and mother. Her children attend a good school, and she is a governor. Her husband works in the City. She earned a first-class degree in chemistry and worked in the Department of Pharmacology at Bath University until her children were born. The family live in a four-bedroom, two-bathroom townhouse in Hoxton. You don't get much change out of eight-hundred grand for a place like that these days. Her role in the operation is to procure the additives they need and cut the basic cocaine product to make it go further and enhance the user's experience. She must be good at her job based on the thriving trade Waqar Ali has developed."

"Thanks, Giles," said Phoenix, "I'll leave you to set the wheels in motion. We're diverting to Hoxton immediately. We'll get there within minutes of Waqar Ali arriving. Heaven only knows how soon the police will arrive once your agent has alerted them. If we can, we'll block the BMW to cut off Ali's escape. I can rely on Rusty to make it seem he's got a genuine problem with the car."

Rusty shrugged his shoulders. "Take your pick," he said. "The electrics just died on me, governor, or I'm lost. Can you tell me how to get to Heathrow? What will you be doing while I'm acting my backside off?"

"I'll get inside the house if need be. To prevent Ms Naru from flushing the evidence down the loo," said Phoenix. "We need the police to catch them in possession of the drugs to make this work."

The agent called back.

"The Met is on their way. After this morning's incident, you'll also have an Armed Response Unit on the site. They're not taking any chances. Ali is turning right at the next junction. That takes him into the street where the Naru's live. I can see a police van in my rear-view mirror. They're making a silent approach, thank goodness. Are you getting close now?"

"We're entering the street from the opposite end," said Phoenix. "Ali's sat in his Beemer, waiting for the electronic gate to open. It's just a bar, though. Not a solid wall of steel. OK, the car's on the driveway. Ali's out of the car and is walking to the front door. What's your position, over?"

"I've stopped on a double yellow," said the agent, "the police vehicles have passed me. They'll be on the Naru doorstep in ten seconds. Right, I'm off before I get a ticket. Good luck. I'll report to Giles and tell him I'm going off watch. One way or another, my job is done."

"Thanks for your help," said Phoenix. He and Rusty then watched as the police vans pulled up across the driveway of the townhouse. Eight to ten men leapt out. Several were armed and dressed in helmets and protective vests. Others wore hi-viz jackets, and one of their numbers carried his big red key.

Waqar Ali had been inside the house for no more than fifteen seconds after Aisha Naru had answered the doorbell when the front door almost exploded behind him. Aisha, Naru screamed. Waqar dropped the bag he was carrying. It was over in less than a minute.

A car horn sounded behind the saloon. Rusty pulled forward and gave a wave to the impatient driver.

"Reminds me of this morning, mate," he said. "Instead of watching something exciting happening right under their noses, most Londoners want to get on with their day. In the country, towns come to a complete stop if something like this occurs. Up here, they're so blasé. Seen it, done it; I'm not sure I could ever live up here, mate, could you?"

"I'm a country boy at heart, Rusty," said Phoenix, "well, we've got rid of the top two people in the chain. That should cut the head off the snake for that drug operation. The Met will have a positive result to balance up this morning's case of mistaken identity. We must ensure the icehouse keeps the Olympus name out of the frame; then we're home free."

"Not yet, Phoenix," said Rusty as he tried to find the quickest route back to Chiswick, "there's the small task of collecting Dwight Thacker."

"I think we can award ourselves a night indoors. Let's get two large pizzas and a six-pack of cans of lager from the supermarket near the safe-house. What do you say?"

"Sounds good. Don't worry. I won't tell Athena if you don't tell Artemis."

"You've got a deal," said Phoenix, "tomorrow is another day, as someone once said."

Chapter Seven

Friday, 7th March 2014

Rusty's alarm awoke him with a start at five o'clock. What unearthly time was that? Light dawned in his head, if not outside. Phoenix had given them the evening off after two successful missions yesterday. Then, after a few hours of eating, drinking and watching a DVD, he suddenly announced they were making an early start today.

Phoenix was washed and dressed, working in the lounge when Rusty descended the stairs.

"You never really switch off, do you, Phoenix?"

"I'm trying to be the future dutiful husband, Rusty. Thacker needs to pay for his crimes. I want to be free of him. Athena and Hope expect me to give them one hundred per cent of my attention this weekend. That film let me firm up my plans for the next twenty-four hours."

"It wasn't great, was it?" agreed Rusty. "I wonder how many other agents have suffered it here over the years since it came out?"

"It was so bad they may have forced hostages they brought here to watch it before interrogating them. That would have softened them up nicely."

"Think about how good 'Scarface' was and 'The Untouchables'. It's strange how that one was such a turkey. I guess every director is allowed one mistake."

"You'd better get a move on, mate," said Phoenix, "I want us on the road by dawn. Can you be ready in forty-five minutes? When you've showered, get these clothes on, and we can leave."

"No problem," Rusty replied; and went back upstairs at the double, carrying a uniform.

Phoenix drove the transit van to Brentwood. The traffic was light. A band of rain had moved southeast across their route, and the M25 was slick and shimmering. The skies overhead promised a drier, more pleasant trip home to Larcombe Manor.

"They say the sun always shines on the righteous, don't they, Rusty?" said Phoenix with a smile.

"So, this passing shower was for Dwight Thacker then, was it?"

"A nasty piece of work, our Dwight. We'll arrive in Brentwood just after seven. He won't be expecting an early morning call. I contacted the ice house while you caught up on your beauty sleep. One of the night-shift crew gave me details of the floor-plan of the B&B where Thacker is lodging. The junior manager is Scottish. I know you can manage that. They offer early-bird breakfasts for sales reps keen to get on the road. Many have been in the area for a week and want to get home to their families. We shouldn't have any trouble gaining access."

"We must assume Thacker won't come quietly," said

Rusty, "what did you pack in the bag you brought with you?"

"Something to subdue him long enough for us to transfer him to the van. I don't suppose you bothered to inspect the kit in the back?"

Rusty had to admit that he hadn't.

"I asked for a specific set of items," continued Phoenix. "We wouldn't have had enough room in the Mercedes or the family saloon. We didn't need them until today, so it was the most sensible option."

Rusty turned around and peered into the dark interior.

"Gotcha; I wondered why we were sporting these natty green uniforms."

"They will be authentic enough to fool the staff and customers we meet. Most will be half-asleep at any rate."

The rain clouds dispersed as they drew up at the traffic lights one hundred yards from where Dwight Thacker slept. A few glimpses of blue sky were emerging.

"I reckon it's going to be a good day, Rusty," said Phoenix. "As soon as I get parked, you jump out and remove the collapsible patient trolley from the back. I'll bring the rest. Thacker is on the first floor, in room three. We'll take the stairs to avoid hanging around in the foyer inviting questions. You knock on the door, tell him it's room service, and we rush him as soon as he opens his door. Sound good?"

"Och aye. What if Thacker's a sound sleeper? He could be armed too; what do we do if he starts shooting?"

"Room service would have to be pretty rubbish if he opens fire when someone makes a genuine mistake over who ordered breakfast in their room."

They had reached the B&B. There were several vehicles in the small car park at the front. An overweight, middle-aged man was loading his suitcase and hand luggage into the boot of a Vauxhall Zafira. One of the early birds was leaving.

Phoenix reversed their van up to the steps leading to the front door. Rusty climbed out and opened the back doors. He removed the trolley and ran inside the building. The Vauxhall driver stood and watched for a moment, his hand hovering over the driver's door.

"Alright, mate," he asked Phoenix, "is there an emergency?"

"Suspected overdose," he replied. He followed Rusty upstairs with his bag. The sales rep from the Midlands got into his car and drove back home to Sutton Coldfield.

Phoenix joined his colleague outside room number three. He opened the bag and removed a bottle of chloroform and a cloth. When he was ready, he nodded.

"Room service, sir," cried Rusty, knocking loudly on the door.

Dwight Thacker stirred. Last night's dark rum fogged his brain. Was that someone outside the door? He hadn't ordered breakfast. He turned over and buried his head in the pillow. It would take an hour or two more sleep to get him ready to face the world.

Rusty knocked again. "Hello, are you awake, sir?" he called.

Dwight was angry now. Why couldn't this bloke leave him alone? He jumped out of bed, naked, and looked for a towel to cover himself. Then grabbed it and rushed to the door.

"What the fuck's the matter with you, man?" he shouted as he wrenched the door open. "I never ordered any breakfast...."

Phoenix was through the door in a second. Dwight still

held onto the towel, in no position to defend himself. Rusty followed his colleague into the room and closed the door behind them.

Phoenix struggled to overpower the younger man. Rusty put the trolley against the door and joined in the fun. Thirty seconds later, Dwight was sleeping like a baby.

Phoenix nodded towards the trolley. Rusty set it up, and they loaded their patient onto it.

"Pass me the oxygen mask from the bag, please, Rusty," said Phoenix, "we'll use this to disguise the fact we're keeping him sedated. If we bump into anyone when we leave, an overdose will be the easiest story to get them to swallow. Later they may wonder who called the paramedics, but nobody will bother us in his room for a while. Finally, we'll collect Thacker's belongings and take them back to Larcombe."

Five minutes later, Phoenix left room three and called the lift. He held the door for Rusty, who had to stand the trolley on its end to squeeze their passenger into the compartment.

"He's hardly going to complain, is he," said Rusty. "Anyway, the stairs would be a bugger to negotiate."

As soon as the lift doors opened, the two agents got the trolley back on four wheels and made a sharp exit from the B&B. The trolley was in the back of the transit before anyone inside noticed. Rusty looked back as he opened the passenger door. There were two faces at the ground-floor window. They were finishing their breakfasts, but they didn't let the sight of two paramedics in an unmarked transit spoil their day.

The time signal on the radio in the van announced it was seven-thirty.

"We should pop into the safe-house to collect our odds

and ends of equipment. Try to leave it as neat and tidy as we found it. We'll be home in time for elevenses," said Phoenix, "and the sun is coming out. Happy days."

"I was right about Thacker having a gun," said Rusty. "We've got his gun and ammunition, five hundred quid's worth of drugs, and several grand in cash on board. So please keep to the speed limit on the way back, mate."

"Don't worry. I'm in no rush. Everything went to plan. The charity shops in Bath will benefit from the other items we collected," said Phoenix. "His clothes, watch, and jewellery will brighten up the contents of the bags we drop off on their doorsteps."

"Can we change radio stations halfway back, Phoenix," said Rusty, "you know this heavy metal stuff gives me a headache."

"When we reach Reading services, I promise," laughed Phoenix, "a headache? I find it relaxes me. It always has."

Phil Hounsell and Wayne Sangster met in the HSS offices when heavy metal switched to middle-of-the-road tracks, which was more Rusty's style. It was an uncomfortable meeting because the work had dwindled. Phil wondered how much longer he could afford to keep Jake and Dusty on the books. He and Wayne looked through the firm contracts they held to come up with a solution. Things didn't make for pleasant reading. Wayne looked at the glum expression on the face of his boss.

"Did you read in the papers about those guys who got shot in Hackney?" he asked. "No loss, of course, but it looked like a professional hit by a rival gang."

"The Met seemed keen to divert the public's attention away from the growing strength of the gangs," said Phil, "that was implicit in the statement they released. For a time, it has been apparent the stronger ones are either eliminating the opposition or squeezing them out of business. There's trouble brewing."

Phil sat back from the desk with his contract file on his lap. His thoughts strayed to Carrie Ditchburn. There had been nothing in the newspapers regarding her former boyfriend yet. He had passed on the information to Olympus, hoping for a response. But maybe they weren't interested.

He realised Wayne was speaking again.

"What chance do the police have against the threat these gangs pose? The Met is losing up to fifty officers a week. The cuts they're making to save money are biting. Then there's their obsession with priorities. The focus now is on radicalisation. They shelved everything domestic for that. As a result, these gangs have become even stronger."

"Radicalisation, the relentless pursuit of historic sex offenders, and hammering the poor old motorist," said Phil, counting out the priorities on his fingers. "I hear you, Wayne. It's the same tune they've been dancing to for years."

Wayne was on his 'high horse' now.

"The gangs deal in drugs, extortion and violence, and their experiences harden some younger members before they ever landed on these shores. A fifteen-year-old from any one of several African countries may have escaped from a brutal regime where his family got butchered before their eyes. We might believe our streets are tough, but they're nothing compared to that."

"There was a quirk concerning the drive-by shooting in Hackney," said Phil, "something didn't sit right with me about that. When we investigated the occasional gang death in the Avon & Somerset Police, we saw a few fatal drive-by shootings. It's more common for a shooter to walk right up to the victim. It's not death from a distance, but up close and personal. Executions in broad daylight, too, are a rarity. The gangs are more concerned with their business dealings than trying to prove they're tougher than their neighbour. Something as blatant as those deaths are bad for business. Nobody wants to buy drugs from their local dealers; everybody stays well away until the police presence withdraws. There was another motive for those killings. I'd bet on it."

The phone rang. Wayne answered.

"Hounsell Security Services, Wayne speaking. How may we help you today? Yes, the boss is here; I'll connect you."

Wayne handed Phil the phone with a shrug to show it wasn't anyone they knew.

"Phil Hounsell speaking."

"Good morning, Orion," said Hayden Vincent, "my employer asked me to get in touch. The report you submitted recently was beneficial. Feel free to pass on any further information you believe might be in our mutual interest. You must forward correspondence to the following email address. That address will be your contact with my employer in the future. Rest assured, positive results bring financial benefits. Enjoy your weekend."

Phil noted the details Hayden provided. There was no clue in the name to tell who or what this man represented. Phil slipped the sheet of paper into the top drawer of his desk.

"Another job, boss?" asked Wayne.

"It seems that's up to us, Wayne," Phil replied.

"Very enigmatic," said Wayne, "so, what's left to sort out here this morning, then?"

"Not much. I think we'll have to tell Jake and Dusty that we won't need them after the end of April. The missing person's jobs, plus our security contracts, will keep the two of us out of mischief for the foreseeable future. This means you won't have to sign on nor have a change of uniform for a while."

"The way that misper's job in London ended was sad, wasn't it?" said Wayne. "Not just the fact Carrie died, but the aftermath made it sadder."

"Thacker getting away without a scratch, do you mean?" said Phil, wondering whether the earlier phone call suggested he hadn't.

"He'll get his comeuppance one day, boss; no, I looked at Carrie's Facebook page the other evening. There were hundreds of messages of condolence from children she went to school with, pony club staff and former members from around Cheltenham. People she worked with in restaurants across London. Some came from parts of the country she had never visited. If only a few of those kids had shown her they cared when she was alive, she might have gotten away from that shitbag Thacker and turned her life around."

"Too true. We need to show those around us love, Wayne. So, I'm going home to my family to show a little love. Take the rest of the day off and do the same. See you Monday morning."

The two colleagues left the HSS offices and headed home.

Phoenix and Rusty were also almost home. The Roman city streets were always busy, but Phoenix turned the van through the stone pillars at the end of the driveway to Larcombe not long after eleven, as predicted. He went directly to the ice-house. They had made a brief stop at Reading services for a comfort break and checked that their patient was still out for the count. While they were there,

Phoenix had called Henry Case to tell him when to expect company.

As soon as the van pulled up, Henry emerged from the ice-house with Pete Thomas and Barry Longdon. Rusty got out of the van and opened the back doors. They removed Dwight Thacker and his trolley. The two ex-SAS men from the armoury wheeled the unconscious Thacker into the lift and took him underground. They laid the Skorpion, spare ammunition, and other miscellaneous items Phoenix had requisitioned at Thacker's feet.

"A successful mission, Phoenix," said Henry Case, "well done, you two."

He patted Rusty on the shoulder.

"A shame your prisoner wasn't awake before he booked into Hotel California. It's a beautiful day, and he won't be returning to the surface alive. Well, I mustn't keep him waiting."

Henry left them and entered the ice-house. Phoenix and Rusty took the transit to the transport section and returned it.

"Just feel the warmth of that sun, Rusty," said Phoenix, as they strolled across the lawn towards the main building, "it's great to be alive, isn't it?"

"Have fun this weekend with your future in-laws," said Rusty.

"Why do you always have to kill the mood?" grinned Phoenix. "You and Artemis enjoy what time you have together too. I'll see you at the meeting on Monday morning."

Rusty went upstairs to his apartment. Artemis was still on shift. He decided to catch up on last night's lost sleep. Who knew? He might need his energy tonight when she finishes work.

Phoenix found Maria Elena playing with Hope when he walked into their quarters. The nanny told him Athena was in the administration office and wasn't expected upstairs until noon. Phoenix kissed his daughter and told Maria Elena he was letting his partner know he was home.

He found her sitting at a desk cluttered with files. Athena appeared stressed. When she spotted who it was barging through the door without knocking, her face lit up with a gorgeous smile.

"Phoenix, you're home safe, thank goodness."

"Early, too," he added.

He went through the details of the past few days.

"We have to be content with the results we've achieved," she said when he had finished. "We have severely restricted the activities of one gang, eliminated the head of another, and in time, we will punish the man responsible for a young girl's death. It's not perfect, but it's a start."

"Have I missed anything else since I was away?" asked Phoenix.

"Me, I hope," said Athena, getting up and coming to him. They kissed and embraced. Phoenix turned to look at the desk.

"Will it muck up your filing system if these files end up on the floor?"

Athena shook her head. She dragged him with her and sat on the edge of the desk. Phoenix lifted her skirt. The phone by Athena's right hip emitted an urgent ringing sound.

"Olympus business," she gasped. "I've got to get it."

"You were going to," groaned Phoenix. The ringing became more insistent.

Athena answered the call. It was Hayden Vincent, reporting in from Shrivenham.

"Good morning, Athena. I've established contact with Orion. As soon as Phoenix can confirm the information he gave us proved beneficial, you can authorise payment. To let you know, Kelly and I are ready to move to Larcombe at the end of the month. The checks on the agents replacing us in the Shrivenham house came back today. They cleared them for duty."

Athena was in control of her breathing now. Phoenix slumped in her chair, waiting for the conversation to end. The moment had passed.

"Thank you, Hayden," she said, "the information proved to be every bit as valuable as Orion hoped. I'll transfer a suitable sum into the HSS bank account later. We look forward to having you join us at the start of next month. Give Kelly my love. Bye for now."

Athena kept the distance of the desk between her and her partner.

"Shall we go to relieve Maria Elena, spend time with Hope, and have lunch together?"

"Is that your best offer?" Phoenix replied.

"For now, darling," Athena said, grabbing his hand and leading him back to their rooms. "After Hope takes her afternoon nap, maybe we can take a siesta too?"

"Blimey, is Maria Elena joining us?"

Athena gave Phoenix a hefty thump on the arm.

"No, she's got the hots for Giles Burke. You won't have seen those two flirting in the swimming pool. Minos caught them when he was over there exercising on Wednesday evening. You see, you don't know everything around here."

"I haven't swum for ages, not since Hope was born. I enjoyed spending time in that pool. I'll never forget you in that silver-grey costume, back in the days when you were ignoring me, pretending you weren't attracted to me."

Phoenix stepped smartly to his right, avoiding another playful punch.

"Maybe we should forget that siesta and take Hope to the pool together?"

Athena laughed. "Golly, we're as bad as an old married couple. Remember when we used to spend the whole weekend in bed?"

"You might as well tell your parents not to bother travelling tomorrow," said Phoenix. "If we're already exhibiting symptoms of married life, then it will be a wasted journey."

"You don't get away with it as easy as that, mister," said Athena. "They're staying here for two nights, and I'll bet my mother mentions the word wedding before she's been here an hour."

"If we could persuade her to accept that we want a quiet wedding, with the minimum of family and friends, then the sooner it happens, the better, as far as I'm concerned."

Athena stopped dead in her tracks.

"Was that a proposal?" she asked. "Not very romantic, but if so, the answer is yes."

"Now we only have to convince your parents to agree to our wishes and find a way to get married without revealing my identity. Answers on a postcard."

Phoenix had slipped his arm around Athena's waist. They reached their apartments and went to the lounge where Maria Elena sat. The young nanny looked up and caught them clinging to one another.

"You two look happy. Have you had good news, perhaps?"

"We're getting married," said Phoenix, scooping up Hope and holding her over his head at arm's length.

"Congratulations," cried Maria Elena, "I expect you can't wait to tell everyone?"

"We'll inform those who need to know," said Phoenix, "we don't want a fuss. So, keep it under your hat, okay?"

"Under my hat?" Maria Elena cocked her head to one side; clearly, it was a phrase she hadn't come across. Then she smiled a broad smile that lit up the room. Phoenix saw immediately why Giles Burke had fallen for her.

"Ah, you want me to come to the wedding, and I can wear a beautiful hat. I will care for Hope during the ceremony; she will look gorgeous in a gown, no?"

"Yes, I believe she will," said Athena. "Phoenix meant we don't want you to tell anyone outside Larcombe Manor of the wedding. Do you think you can do that? Not even your parents, back in Estepona."

"If that is your wish, then this is what I shall do," Maria Elena passed her hand across her mouth as if she was fastening a zip.

"You're learning," said Phoenix with a grin, just as Hope was sick on his shoulder. "You, young lady, I can see, don't enjoy being chucked in the air a short while after your feed."

Hope gave him a toothless grin.

"Let's get us both washed. Then we'll have a play before we eat. Make the most of the calm before the storm when your grandparents arrive tomorrow."

Maria Elena left to prepare lunch. The phone rang, and Athena answered. She listened for a while, then ended the call.

"Trouble?" asked Phoenix.

"Henry," Athena replied, "he's injected Thacker with a high dosage of his product. The effect was immediate. Death will follow in the next hour."

A New Dawn

"Remember to keep Maria Elena busy indoors tomorrow morning," said Phoenix. "Warn Giles, too, just in case they spend nights together. We don't want her slipping away from his room in the stable block and catching sight of the burial party taking Thacker across to the pet cemetery."

Athena nodded. She was pensive. Phoenix sat by her and cradled Hope in his lap.

"Thacker was a nasty piece of work. He ruined dozens of lives, not just the girl that the ex-copper mentioned. So don't shed any tears over him."

"You're right, as always. I think I'll reward Orion with a sum of ten thousand pounds. Do you think that's appropriate?"

"I'm sure the Ditchburn family would approve," said Phoenix. "I'm still struggling to come to terms with having my nemesis becoming an Olympus contractor."

"You think you've got problems?" said Athena. "I'm struggling with the thought I've got to tell Mummy and Daddy I'm not getting married in a cathedral, as they planned, but in a small family church at the Manor where the Hunt family were baptised, married, and buried."

"Erebus would have approved," said Phoenix, carrying Hope over to the side table where the photograph of William and Elizabeth Hunt had pride of place. "I think we would have his blessing."

"It will be the beginning of a new dynasty," said Athena, joining her fiancée, "the Fox-Bailey's will be legitimised.

"A new dawn," they said in unison.

Chapter Eight

Saturday, 8th March 2014

Geoffrey and Grace Fox left Paddington at half-past ten, and their train pulled into Bath Spa station at noon. As Geoffrey helped Grace onto the platform, their daughter Annabelle Grace Fox stepped forward to greet them.

"It's wonderful to see you both," she cried as she embraced her parents, "we've been looking forward to this visit."

She gestured to the driver to carry her parents' cases to the waiting car. The Foxes were to be treated to one of the better limousines from the Olympus transport section today. Not a standard vehicle, with an image of Mt. Olympus, emblazoned on the door panels.

"On your own then, darling?" Grace asked.

"Phoenix is looking after Hope; we've given nanny the day off."

"Phoenix didn't strike me as a 'hands-on' father," said

Geoffrey, "he is at home then? Not traipsing around the country on behalf of the Olympus charity?"

"They're both at Larcombe Manor waiting to see you," said Athena. The car negotiated the Saturday morning traffic, wending its way out of Bath into the green, sunny countryside.

Geoffrey gave a low whistle of appreciation as the car swept up the driveway towards the Georgian manor house.

"What a magnificent place to live and work, darling. I can't wait to explore."

"Sorry, Daddy," said Athena, "you may not have much time to wander around on this visit. It's the three of us you've come to see. We've got lots to discuss."

The car drew up in front of the building. Phoenix stood on the steps with Hope in his arms. His daughter was in her best new clothes.

He had just told her in no uncertain terms that puking on this outfit once her grandparents arrived was out of the question.

Hope had given him the are you serious look.

"Now, that's a look I've seen before," he chuckled, "you've inherited that from your mother."

Geoffrey and Grace Fox got out of the car and gathered around their first grandchild. Phoenix kissed Grace on the cheek, handed the pristine infant over, and then shook Geoffrey by the hand.

"Welcome to Larcombe, Geoffrey," he said.

"Good to see you, Phoenix," Geoffrey replied quietly. "I wondered whether you might have been on one of your adventures."

The two men stood and watched the three women in their lives. Grace, Annabelle and Hope were in a world of their own. The driver emerged from the house to inform

Athena he had left their guests' cases in their room. Phoenix invited everyone to join him inside.

He was only too aware of the older man's suspicions.

He knew the rest of the weekend would be difficult as he dissuaded Geoffrey from poking his nose into what lay behind the charity smokescreen. Minos had briefed the staff to ensure no overt signs of Olympus over the next forty-eight hours.

Phoenix was free to show his future in-laws around the manor house, the orangery and the gardens. Everywhere else had to be out of bounds.

The elegant Georgian furniture in the rooms on the ground floor and the superb ceiling-high windows lifted the surroundings above the descriptions that Phoenix offered.

"This is where we hold meetings with guests and where we eat; if the senior charity officers are in residence. There are charity offices there on the left; further on are the kitchens."

They climbed the magnificent staircase. Geoffrey stopped to admire the paintings.

"What a history this place must possess, Phoenix, if these walls could talk, eh?"

Phoenix let the comment pass. He carried on with his guided tour.

"More meeting rooms and offices on the left. They each have a terrific view over the grand patio and the lawns at the rear of the building. On your right are the apartments occupied by our senior staff. Your room is at the far end, opposite our suite of rooms. Again, you have a spectacular view of the trees and lawns at the front of the estate."

Phoenix opened the door to the rooms they had inherited from Erebus.

"Sir William Hunt and his family enjoyed living in this corner of the building. We love it too."

Geoffrey Fox walked through the reception room to the lounge. He stood at the window and surveyed the view.

"Magnificent," he said, "what are the buildings I can see, Phoenix?"

"We'll take a walk over there after lunch if you wish," said Phoenix, "but much of what's left to see is mundane, I'm afraid. The main house is the jewel in the crown."

Athena sat with her mother, holding onto Hope, when the two men turned back to the room and joined them.

"What a lovely home, sweetheart," said Grace to her daughter. Then, turning to gaze at the child in her arms added, "Aren't you a lucky baby to grow up here?"

"I've asked the staff to prepare lunch for us, as Maria Elena is off today," said Athena. She walked through to the kitchen, and Phoenix joined her.

"Need a hand," he said, coming up behind Athena and slipping his arms around her waist.

"I need a drink," she said, pressing herself back against the body of the man she loved, "every step is like walking on broken glass. We need to tread so carefully."

"I warned you," scolded Phoenix, "but you insisted on bringing them here. Don't worry. We'll get through it. If you break the 'W' news to them, sooner rather than later, that might take Geoffrey's mind off what's happening elsewhere in the grounds."

They carried the food and drink through to the lounge. Hope was keeping their guests amused; she was a quick learner.

"Let's have lunch," said Athena.

When they sat, relaxing afterwards, Athena and Grace left to get coffees for the four of them. Hope was nodding off in her grandfather's arms, and Phoenix took her to her bedroom for a nap.

"This looks serious," said Geoffrey when the four of them were seated, with the coffee cups on a silver tray on the low table in front of them.

"We have an announcement," said Athena. "Phoenix has asked me to marry him, and I accepted."

Grace hugged her daughter and wiped a tear from her eye. "That's wonderful news, darling."

"Don't cry, Mummy. You'll start me off too," said Athena.

Geoffrey Fox gripped Phoenix firmly by the hand. "Welcome to the family, Phoenix. Not before time, of course, but young people have different ways these days."

Once the initial excitement had quietened, Athena explained their wish for a private ceremony. Geoffrey and Grace exchanged glances but didn't protest.

"As it's a sunny afternoon, we'll put Hope in her buggy when she wakes up, and then we'll take a stroll around the grounds. We can visit the church and the other places of interest; then I'm sure you want to see your rooms. Perhaps you want to put your feet up and nap before we dine this evening?"

"Whatever you decide, darling," said her mother. "If I can push the buggy when we're walking, then I don't care about anything else."

When Hope was ready for more fussing over from the grandparents, they ventured out into the Saturday afternoon sunshine. Phoenix showed them the orangery and the walled kitchen garden. Grace and Geoffrey admired the spring flowers, mature bushes, and trees that were Erebus's legacy to Larcombe.

Geoffrey pointed towards the distant buildings as they crossed the lawns to the tiny family church. "What goes on over there, Annabelle?"

"Oh, the old stable block houses accommodation for the ex-servicemen we have here. Many of our carers and trainers live on the estate. Other guests are here temporarily while they receive treatment for their PTSD. At the far end, what was once a row of estate workers' cottages have been converted into a swimming pool, recreation areas, and a staff restaurant."

"Is that an ice-house in the corner?" asked Grace Fox. "I've read about them but never seen one, except in photographs."

"It's derelict," said Phoenix, "we ought to get it condemned. I keep meaning to get it fenced off, especially with Hope likely to go exploring in years to come."

They had reached the other side of the lawn and stood inside the porch of the family church.

"Have you given any thought to a date yet?" asked Grace.

"Saturday, the nineteenth of April," replied Athena, "on Easter Saturday. I know it's only weeks away, but we don't want anything elaborate."

Phoenix swallowed hard. A little warning wouldn't have gone amiss, he thought. He recalled his past two wedding services; one a brief affair in a registry office with a pregnant Karen and the other on a secluded beach in The Gambia with Sue Owens. No matter how basic it might be, this would be his first church wedding.

They moved inside the church. The six short rows of pews defined the numbers the church could accommodate. Everything else one would expect was in evidence, an altar, a pulpit, and a font. The stained-glass window above the altar depicted St. Michael slaying the dragon.

"It's spartan," said Geoffrey, "but no doubt it was sufficient for the Hunt family and its estate workers to worship. There's no cemetery here, though, Phoenix?"

"After any funeral service held here, at least for the past two centuries, bodies have been buried in the city's main graveyard."

He decided Geoffrey needn't to learn of the site where family pets were laid to rest. Traces of Dwight Thacker's unmarked grave might still be visible.

They left the church, and Phoenix paused to stare across the valley to the crematorium and cemetery where the Hunt mausoleum stood. He thought of his mentor, Erebus, and imagined that he would have approved of his marriage to Athena and their chosen venue.

The truncated estate tour was soon over, and they returned to the house. Geoffrey and Grace retired to their room to unpack and relax until the early evening. Finally, Phoenix, Athena and Hope returned to their apartment.

"Well, that went as well as we could have hoped," said Athena.

"I have several questions," Phoenix said as he removed Hope from her buggy, "firstly, have you invited anyone else to dinner this evening?

"I wanted Rusty and Artemis to be present. He's going to be your best man. Is that okay?"

"That's fine. Secondly, have you decided on a bridesmaid or a maid of honour? The natural choice is Artemis, but we need to find two different witnesses for signing the register."

"I have mentioned it to Artemis, and she was more than

happy to be my bridesmaid. I suppose your concern is regarding the small matter of your name?"

"A simple ceremony can dispense with the elaborate order of service sheets. We can get the banns read in the family church. There's no need for anything other than our first names to be used during the service. It's the official document where we need a surname. We must avoid Artemis, and the wider public from ever seeing that, whatever happens."

"I'll discuss things with Henry Case; I'm sure we can overcome your concerns," said Athena. "Were you comfortable with me fixing the date so soon? Mummy's question panicked me."

"My diary was free that weekend, anyway," said Phoenix with a relaxed wave.

Rusty and Artemis joined them for dinner. Athena made the introductions to Geoffrey and Grace Fox.

Sunday, 9th March 2014

On Sunday morning, Minos and Alastor heard of the forthcoming wedding, and both men agreed to perform the role of witness. It was something to make them feel important.

After a lazy morning and brunch on the patio, Phoenix asked if everyone was ready for a trip to the coast.

"It's another warm, sunny day," he said, "why don't we drive to Lymington to visit 'Elizabeth'?"

"Is this a family member, Phoenix?" asked Geoffrey.

"Elizabeth was Sir William Hunt's wife. He was the

founder of the charity. We inherited the yacht he named after her when he passed away. We thought of selling her, but for the moment, we love her too much to part with her."

"Do you sail, Phoenix?" Geoffrey asked.

"Heavens, no," said Phoenix, "but we have several ex-servicemen here who can sail her. We're hoping to go sailing in the future to give Hope her first overseas trip."

"Not a honeymoon voyage?" asked Grace.

"We're too busy with work to have a holiday in April," said Athena. "Hope will enjoy it more when she's a little older."

The trip to and from Lymington passed without incident on this occasion. They spent two pleasant hours looking over the yacht or trying to spot a more elegant one moored in the marina. It was a difficult task.

Later, Athena drove back to Larcombe, avoiding as much of the New Forest as possible. That stretch of the road held dark memories. Phoenix noticed a popular country pub, and the food was worth the wait. They arrived home at around eight o'clock in the evening.

Hope was exhausted and soon put to bed. Phoenix poured a large glass of Erebus's favourite brandy for him and Geoffrey; a white wine for the two ladies was his next order. The room fell silent as the effects of the day caught up with them.

"It's the ozone, Geoffrey," said Phoenix, "not the alcohol that's produced this lethargy."

"And the advancing years, Phoenix. Particularly for Grace and me. We've packed a lot into this weekend. Thank you. It's been most enjoyable. We'll take home happy memories of our time with you two and Hope."

"We're together again in a matter of weeks," said Grace, "and the wedding will give us even greater memories on which to reflect. I realise now, darling, seeing the three of you together in your lovely home, that it's not important to have the big, expensive wedding I always dreamt of for you. Instead, the declaration of your love for one another before God and those closest to you will make it far more significant. Nothing else matters."

"I couldn't have expressed it better, my dear. I think this is as good a time as any to call it a night," said Geoffrey.

Athena went to her mother and clung to her.

"Thank you, Mummy. I knew you would understand."

She kissed her parents, and Phoenix promised to accompany them to the station in the morning.

"I'll drive us into the city," said Phoenix, "we've got a meeting at nine. Your train will have arrived in London by then. We'll see you in here for an early breakfast; I'm sure Hope will be awake. You can say your goodbyes to her properly."

Athena took Phoenix by the hand when they were alone and led him to the bedroom.

"Time to demonstrate the love we have for one another, Phoenix," she whispered, "try not to wake the neighbours."

"Considering the speed with which Geoffrey rushed your mother away after her little emotional speech, I think he had the same thing on his mind."

Athena gave him a playful punch, but nothing changed her plans for him tonight.

Monday, 10th March 2014

Little Hope slept through until dawn. By the time she had been changed and fed, Athena decided she may as well get herself up and dressed. Phoenix lay in their bed for a few minutes longer until he joined them in the kitchen. Hope sat happily bouncing in her rocker, watching her mother making breakfast.

"Coffee, darling?" asked Athena.

"Hot and strong, please," he replied, pulling her towards him.

"Easy tiger," said Athena, "Hope is watching, and Mummy and Daddy will be here soon."

The Foxes tapped on the door at just before seven. Soon they were in the Olympus limousine and heading for Bath Spa. There were the expected tearful goodbyes as Athena waved her parents off on the train. Phoenix stood with Hope in his arms, watched, and then gave a brief wave.

"A successful mission," he said as they returned to Larcombe.

"Yes, it was," said Athena. "Just one thing I must remember to do when we get home. I must call Sarah Gough; we were at university together. She first worked in marketing in London, and our paths often crossed in our twenties. When Sarah reached thirty, she felt she had received a calling and entered the church. I'm sure she will officiate for us if she's free, and I know I can trust her. She was one of only a handful of my friends who knew where I had gone to work after I quit the publishing business."

"We're almost there then?" asked Phoenix, as the Manor loomed in the distance, "apart from me deciding what I'm wearing."

"Daddy's a comedian, Hope, isn't he?" said Athena.

Hope was asleep. Grandparents can be so tiring.

An hour later, at the offices of HSS, Phil Hounsell was staring at the computer screen with a smile on his face when Wayne arrived for work,

"Something's brightened you up since Friday, boss," said Wayne.

Phil was looking at the HSS bank account. A ten-thousand-pound credit from a Cayman Islands account had boosted the balance significantly. Perhaps Jake and Dusty could stay on the books for a little longer.

"Oh, we got paid for a job I'd forgotten about," he lied.

Phil realised the timing of the phone call on Friday had been more than a coincidence. Olympus had followed through on his information. There had been nothing reported in the media. Nevertheless, Dwight Thacker wouldn't ruin any more lives. It would prove lucrative if this were the measure of compensation HSS could expect to receive for passing on tips.

Taking the money tugged at his conscience. Although he upheld the rule of law over the years, things had moved far from the principles he had joined to defend. This path guaranteed the criminal paid the full price for his crime. He could live with it.

"Do you want to speak with the others when they drop by later?" asked Wayne.

"No rush," said Phil, "let's see how things go for the next three months; we can review the situation then."

As their wedding day approached, Athena heard from her friend, the Reverend Sarah Gough; she was only too happy to oblige. The banns were read for the first time on the last Sunday in March, both on the estate and in Annabelle Fox's parish church in Pimlico.

Decisions had been taken on the outfits to wear. Phoenix and Rusty would wear dark suits with buttonholes from the Larcombe gardens.

Athena selected a long gold dress. Artemis had chosen turquoise.

Erebus would have smiled. These colours had linked the two goddesses since the mists of time.

The array of spring flowers in the bouquet Athena was to carry would be cut fresh on the day. Maria Elena Urbano would take the arrangement, still sprinkled with morning dew, to the church to hand them to her mistress as she passed through the porch.

Monday, 31st March 2014

At the start of the week of the Curzon Street meeting, the focus at Larcombe was firmly on Olympus matters. Minos updated his previous report on the deaths of several women following cosmetic surgery procedures.

"In January, a dancer Candy Jacobs, 21, died of heart failure in a Birmingham hotel after silicone fillers leaked into her bloodstream. In February, Daphne Richards, 29, died in Wolverhampton from medical complications. She was married with two sons, aged seven and five. When she was taken ill, Daphne Richards had been undergoing liposuction and buttocks augmentation procedures at a private clinic on the city's outskirts. She was rushed to the hospital but died in the ambulance. In addition to these deaths, I have examples of cosmetic procedures that have been botched, leading to patients being in the hospital for treatment. Doctors have had to deal with blood clots and to carry out corrective surgery."

"What drives these women to take risks with these procedures?" asked Giles Burke.

"Many of them desperately want to look younger, I suppose," said Alastor.

"Are these doctors licenced?" asked Phoenix.

"It's big business, that's for sure," said Minos, "and we know big money will attract rogues. The so-called interventions industry is worth three billion pounds annually in the UK. Demand has expanded so fast; existing regulations are inadequate. Expert cosmetic surgeons carry out the work on the surgical side, namely facelifts, liposuction, or breast implants. But when you're talking about fillers or Botox, then staff in beauty clinics often carry out these procedures, even if not medically trained."

"Are the authorities aware of the problem?" asked Athena.

"Legislation is on its way. There will be a great deal of tightening up in the regulations," Minos explained, "one of the main areas of risk is a lack of informed consent."

"Many treatments are advertised as special offers, buy one get one free," said Henry Case. "The customer is pressured into making a decision. It's akin to the double-glazing salesman's spiel."

"Were you thinking of having a 'nip and tuck' Henry?" asked Phoenix, "you seem to know a lot about it."

"It's no laughing matter, Phoenix," said Henry, "people are dying. Sometimes the expectation the customer has is unrealistic. They need to be aware of the risks involved."

"Have we identified the person responsible for the two deaths in the Midlands?" asked Phoenix.

"Not so far," replied Minos, "the first victim booked the hotel room in her name. The private clinic had closed before the local police followed up on Daphne Richards's husband's complaints. Tracking the person who had rented the premises proved to be beyond them."

"We're working on that aspect, Phoenix," said Giles, "we're confident we'll have a name for you by the end of the week."

"Good," said Phoenix. "I look forward to meeting them."

Chapter Nine

Thursday, 3rd April 2014

Maria Elena raised Hope against her shoulder to see her parents as the car taking them to London moved away from the main building. She lifted the infant's chubby little hand in a wave.

"They'll be back tonight, Hope," she said, "if their day goes well, they'll be home before bath time."

As Hope fought back the tears, the pouting bottom lip told everyone that this statement didn't convince her.

Athena and Phoenix discussed the forthcoming meeting in Curzon Street in the car. Zeus, Hera and the other Olympians would gather there for an important meeting.

"What was on the agenda you received, Athena?" asked Phoenix.

"The first items concern finances, ongoing missions, and the announcement of a recruitment drive. This meeting has a greater focus on home matters rather than abroad. The threats may originate abroad at first, whether from Russia, China, or terrorist organisations throughout the Middle East, but the potential impact on the UK is causing Olympus concern. The final item will be the unmasking of our new Olympians."

"Will they be present?" asked Phoenix.

"Not on this occasion. Because of the unsuccessful coup by the Titans, Zeus is ultra-cautious. He has selected four names for approval. The final vetting process will pass to us. Any flaw in these candidates' personality has to be exposed."

"That's fair enough; you did a good job on Demeter and the others. With the help of Minos and Alastor, you can dig into their closets and find their skeletons."

The driver dropped them at the London Executive Offices in Curzon Street at eleven o'clock.

"There's time to freshen up, get ourselves a coffee, and wait for the others to arrive," said Athena as they glided to the first floor in the lift.

The venue was as professional as they remembered. Phoenix and Athena followed the signs to the room Olympus occupied on these occasions. The eight high-backed comfortable chairs were spaced evenly around the long, light-coloured wooden table — four chairs on either side.

"No doubt the security sweep has been done," said Phoenix, taking the opportunity to switch off his mobile phone. He knew the protocol at these meetings well.

"The name cards have altered," Athena remarked. "We're sat opposite Zeus and Hera.

"Two united fronts," shrugged Phoenix. "Zeus is keen to consign the Titans to history.

A New Dawn

The two colleagues sat together and drank their coffees, and waited.

Their fellow Olympians arrived as the clock on the wall clicked around to half-past eleven. Hera and Zeus, the elderly married couple, came together. The reserve they had shown at earlier meetings was gone. Their greetings were warm and sincere. They were soon seated with their refreshments, keen to hear news from Larcombe. Not on Olympus affairs, just how little Hope was.

Sir Malcolm Dunseith, the Privy Counsellor, soon joined them. Dionysus had a few problems with his vines and was worried last year's vintage wouldn't be as popular as his previous crops. Zeus and Hera were sympathetic.

Phoenix listened; farming folk always have problems. The weather's too dry, too wet, too hot, or too cold. Finally, the door opened, and in breezed Aphrodite.

Elizabeth, the Duchess of Lochalsh, looked flushed.

"What on earth's the matter, dear," said Hera, rushing to her side.

"Never again," she said, "Sir James offered me a lift from Scotland today. He said it seemed silly for me to travel south alone when he was flying south. I thought it was an excellent suggestion, but being buffeted by high winds and sitting in a two-seater plane no bigger than a baked bean can is horrendous. Despite how rotten the service is these days, I'd prefer to suffer a train journey. I'm only just recovering. I wish we had a drop of scotch to liven up this coffee."

Heracles arrived a minute later with Apollo. Sir James Grant-Nicholls had spotted Troy Gardner, the former boxer, downstairs and waited for him. Although they were not ordinarily close companions, Athena imagined Heracles had used the tactic to keep his distance from Aphrodite until she had calmed.

Elizabeth had recovered enough to ask after Hope. As Athena was repeating the update she had given Zeus and Hera, the Duchess was scrabbling around in her bag.

"Wonderful, Athena. I know I brought something for her. It's in here somewhere. Ah, here we are."

She handed over a beautifully knitted cardigan.

"I made it myself, dear; I enjoy knitting. It keeps my hands warm in the winter. My castle is so difficult to keep warm, you know. I pray it will fit."

"She'll grow into it," whispered Phoenix, which caused Athena to stifle a giggle.

Minutes later, Zeus called the meeting to order. He outlined the agenda and suggested they broke for refreshments after the first three items. His first report concerned Olympus' finances. Despite legal hurdles, Olympus finally acquired significant sums from the estates of Demeter, Poseidon, Hermes, and Nemesis. As for properties they owned, they had altered and refurbished the infamous mews cottage and Poseidon's house in Elmbridge. They added to the number of safe-houses available to Olympus. New funds were necessary to meet the increased threats at home and abroad.

Phoenix listened intently to the accounts of successful missions on the continent of Europe and North Africa. He had the recent trip to London to remember; it brought home to him how much he'd missed the intensity of their direct actions in the months since Hope was born. Athena noticed him leaning forward in his chair, his brow furrowed in concentration. It was good to see the fire was still burning. The risks were high, but the vigilante killer she loved needed the thrill of the chase and the ultimate kill at the end. Olympus needed many others like Phoenix.

Zeus outlined his solution to that problem. Recruits were coming from service members returning from action in Afghanistan. Also, from postings in Germany, now that bases were abandoned in that arena. So there could be no poster campaign or recruiting vehicle visiting various town centres. Instead, it was a stealthy process where existing agents used their contacts, still serving, to ask them to 'flag up' men and women with the right qualities.

"What numbers are you looking for, Zeus?" asked Heracles.

"A minimum of fifty; we would prefer one hundred," said Zeus. "They will be trained at Larcombe Manor."

"Our senior trainers will be in place in a few weeks," said Athena. "We will be ready for the first intake by June."

"Excellent," said Dionysus, "the more, the merrier."

"Let's break there for the moment," Zeus said. So the Olympians moved to the side tables holding their buffet lunch. As they ate, drank, and chatted, Hera moved over to Athena.

"The atmosphere is so much improved, don't you think?" she whispered. "That tension, and malice, that one could sense around the room has gone. But, of course, I still have nightmares over what happened to Demeter and the others. Zeus kept telling me it was unavoidable, but we had been working together, side by side, for years. No one had a clue they were thinking along different lines from the rest of us. Erebus would have spotted it, I'm sure. He saw everything."

Athena didn't wish to dwell on the past. The Titans had paid the price for their treachery, and there could be no regrets. It was essential to keep moving forward.

"Phoenix and I have more news," she told Hera to change the subject. Phoenix heard his name and paused, with a salmon sandwich halfway between his plate and mouth. The noise of chatter dulled until you could hear a pin drop.

"Phoenix and I are getting married later this month," Athena said. Her announcement echoed around the room.

The noise level rose again as their fellow Olympians congratulated them both. Everyone wanted to know when and where it would take place. Phoenix put his sandwich back on his plate.

"Thank you for your good wishes. It's later this month and will be a quiet ceremony with a dozen family and friends. That's enough about us; let's finish lunch and get back to that schedule."

Zeus took the hint, and the meeting reconvened around the main table. He had one major item to outline before he revealed the names of the four candidates he'd selected. The topic ahead of them was organised crime and the growth of the super gang.

"Organised crime has traditionally been governed by homegrown organised groups involved in many illegitimate businesses. We are a multi-ethnic society; therefore, criminal enterprises come from various ethnic backgrounds. They might originate on these shores, and White British groups still dominate. Outside the indigenous British syndicates, foreign gangs from Eastern Europe, Asia, the Indian subcontinent, and the Caribbean also operate here. Seven thousand organised criminal groups cost the country 3.5 billion pounds annually."

"It's not as if we weren't aware of these figures, Zeus," said Apollo. "We've fought to keep them at bay for eight years."

"We've eliminated just a fraction of their number," said Phoenix. "Several of the worst criminals have indeed learned crime doesn't pay, but the authorities have as good as conceded defeat to the gangs. We are too few to do more than irritate them now and again. Apollo's right; this is old ground. What do you think has changed?"

"Street gangs are putting their differences aside," Zeus explained, "to form a national super gang. We've read Athena's recent report on your actions in London, Phoenix. You hid the identity of our hand in the death of a vicious gang leader by manufacturing evidence that pointed to a rival. Clever though it was, it's a device that will soon be outdated and unbelievable. This emerging trend towards a super gang would see control of the lucrative drug trade pass into the hands of a vast network."

"Where is the centre of this threat based? Who's leading the setting up of this network?" asked Apollo.

"It doesn't work that way, Apollo," Zeus continued. "There have always been loose connections between the major cities of London, Birmingham, and Manchester. In those cities, the growing network gradually absorbs local units into their number. Either by force of argument or violence. The day will come if this threat remains unchecked, when only a few hundred gangs exist, rather than the seven thousand I quoted earlier."

"Creating the nationwide network would be relatively simple," said Phoenix. "We have received reports at Larcombe of a shift in how the less local gangs operate. Many are actively doing business together, despite their traditional or ethnic differences. It makes sound economic sense. Violence attracts attention from the police; many of their numbers end up behind bars, even if only for a short period. What they want to do now is make money. It makes much more sense for them to work together."

"Why were these loose connections established in the first place?" asked Aphrodite.

"A lot of drugs and firearms find their way to the Midlands first," Zeus answered, "so the gangs there formed alliances as they trafficked the goods around the country."

"The street-level gangs will still do the legwork and take most of the risk," Phoenix added, "but the aim would be to keep adding pieces to the jigsaw. As the elements are locked together, they could create a country-wide power base of frightening proportions."

"As Phoenix remarked, many of the main ethnic gangs have linked up with gangs of British criminals to enable them to work more efficiently," said Zeus. "The National Crime Intelligence Service reports that gangs share the risks of smuggling drugs across multiple borders. Each stage is handled by whichever gang has the greatest experience. That creates challenges for the police because the chain doesn't collapse if they identify and arrest an individual gang. The next gang immediately fills the gap in the network in the pecking order."

"This network stretches beyond our borders, then?" asked Heracles.

"Russian gangs are the most powerful across Europe," said Zeus, "they specialise in financial crime and money laundering. The next biggest threats within Europe and on our shores come from the newer EU member states. We only have to recall the deadly battle at Eton Wick that saw us lose several valuable agents. The Bulgarians have a strong presence here, and the Albanians are only months away from joining the party."

"What's their speciality?" asked Hera.

"The trafficking of drugs and people and taking over the vice industry wherever they infiltrate," replied her husband.

"Nasty," said Hera with a shudder.

"That's something to look forward to," said Athena. "However, I believe we need to concentrate on the brains behind this network. Earlier this month, we discussed this at Larcombe Manor. The methods gangs are using to distribute drugs are increasingly sophisticated. That takes a good deal of organising. The heads of these gangs are highly intelligent. If we can play any role in the fight against the completion of the jigsaw Phoenix alluded to, then these men must be our target."

There was a unanimous agreement with Athena's suggestion in the room. Zeus paused for a moment before continuing: -

"We must make that our priority, Athena. I agree with the logic. There's just one problem we must be prepared to face. If we stick our heads above the barricades, we risk getting shot. These gang bosses are intelligent. It won't be long before they realise someone is targeting their number. They use violence daily to ensure their business operations continue unchecked. The hunter will become the hunted."

The room was silent for a time.

"I think that was long enough to produce a viable alternative," said Phoenix. "It was a straight choice of 'fight or flight'. We have elected to fight."

Athena felt that everyone around the table had been holding their breath. After Phoenix had spoken, it seemed as if everyone breathed out simultaneously. The die was cast.

"This will be a major topic in our direct actions for the foreseeable future," said Zeus. "Let's finish today's schedule with brief descriptions of our new Olympians. I hope you will agree that I've chosen well. Then it's over to you, Athena. We will await your final approval."

Zeus displayed a series of photographs on a screen at the end of the long table. As the lights dimmed, the Olympians turned to view their potential colleagues.

"This is *Ludovic Tremayne*, 46 years old. He is a director on the boards of several oil and gas exploration companies. Before that, he completed eighteen years of service with the British Army. He was attached to various campaigns in Eastern Europe and the Middle East. While with 22SAS in Iraq, he received the Conspicuous Gallantry Cross. He married Rosalind Wilson, 44, in 1990. They live in Cradoc, near Brecon, and have two children. His code name would be *ACHILLES*. To match his war hero status,"

"What a handsome man," said Aphrodite, "does he have the funds we seek?"

"He is from a noble family," said Zeus. "While he may not bring as much money to this table as others among us, he has invaluable hands-on knowledge of counter-terrorism techniques.

Our second candidate is *Jean-Paul St. Clair*, 56 years old. He was born in Paris, but his family moved to the UK in the early Sixties. He studied at the Royal College of Art and is a renowned industrial designer and inventor. He sold his group of plastics companies in 2009 for a shade under three billion pounds. His wife Simone was born in 1979; she is a former glamour model. They have a flat in Paris, a ski chalet in Chamonix, and a country house near Redbrook, Monmouth. They have no children."

"What code name might we assign to him?" asked Heracles. "I've met him; he's a tough businessman, despite the impression he gives of being merely an 'ideas man'. Full of Gallic charm, but as hard as flint when he needs to be."

"Sounds as if he's just our man," said Phoenix.

"*DAEDALUS*," said Zeus, in response to Heracles's enquiry, "he continues the flavour of the people I have been hunting; we need to inject more youth and diversity into the upper echelons of the organisation. Of course, they must still support everything we stand for, but new blood will keep us from becoming stale. None of us is getting any younger."

"Excuse me, but some of us don't consider ourselves old," said Athena, smiling, "but I agree with you. So far, both names you've proposed bring particular talents which would offer much to Olympus."

"We have two men and two ladies on our list," Zeus continued. "This is *Piya Adani*. She will be forty in October. Her family arrived from Kenya in the early Seventies. She was born in Leeds and educated at the Grammar School. She completed a Business Management degree at Leeds University, studying part-time while helping her father in his business. From humble beginnings, selling Indian food from a market stall, her father expanded his range of products, and over the next twenty-five years, the business continued to thrive. When her father died suddenly in 2003, Piya took control. Under her stewardship, the company has doubled in size. Several conglomerates were keen to add her business to their portfolio. Piya stoutly rejected their offers over eighteen months; in October last year, she sold the business for seven hundred and fifty million pounds."

"Do we know what changed her mind?" asked Phoenix.

"The people she sold to didn't make the highest bid. Yet, they agreed to every stipulation Piya made regarding the future security of her workforce. They guaranteed the continued integrity of the product and maintained her father's company ethos. She wanted to protect everything they had built. Once she was happy the legacy was secured, she felt it was time to move on, to have fun. Ever since she left school at eighteen, she has worked tirelessly, dispensing with holidays and social life. She's single; but 'lives in hope', to quote from her Facebook page."

"What can she bring to the table, apart from her obvious wealth?" asked Apollo.

"How convinced are we that she shares our ideals?" added Dionysus.

"Piya brings youth and vitality; as a British-born Asian, she would provide a balance that we may not possess at present. As for her ideology, Athena and her team will test those to the limit. However, her record in the local community over the past decade suggests she won't let us down. She would become *AMBROSIA*.

Finally, we have *Dawn Prentice*, born in Cambridge in 1976. As the only child of a West Indian immigrant couple in an English university city, she sided with other outsiders and rebels. Bob Marley was her idol. She studied Politics at Reading University. Her gap year took her to the Far East, where she fell in with a crowd of fellow ex-students who introduced her to drugs. Dawn dropped out and only returned to the UK when deported from Australia. Her first stay at a rehab clinic was in 2001. She finally got herself clean by 2005. She had lost seven years of a meaningful working life to addiction. Dawn has worked for a charity that has helped recovering addicts for eight and a half years. Her parents won a massive Euro million jackpot in 2010 but died a year ago in a freak paragliding accident while on a third 'around the world' tour. Dawn is keen to use her parent's windfall in areas that help combat the spread and use of drugs. Her code name would be *AURORA*."

"Is she married; does she have children?" asked Hera.

"Neither; she has no family living in Britain," replied Zeus. "As for relationships, there were only a few since her first year at Reading. She lives alone in Notting Hill. Those are the preliminary details for our four candidates. Over to you, Athena."

"When is the next meeting, Zeus?" Athena asked.

"The first week in July," he replied, "if you can complete your checks as soon as possible, I can invite them to attend our meeting in Manchester."

"Ah, closer to home," said Aphrodite. "I can take the train."

Heracles seemed to be disappointed but held his tongue.

"We'll bring this meeting to a close," said Zeus, "many thanks for coming here today. We still have much to achieve. My final words, though, are for Phoenix and Athena. Best wishes for your wedding. I'm sure you'll be happy together. The Olympus Project is fortunate to have you among its number."

Athena and Phoenix thanked Zeus, and everyone said their farewells. Then, Athena pulled Phoenix to one side as they waited for their driver to bring the car around to the front of the LEO building.

"Just watch them, Phoenix," she whispered, "they are leaving in groups. Zeus and his wife, Hera, led the way. The other four were side-by-side, only a few steps behind. What a difference to our first meeting."

"The eight of us overall formed a cohesive unit today. We covered a lot of ground, and there was a positive exchange of views. The dynamic will change again if the four candidates survive the vetting process. We must take care they are absorbed into the Olympus family. We can't risk developing an old and a new faction. Look where that led before."

Minutes later, they were en route to Bath and home.

"When Zeus said he was aiming for 'fresh blood', he wasn't kidding, was he?" said Phoenix.

"Change is continuous, Phoenix," said Athena, "the only constant is evil."

Chapter Ten

Friday, 4th April 2014

When Phoenix and Athena arrived for the nine o'clock meeting, they discovered Giles and Artemis had been active in the ice-house. They had promised to deliver a name for the person responsible for the deaths of Candy Jacobs and Daphne Richards within the week. The smiles on their faces gave the game away.

Athena opted to stick to her schedule. She opened proceedings with a brief summation of yesterday's Olympus meeting events. She sensed Phoenix growing impatient. The Two Stooges, too, looked as if they had heard a whisper that something important was imminent. Athena was keen for her authority to be recognised; these meetings could descend into a 'free-for-all' if she didn't maintain discipline.

Athena invited Minos and Alastor for their input. They seemed reticent for the first time in living memory. Often, she had to persuade them to cut things short to avoid meetings running through until lunchtime. Those few snatched hours with Hope were precious, especially when she was so tiny and vulnerable. Athena didn't want Maria Elena to become more of a mother figure to her daughter than her.

Athena's attention had drifted away for a few seconds. She realised Phoenix had asked if she was alright.

"I'm fine, Phoenix; if you have nothing to offer, gentlemen, we should move on to news from the surveillance section?"

"We have found our man, Athena," said Giles. "In the past three days, we have uncovered a terrifying trail of death across several countries. Arjun Krishnan, fifty-eight years old, a self-styled GP based in Solihull, in the West Midlands. He arrived in this country three years ago from Baltimore, Maryland. Krishnan had portrayed himself there as a psychiatrist for over a decade. The trail leads back to his native Mumbai, when he began a new career treating patients without medical training. Krishnan had lost his job in the filmmaking industry due to complaints of sexual harassment."

"The fake doctor set up a makeshift medical practice in Dharavi," said Artemis. "Which is a slum where half a million people exist, crammed into five hundred acres. When Krishnan fled to the US, he faced numerous charges of practising medicine without a license; fears grew that he was much more dangerous than anyone suspected. The authorities now believe the fake doctor was responsible for the deaths of up to thirty people. They died because of an overdose of prescription medicine. Hundreds of people visited Krishnan daily; the queue outside his shack was filled with sick men and women to whom he would always supply pills from the internet. It operated like a sweet shop. He shovelled pills into a bag, and they handed over a few coins."

"When the authorities started asking too many questions, he fled to the States," said Giles, "he had family in Baltimore, an elderly aunt and uncle who took him in. Krishnan told them he had re-trained as a psychiatrist after he had quit the film industry. They helped him financially, enabling him to set up a practice in the city. He repaid them by overprescribing them with antibiotics. They died six months apart in 2008. After his uncle died, Krishnan persuaded his aunt to alter her will. When she died, he inherited everything. That raised concerns in the neighbourhood. He continued to dish out opiates and psychoactive drugs at the practice, which provided a far more lucrative income than in his home country. Krishnan grew very rich very fast. By 2010, over a dozen deaths of patients were linked to controlled substances prescribed by the fake physician. Baltimore PD received complaints from relatives that they believed Krishnan had given their loved ones drugs without a legitimate purpose. The police were wary of overreacting. Many of Krishnan's patients were addicts, and tens of thousands of their fellow Americans abuse prescription drugs daily. Before they could act, Krishnan moved again."

"When the police raided the practice's offices," said Artemis, "they found them empty. He had sold the house, liquidated his assets, and flown to London. Then, a few months later, he turned up in Solihull. We heard of two deaths he was responsible for from Minos but other incidents over the past three years. This guy is another Harold Shipman. After six months, he branched out from general practice and rented accommodation for a beauty clinic. The money amassed in the States allowed him to set up a slick-looking cosmetic surgery business with state-of-the-art equipment."

"How could he get away with it for so long?" asked Athena.

"In general practice, he chose victims well. Often, they were widowed and lived alone," said Giles. "Residents were unconcerned when one of their elderly neighbours passed away suddenly despite not suffering from any known illness. The local community accepted Krishnan, and patients described him as a hardworking doctor if he was a little abrupt and arrogant. His behaviour never raised suspicions from other healthcare professionals working in the area. At the beauty parlour, he pandered to his female clients' vanity. Even if treatments didn't prove fatal, they were unlikely to admit they had undergone treatments that left them in pain. Undertakers confirmed to our agents that Krishnan's patients died at a higher rate than other GPs, but he always reassured them there was no cause to be concerned. Despite evidence to the contrary, he maintained the aura of a caring family doctor. Krishnan enjoys exercising control over life and death; in the decade and a half he's been operating illegally, he's become addicted to killing. We could be talking about anything between fifty and one hundred victims."

"He's got a way to go to catch up with Dr Death," grunted Rusty.

"I think it's high time we closed his little shop of horrors, don't you?" said Phoenix.

"Not so fast, Phoenix," said Henry Case, "it won't be that simple. In Brentwood, you could collect your target and bring him here so we can dispose of him. Arjun Krishnan is a slippery devil; he evaded the law in Mumbai, and Baltimore, don't forget."

"Giles began this report with 'we've found our man'," said Rusty, "well, have you or haven't you?"

"We know he carried out these murders, but he's not attended the surgery, or the clinic, in the past few days."

"Has he travelled overseas?" asked Athena. "Please tell me you've checked border control?"

"There are no records of Dr Arjun Krishnan leaving the UK by train, plane or sea crossing," said Giles.

"He may have used a fake passport and changed his appearance. He's not short of funds. We've got surveillance agents, both on the ground in the West Midlands and the ice-house hunting him. We need time."

"Make him your priority, Giles," said Athena.

"I think we may have covered enough ground this morning," she continued. "Minos and Alastor, please take these four files. We need as comprehensive an investigation into these people as you did for me on our fellow Olympians last year. We need to know every scrap of information about them from birth. No matter how insignificant. There can be no slip-ups with this vetting procedure. If they add to our number, they must be 'squeaky clean'."

"Leave it with us, Athena," said Minos.

Phoenix and Athena went upstairs to their apartment. Athena wanted to spend time with Hope before returning to work this afternoon. Phoenix was keen to start work on removing the threat of Arjun Krishnan, but his hands were tied until he knew where to base his plans.

"We can't let this guy slip through our fingers," Phoenix seethed, "perhaps I should go to the ice-house myself?"

"Let Giles and Artemis do what they're employed to do, Phoenix," said Athena.

Along the corridor, Rusty Scott was also seething. It was frustrating not having a location to go with the name of the killer they sought. Artemis had returned to the ice-house with Giles and Henry. He hated waiting. It didn't help that

Artemis wouldn't be finishing her shift for another six hours. Rusty decided to use up his pent-up energy in the swimming pool. One hundred lengths used to be a regular session for him in the old days when he was still unattached and required to train recruits in addition to direct actions when they arose. As he gathered up his swimming shorts and towel, he wondered whether he could even manage fifty lengths.

Athena was feeding Hope while Maria Elena had gone into the kitchen to prepare lunch. Phoenix decided he wasn't hungry.

"I'm going for a swim," he said, "ask Maria Elena to put my grub to one side. I'll eat when I get back."

"Okay, darling," said Athena, "have fun, but don't forget what I said. Leave the ice-house staff to search for Arjun Krishnan."

Ten minutes later, Phoenix was at the poolside. Rusty powered up the middle lane. It took him back to the early days at Larcombe. Three years on, and Rusty was blowing harder than Phoenix remembered. The years were finally catching up with him. They were catching up with each of them. Rusty saw his pal towering over him and stopped.

"I'm here because I'm frustrated with the wait," he said.

"Me too," said Phoenix, "there are only two weeks until the wedding. So I want this mission planned, executed and tied up with a ribbon well before the big day."

"There's not much we can do, mate. Why not get changed and join me? I hoped to do a hundred lengths, but what do you say to each of us doing forty?"

Phoenix swallowed hard.

"I'll do my best."

"I'm knackered," said Rusty, almost an hour later, as

they made their way painfully back towards the manor house.

"You can take a nap. Artemis won't be home for ages. I've food waiting for me, and Hope will be awake. Maria Elena deserves a break. I'll probably nod off thirty minutes after Athena gets back. That will be popular. Remind me never to go swimming with you again."

In the ice-house, Giles and the surveillance team scoured the country for signs of the fake doctor. There continued to be no sightings of him at international airport terminals, railway stations, or seaports. Comparing the image of every sixty years old man to the photo of Arjun Krishnan retrieved from his offices in Solihull was left to Artemis. It was going to be a long day.

Giles was alerted by another agent trawling through CCTV images from Birmingham New Street station. That was his most likely starting point if he had left the West Midlands.

"Got him; Krishnan caught a train on Monday lunchtime. Just checking; at that time, it was to Liverpool Lime Street from that platform."

"That will cut the numbers you're sifting through, Artemis," said Giles, "concentrate on Liverpool as a departure point."

"How many stops does that train make?" asked Artemis.

"Eleven, in total," the agent answered, "I'll check that he didn't get off along the route."

"Where might he have gone to from Liverpool, I wonder?" said Giles.

"We can't assume he isn't planning to flee the country," said Artemis, continuing to flick through images. "He may have travelled north to throw the police off the scent; if he suspected someone was on to him. On the other hand, he could be heading to Scotland or Ireland. Can we get someone to check whether he changed trains at Lime Street or left the station?"

Giles assigned another agent to that task.

"I'll check his financials," he said to Artemis. "If he felt the time was running out, Krishnan may have just panicked and made a run for it, but if he had a few days to prepare, he might have transferred funds to wherever he plans to set up in business. next."

The next hour was productive, if not conclusive. Krishnan had spent the entire ninety-minute journey on the train he boarded at New Street. When he left the carriage at Lime Street, Artemis spotted him in the street outside the station, hailing a taxi.

"Our man might have gone towards the city centre, I suppose. My guess is he's taken the Birkenhead Tunnel. Let's search for him at the ferry terminal."

The agents soon discovered Krishnan left on the Dublin ferry in the middle of Monday afternoon. Thus, he had a four days head start on his pursuers. On Monday morning, Giles found that the doctor withdrew twenty thousand euros from his bank account in large denominations. The balances on his various accounts were transferred to the Central Bank of Ireland on Tuesday morning.

"We lost him after he climbed into that taxi," said Artemis, "But we know he was spooked either by concerned relatives of his victims, the local police, or our agents. He secured enough cash to make his initial escape and to find a remote hideout in the Republic. That's where our search needs to concentrate now."

"With his money transferring to Dublin, it suggests he's setting up a clinic in the city," said Giles. "We could scupper his plans by an anonymous tip-off to the Garda. They would freeze his bank accounts, denying him access to funds. You're right, though. He has plenty of cash to stay off-grid for days, even weeks."

"Freezing his bank accounts would only confirm his suspicions that the authorities are on to his little game," cautioned Artemis. "He would use the cash to alter his appearance and fly further overseas. Perhaps, even back to India. It will be tough to track him in a city of half a million. A nightmare on a sub-continent with one and a half billion people."

"Fair point, Artemis," said Giles. "Our best hope is that Krishnan is hiding out in one of the small country towns within a fifty-mile radius of the capital."

"Good luck with finding him on CCTV in the outback, Giles," said Artemis, "we need people on the ground."

"We have only a handful of agents in the Irish Republic," said Giles, "nor do we have the same access to CCTV as we do for the UK. We need to contact Fintan O'Sullivan in Wexford. He will have the contacts we require to search effectively."

"Fintan's only two hours away," said Artemis, "he could set up a central command post in Dublin. From there, he can direct operations. He can keep in constant touch with us at Larcombe, plus coordinate the search patterns for the agents already in the country. Where are the nearest agents?"

"The few we have are in the major coastal towns," said Giles. "We'll get them to carry out swift surveillance in their region, then head towards Dublin. Fintan can give them new information as we receive it. After that, the noose will tighten, and if the Gods are with us, we will trap Arjun Krishnan in whatever hidey-hole he chose."

"Poor Rusty," sighed Artemis, "he'll be disappointed

again. Unfortunately, I can't see us finishing on time tonight."

"Someone else will be disappointed too," Giles said, somewhat embarrassed.

"Oh? Were you meeting you know who?"

"We were going to have dinner together, and then she was coming to my quarters."

"They always say the quiet ones are the worst," said Artemis. "They used to say that of me, so I'm a fine one to talk. I'm pleased, Giles; you're a good man. You deserve to find someone."

"It's early days," said Giles, "but it's going well so far. The difficult part is keeping it from Henry. He was keen on Maria Elena too, as you know. He doesn't realise that we see one another."

"Ah, I see," said Artemis, "well, he won't hear a thing from me, I promise you. Poor Henry, all that money on cologne went to waste."

The two colleagues ploughed on with the search routines. The rest of the team was due on the surface, but the night crew began their shift. They would soon discover it would not be a quiet Friday night.

Over in the Republic, Fintan O'Sullivan was driving towards Dublin on the M11. He had phoned ahead to book himself into a hotel overnight. In the morning, he would head to the internet café on Grafton Street. It would serve as his base until the other agents converged on the city. Fintan was used to surveilling criminals for Olympus, but the direct actions were always the responsibility of a high-up official from Larcombe Manor. He never carried a weapon, nor did his fellow agents. Fintan prayed this doctor they were chasing wasn't a violent man.

Artemis had asked one of her colleagues going off shift

to call Rusty when they reached the surface. Her partner was lounging on the settee, with his aches and pains, watching TV, when his phone rang. After listening to the message, he slammed the phone onto the table. He poured himself a large whisky.

"Looks as if it's supper for one again," Rusty groaned, "let's hope this overtime pays dividends."

Athena and Phoenix were relaxing in their rooms too. Hope had been put to bed an hour earlier. Athena heard from Giles that the trail had led them to Ireland. If things went well, they would have better news soon.

"How soon?" asked Phoenix tersely.

"We'll have an agent in Dublin from first thing tomorrow keeping Giles informed of progress. The Irish agents are moving in to prevent Krishnan from escaping. As soon as we find him, someone needs to fly in. Rusty can go if you prefer."

Phoenix levered himself awkwardly from the chair.

"What on earth is up with you tonight?" asked Athena.

"Rusty and I went swimming this afternoon. I think we overdid it."

Athena laughed, "No doubt, you pushed each other further than was good for you. You two are so competitive, and I bet the frustration of being unable to get after Krishnan contributed to the over-ambitious exercise."

"I'll be okay tomorrow," said Phoenix, "how do I get over there?"

"Olympus has a helicopter at Cardiff airport. Why don't I drive you over now; I called to warn Biggles, and he can fly you tonight. You can carry whatever weapons you wish to take for the mission. He won't bat an eyelid. Biggles has flown more missions in hostile territory than you've had hot dinners. I'll get him to log a flight plan from Rhoose to

Dublin. He can land at the airport as scheduled after dropping you off further along the coast. Nobody will be any the wiser, I promise you."

"How am I getting out again afterwards?" asked Phoenix.

"As soon as you call him, he can schedule a return trip. You need to be at the rendezvous point so he can move in, hover, pick you up, and fly out in less than a minute. Have you decided what to do with Krishnan?"

"Biggles won't be picking two people up; that's a given," said Phoenix, "if we're leaving soon, what do we do with Hope?"

"I'll ring Maria Elena; it's not that late. She should still be up. I'll ask her to babysit."

Athena rang their nanny. There was a tap on the door two minutes later, and Maria Elena entered.

"Everything alright?" Athena asked. She thought Maria Elena looked glum.

"I hope so," she replied. "I was looking forward to going out tonight, but it got cancelled. Giles is always so busy."

Phoenix guessed who she meant. If Giles was still underground, Artemis was too, and Rusty would be spitting feathers. It didn't seem they needed his pal on this mission, though.

Thirty minutes later, Athena was driving them towards the M4. Phoenix had packed a bag with a change of clothes, passport, maps, compass, combat knife, pistol, and ammunition. Phoenix hadn't been able to plan for this job as he was used to; even now, he had no idea where to search for his quarry. The gun might be impossible to use. On the other hand, the knife could be the best option. Phoenix worked through possible scenarios as they sped past the lower volume of vehicles on the motorway at such a late hour.

As they left the motorway and weaved down the country road that led to the airport, his mind turned to other matters.

"Why on earth is this pilot called Biggles? Is he a throwback to the Thirties?"

"I knew you would ask me that," she replied, "it's embarrassing. Biggles is not a square-chinned hero with an old leather flying helmet, but he's quite mad. Flying with him will be an experience, by all accounts, but men who have talked of how he rescued them from hell-holes worldwide swear he's the best damn pilot that ever flew a chopper."

"I get that bit, and I'll steel myself for a few bumpy moments, so what's embarrassing?"

"His name is Les Biggar; he's from Aberdeen and in his early fifties. His nickname when he was in the RAF was Big Les. It morphed into Biggles over the years as he became the legendary pilot he is today. The big part didn't come from his surname."

Phoenix laughed, "Barrack-room humour; boys will be boys. I can't wait to meet the guy."

"You won't have to wait long; here we go."

Athena drew the car to a halt. A tall, rangy-looking man loomed out of the dark and pointed to a gate to her left.

"Follow me through here, ma'am."

He swiped a passkey over the panel on the gate, and it swung open. Athena drove through, and Les Biggar pointed to where she should park. The helicopter sat on the tarmac, yards from its hangar.

"It looks tiny," muttered Phoenix as he grabbed his bag and got out.

Athena kissed him on the cheek and wished him a safe journey.

Les Biggar didn't want to waste any time chatting. He took the bag from Phoenix, stowed it behind the passenger seat and told him to get in and belt up. He spoke briefly to Athena, and then she drove through the gate and back to Larcombe.

"Call me Biggles, Phoenix," the gruff Aberdonian said as he climbed on board, "let's get this thing airborne."

"Flight time will be around forty-five minutes," Biggles shouted.

"No rush," replied Phoenix, regretting having agreed to sit next to the pilot. He could have sat in the rear seats with his eyes tight shut. Then he wouldn't have had to endure the seat-of-the-pants flying style this madman favoured.

"Right, let's get this straight," shouted Biggles. "I'm dropping you in the grounds of Shanganagh Park. It's twelve miles south of Dublin. When I tell you it's time to leave, grab your bag and get out. Crouch low until I'm clear. I will only be on the ground for five seconds. Then I'm up and away to the airport. Got it?"

"Got you," replied Phoenix. "This shouldn't take long. I've got people to help me find a fake doctor called Krishnan. He's a killer. I'll call you when I've completed the mission and need a ride home."

"Not so fast, Phoenix. I'm not flying in daylight; I don't need anyone clocking the details of this chopper. So, you find this guy, carry out your mission, and then get back to where I drop you. I'll scoop you up in the same fashion at eight-thirty tonight. I'll be with you in twenty minutes from

Collinstown. So, I expect to hear confirmation that the pickup is on at least twenty minutes before that."

"I'll be there," said Phoenix.

"You'd better," said Biggles. "I can only stand so much of Dublin's bonhomie. This job needs to complete by tonight."

"No pressure," said Phoenix.

"Not for me," said Biggles.

They spent the rest of the flight in silence. As the helicopter neared the coastline, Phoenix could see the lights of houses dotted here and there and the lights of cars on the motorway. The chopper came in low, skimming over tall trees bordering the estate. It was dark, very dark.

"Grab your kit," shouted Biggles. Phoenix retrieved his bag from the back of the helicopter. With a bump, they landed. Phoenix didn't wait; he opened the door, rolled out onto the grass, and slammed it shut behind him. As he curled up in a ball on the grass, he heard the twin engines roar, and Biggles was up and away. Phoenix waited. The sound of the chopper's rotors was already fading as Les Biggar continued his flight north to the airport. No one there would be any the wiser that the logged flight plan had included an unscheduled detour.

Phoenix assessed his surroundings. Twelve miles to negotiate on foot would be a bind. Walking at night near main roads was dangerous and likely to attract attention. Even if the Garda only stopped to ask if he needed a lift anywhere, it was still a meeting he wished to avoid. He found shelter in the ranks of trees. He rested for two hours. An hour before sunrise, he made his way through the estate grounds until he reached the boundary.

Phoenix called Fintan O'Sullivan. The rough sound of

his voice told him he had disturbed the Irishman's beauty sleep.

"Fintan, it's Phoenix. Sorry, it's so early, mate, but can you collect me? I'm a few hundred yards from the junction to the M50, from M11. I'm near the front gate in Shanganagh Park, the Community Centre."

"I'll be with you by sunrise, Phoenix,"

Five minutes after six, Phoenix set off towards the main road. No traffic was passing, so he scaled the wrought-iron fence and trotted along the grass verge. A car passed him, swung around in the gateway to the Park and came back to pick him up. It was Fintan.

"Top of the morning, Fintan," said Phoenix.

"Bollocks," replied his fellow agent. "I've missed my breakfast coming out here to collect you. So we're off to the Pantry for one of the best Irish breakfasts in the city. They open at half seven in Talbot Street. You're buying."

Phoenix didn't complain. At least he wasn't walking or hitching a lift into the city. His driver had one of those faces with something a bit off wherever you looked. He had broken his nose at least once. There was a small white scar above his top lip. He had one brown eye and one green eye. And when he turned his head towards him, Phoenix noticed his right ear stuck out while his left ear lay flat on his head. His dark brown hair curled over the collar of his jacket. Fintan O'Sullivan was in his mid-thirties, and even Phoenix had to admit; the man was devilishly handsome,

"The nearest internet café to the restaurant is two minute's walk away, so it's perfect," Fintan said. "When we're ready to face the day, we'll get online. I can talk with the ice-house, tell them you've arrived safe and sound, and get an update on chummy. Then I'll check in with the others. They should be closing the net on your man."

"The sooner, the better," said Phoenix.

"Not for him," grinned Fintan. He was wide awake now.

They drove into the city and parked the car. A steady stroll brought them to the door of the Pantry as the sign turned to 'Open'.

"Perfect timing," said Fintan, "two breakfasts, and I take my coffee black."

Phoenix ordered their meals and drinks. He recalled the 'heart-attack on a plate' offerings he had eaten with Frankie and Billy on the Scottish leg of the Maiden's Hair tour. He couldn't believe four years had passed. Then, those meals were transport café specials; but today, when their plates arrived, they ate in silence, with deference to the food's quality.

"That was great," said Phoenix as he finished his coffee.

"It was almost worth being woken up at such an ungodly hour," said Fintan.

He was out of his chair and walking towards the door. Phoenix reluctantly paid the bill and hurried after him. The internet café was indeed only a few doors further along Talbot Street. Fintan had already sat at a terminal when Phoenix walked through the door. Typical of these establishments, nobody looked up from their screen.

Phoenix sat beside his colleague.

"What's the latest?"

"I'm still waiting for the ice-house to respond. My contacts in the Republic are progressing towards Dublin. So far, none of them has found hide or hair of your man. If he's left Dublin, he's hidden way deeper than we would prefer."

"It's likely that he's planning to stay in, or near the capital, to carry on the same business operation he had in the UK."

Fintan nodded.

"Paddy Power has stopped taking bets," he said.

"Giles and the ice-house can't track CCTV from here as easily as they can on the mainland," said Phoenix. "Can you track Krishnan's whereabouts from here?"

"Keep it quiet. It might seem nobody gives a shit what you're up to in here, but when I search for clues, some might construe my methods as illegal. It's better not to raise anyone's unwanted interest."

"Point taken," said Phoenix.

"Giles is ready to deliver the goods," said Fintan.

Fintan and Phoenix viewed the images transmitted from Larcombe Manor. Arjun Krishan was pictured leaving the ferry. Artemis has trawled through the hotels near the terminal without luck. Giles had discovered Dr Krishnan had booked into a hotel a mile from Croke Park for five nights. He was probably finishing breakfast.

"Nearly there, Phoenix," said Fintan. "Sure, it's only a ten-minute stroll to the other side of the Liffey."

"Krishnan's a slippery customer, Fintan; we had better confirm that he stayed there last night. He's not short of euros. He could afford to make a booking, or two, to throw us off the scent. Call the hotel. Ask to speak to him. Try to get the room number out of them. I'll call around if he is there to leave my calling card."

Fintan called the hotel.

"Could I speak to Dr Arjun Krishnan, please? We studied medicine together; I understand he stayed with you last night?"

"Just one moment, sir," said the young man in reception. "I'm sorry, there's no reply from his room. The doctor must have stepped out."

"And which room would that be? I'd love to catch up with him again to reminisce. Then, if you're still working later when I drop by, I'll give you something for your help."

"Room 208, sir. Be sure to ask for Gerard."

Fintan ended the call. He returned to the laptop. Phoenix was always in awe of the ability and inventiveness of those that excelled with computers. His talents were far better than when he left for Africa with Sue Owens, but as he watched Fintan, he realised he was a relative novice.

"What am I looking at?" Phoenix asked his colleague what looked like a map with several blinking red dots on the screen.

"My colleagues have GPS trackers in their Olympus vehicles. I can see their current position. Those that travelled from Kerry, Newcastle, and Galway couldn't check much last night. Since early this morning, they've been working their way towards us. You can tell from the screen; they have perhaps two to three hours to go before they can finish sweeping the path they're following. We could have located your man at that time. The closest operative is Brendan Connery."

"Where did he set out from?" asked Phoenix.

"Naas," replied Fintan. "I'll call him and bring him here. Then, if Krishnan has slipped away, I can re-direct the remaining agents to sweep the areas missed by Brendan."

"Fair enough; check whether Krishnan has returned to the hotel. If he has, stay there and follow him if he leaves. It's far too public a place to kill him there. However, if he's still in the city on foot, we must search nearby. I'll take on that task. When Brendan arrives, he can take your place inside the hotel. You'll be more valuable to us here, with your computer skills. While you're away, I can identify commercial property for sale or rent that might suit his purpose. Show me quickly how to start on that, and you can get away."

Fintan found the necessary links. Phoenix had to tell him to take it slow so he could make idiot notes, but after two minutes, he reckoned he was fit to go.

"I'll be off to the hotel," said Fintan. "You paid for breakfast, so I'd better stump up twenty euros for Gerard, I suppose."

"I thought it was the Scots who were tight," said Phoenix, shaking his head.

With a wave, Fintan left. Phoenix began his search for possible sites that might attract Krishnan. Where would the vain women of Dublin find attractive if a clinic opened on the city's outskirts? He narrowed the search to modern office space, slightly off the beaten track. Phoenix hunted for premises that allowed them to slip in and out for cosmetic procedures; without people poking their noses into their business.

Phoenix had an impressive list in no time. His phone rang; it was Fintan. It had cost him fifty euros to discover that Krishnan was not due back for hours. After some persuasion, Gerard informed him that a hire car had arrived at eight o'clock, and the doctor had driven away.

"Did you get the car hire firm and the make and model?" asked Phoenix.

"It was an Avis compact," said Fintan, "I'm heading back now. I'll check the main routes out of the city to see if we can find where he's headed."

Phoenix continued his search, and his attention centred on one advert. It wasn't an office block or an industrial estate; it was a two-storey house with a sizeable ground-floor extension to the rear. The house needed modernisation, and the price reflected that fact.

"Now that looks perfect," muttered Phoenix, "do it up, live on the premises, and turn the extension into a beauty clinic. That part of the building isn't visible from the road. Unless you knew it was there, anyone driving by would think it was just a private dwelling. Exactly what both Dr Death and his clients want; exclusivity."

Fintan was back from the hotel, and Phoenix showed him the advert.

Fintan took over control of the laptop.

"Brendan's in the car park up the road, by the way. He'll be with us in two minutes. That house is in Shanklin," he said, nodding at the image on the screen, "a half-hour from where I fetched you at the crack of dawn. We'll access the CCTV cameras on the roads leading to Shanklin and see if we can confirm where Krishnan is headed. Although, there might be quite a few hire cars on the road on a Saturday morning."

Phoenix looked at the clock on the laptop. It was amazing how time slipped through your fingers like grains of sand. What if he was wrong? What if Krishnan headed further west? As they drew closer to the city, the agents closing the net didn't know their target was in a car.

"Just in case I've picked the wrong property to home in on, can you ask the other agents to look out for an Avis compact?"

"Will do," said Fintan, not taking his eyes off the screen, "ah, here's Brendan, coming through the door now."

Phoenix shook the agent by the hand. Brendan Connery was short, stocky, and with a mop of unruly black curly hair. Brendan's clothes looked as though he had slept in them.

"Surely, it must be coffee o'clock, Fintan? I've got a throat on me like a bear's armpit." Their fellow agent announced his arrival in a voice so loud that it caused a few people working close by to look up and let Brendan know they preferred the library-like hush that had existed until a minute earlier. Brendan didn't notice.

"We'll get ourselves a drink in a moment and drink it on the run," said Fintan, "if I'm not mistaken, this is your man driving through Kimmage. I think you hit the nail on the head, Phoenix. Krishnan is planning to work from home, as they say. His customers would appear to be paying a friend or relative a social visit. Something of only passing interest to the curtain-twitchers. The nosy neighbours might take more notice if they knew he was injecting stuff in peoples' arses that might kill them."

Fintan suddenly closed the laptop and jumped up from his chair.

"Let's get moving then, lads," he cried, "there are great coffees in a shop on the corner. We'll collect the cars and head for Shanklin."

"What about the others?" asked Phoenix, hurrying after two Irishmen, who were already out of the door.

"I ordered them to stand by and await further orders," said Fintan, "didn't you see the message I sent? It's not just women who can multi-task, Phoenix. So don't let them know; it's best to let them believe they have a monopoly in one skill at least."

"You're not married, are you, Fintan?" Phoenix asked.

"Sure, why would I be married? There are so many women out there; it would be a crime to disappoint them by tying myself to one poor girl. Look around you, Phoenix. Aren't the women here in Dublin the most beautiful in the world? Did you see the fair-skinned beauty's look as she brushed past me?"

Brendan laughed out loud.

"Your first time in the city, Phoenix?"

"My first time in Ireland."

"There's a large park, two miles up the road, created in the seventeenth century, with your name on it, did you know?"

Phoenix had to admit that he didn't. They had arrived at the coffee shop. As they walked towards the car park in Lower Abbey Street, sipping their hot drinks, Fintan was still girl-watching.

"You don't wear a ring, Phoenix. So, you are a single man too. Why not grab yourself a girl and take her to the park? Wander among the trees. Lie beside her on the grass. As she looks deep into your eyes, tell her my name is Phoenix, all this is mine to give you, for your heart,"

"You'd be onto a winner every time, Phoenix," cried Fintan. Both the Irish agents laughed until they reached the car park.

Phoenix knew they didn't realise he and Athena were getting married two weeks today. It was a closely guarded secret. The two reminded him of Bazza and Thommo in the armoury. The humour was a defence mechanism. Olympus agents in the field could put their life on the line with every mission. Phoenix admired the men who walked beside him. He was confident they would be good men to have by his side if things got tough today.

Fintan steered his car down the ramps and away from the multi-storey. Brendan followed two cars behind them. They headed for Shanklin.

Phoenix called Giles.

"We've identified a probable site Krishnan is planning to

purchase in Shanklin. He's there now. We'll be there in twenty minutes."

Giles summarised the latest information they had from the ice-house. He had nothing relevant to the situation in Ireland. Phoenix was watching the road signs signalling they were closing on their destination.

"Pass the usual message on to Athena, Giles; it won't be long now. We should tidy up this job in the next hour or two. I'll ring for the chopper pilot for my lift home later; I should be in Cardiff by half-past ten. Contact the transport department and organise a car, please."

"Consider it done, Phoenix," Giles said and ended the call.

Fintan drove into Shanklin and found the premises. He parked on the side of the road twenty yards past the turning. Brendan swung his car in front of them, parked and strolled to join them.

A muddy dirt track led through open fields to the house, standing fifty yards from the road. At the rear of the property stood a dense line of trees stretching at least one hundred yards in each direction. There was only one car parked in front of the garage to the left-hand side.

"Avis compact," he said, "he's still here. Brendan, block the entrance behind us to cut off his escape. The approach is too open; he's certain to spot us. If he waits until we've reached the end of the drive, he might dash for it. We must avoid a car chase. Or the need to do the deed in the open. Okay, let's go inside."

Fintan turned the car around and drove up the dirt track. There was no movement from inside the house. Brendan blocked the entrance with his car. He closed his eyes; this was the type of operation he enjoyed.

Phoenix removed his weapons from his bag, fitted the

silencer to his Sig Sauer, and nodded to Fintan. They got out of the car. Fintan went to the front door. Phoenix made his way around the right-hand side of the house, checking the windows. Krishnan was not in the lounge or the kitchen. He could be upstairs; or in the rear extension, planning the layout of his lethal clinic.

Fintan rang the bell. There was no answer, so he tried the door. It was unlocked. He pushed it open, standing to one side, even though there was no evidence Arjun Krishnan was ever armed. It was a habit. He edged inside the hallway and cleared each room downstairs methodically. The house had been unoccupied for a while. Only a few scraps of furniture remained. Fintan reached the door that separated the main house from the single-storey extension. His hand reached for the handle.

His phone rang. In the silence that surrounded him, its loud ringtone startled him.

"Jesus, Phoenix, that scared the shit out of me."

"We've got a problem," said Phoenix quietly, "come through, watch where you walk and let me in through the French windows at the far end."

Fintan opened the door to find Dr Arjun Krishnan lying face down on the floor. The doctor was naked and shot three times. The shot that killed him had been through the back of the head. The exit wound at the front suggested his mother wouldn't recognise him.

Chapter Eleven

As Fintan stepped past the body, taking care to avoid the pooled blood, he guessed the shots to the buttocks came first to cause Krishnan as much pain as possible.

Phoenix stood outside the doors. Fintan let him in.

"Krishnan must have pissed off someone. It was a big mistake to mess with," said Fintan. "This was the last thing I expected."

Through the open doors, they could both make out the faint sounds of sirens.

"There's no time to get away using the track from the road," said Phoenix, "phone Brendan, get him to stall the Garda. Grab our bags, then set fire to the car. Wipe clean everything you touched in here. We leave this place as we found it. We'll go out the back way and run through the trees. They'll provide enough cover for us to escape. You can call Brendan to pick us up later."

Fintan did as ordered. It wasn't the first time the Irishman had torched a car. There had been loads of it on the estate when he'd been younger. But, after the call to

Brendan and a clean-up, he was soon outside the rear extension and over the fence. The sirens had stopped. Fintan joined Phoenix, handed him his holdall, and they ran through the thick trees, then out into residential streets, heading for Kimmage.

Back at the house, their colleague was being woken up by two irate Garda officers who were attending the scene of a murder. They weren't happy to find a car blocking the entrance. An officer called the fire brigade while Brendan moved his car.

By the time the officers reached the room which contained the fake doctor's body, the two agents had slowed their run; their escape was complete. They had time to stop for a breather. Fintan's phone rang. It was Brendan.

"I'm driving towards Kimmage. Where do you want me to collect you? What the hell's happening? You were only three minutes. The Garda in Terenure received the call fifteen minutes ago, informing them of a murder."

"Someone beat us to it. The guy was dead when we arrived. Pick us up outside the supermarket in five minutes."

Phoenix and Fintan arrived just as Brendan pulled up to the kerb. They jumped in, and he reversed out of the parking space.

"Where to now?" he asked.

"Somewhere we can relax and think," said Phoenix calmly. "Fintan, when you walked past the body, did anything catch your eye?"

"Apart from the blood, the large holes in his skull and butt cheeks, you mean? No, nothing springs to mind."

Brendan drove them back to the city and returned to the internet café. Fintan wanted immediate access to his toys if he needed them.

"I retrieved this note from Krishnan's left hand," said

Phoenix, "his right hand was splayed open; his left closed. Whoever killed the doctor knew we were coming. They timed the call to the police for us to get caught. We were lucky. If I had closed the doors behind me when I came inside, we might not have heard the sirens until the Garda arrived at the end of the track."

"The note carried our address?" asked Fintan. "You mean someone has been watching us since we arrived here in Talbot Street?"

"It's more worrying than that. You were right when you said Krishnan pissed off a villain, and that's who carried out that brutal killing. We need to find out who ordered the killing. See whether he's connected to one of the doctors' victims. This note was a personal message for me."

Phoenix spread the blood-spattered piece of paper on the front desk. He and Fintan read the typewritten message in silence.

'This one was personal. You should have kept your nose out of my business.
I don't know who you are, but I know Hackney was your handiwork.
G was a comrade.
Have fun with the Garda. H.'

"Shit. I see what you mean, Phoenix," said Fintan, "what this guy knows about Olympus will make them uncomfortable. He thought we would find this and get caught with the body. These London references are direct actions you carried out; I take it?"

"Recent, too," nodded Phoenix. "A month ago, Rusty Scott and I took two gang leaders off the streets, plus members of their crew. 'G' refers to Gavin McTierney, a nasty piece of work. Perhaps there's an Irish connection?"

"It's not unusual for London gangs to have family back in the Republic; we didn't all leave for Britain or America. This 'H' may have links to the underworld, and he put a contract on Krishnan. The woman involved must have meant something to him, whoever he is."

"What concerns me is we pride ourselves on carrying out our missions without raising suspicions from the authorities," said Phoenix. "Somehow, this guy spotted us in London and knew we planned to come to Ireland. I didn't know myself until only a few hours before I left Larcombe. This Krishnan job was unrelated to the drug dealers we targeted in Hackney and Tower Hamlets. Either someone has been tailing us every minute since I killed McTierney, or someone talked."

"Who knew you were flying over to find Krishnan?" asked Brendan.

"Apart from Athena, only Les Biggar, the crazy helicopter pilot who dropped me off at Shanganagh Park."

"They must have got to him," said Fintan. "It's unlikely they got onto you fast enough to have followed you back to Larcombe from the boroughs."

"We diverted via Brentwood for another clean-up job, so no doubt you're right. But, no, this guy must have access to a high level of intelligence-gathering capability. He's done similar searches to those Olympus carry out daily. He's tracked our vehicle movements, found our HQ and had us watched from somewhere outside the perimeter. Early Saturday morning, as our car left for Cardiff, Athena and I were followed. Then they took the registration of the chopper in Wales and found its flight plan. Les Biggar must have received a visit from their contacts here almost as soon as he landed. We should get to the airport; to see if he's OK. He's my lift home."

"Any idea who 'H' might be, Phoenix?" asked Fintan as they walked to the car.

"Not a clue."

Thirty minutes later, they arrived at the airport in Collinstown. Phoenix stayed in the car. Fintan and Brendan went to see if they could find out where Les Biggar parked his helicopter; and if he was somewhere in the surrounding buildings.

Ten minutes later, they returned.

"Call Larcombe," said Fintan, "tell them you'll need transport to get you home."

"An engineer found Les Biggar this morning," said Brendan. "He'd taken a severe beating and was taken to the nearest hospital. Your pilot's in a critical condition."

The drive back to the city was a sad one. Phoenix had to think. Was he stranded? He had the passport he'd used to get in and out of Ibiza after Erebus died; it should stand the scrutiny border control gives Brits returning to home soil. However, this time there was just one small problem. His method of arrival with Biggles meant no record existed of him having ever landed in the Republic. Could he risk it? How vigilant would the Irish authorities be?

Fintan spoke first.

"Look, Brendan can stay close to the hospital. I'll let the others know they can return to their home base; we'll not need their services today. Brendan will get updates on Biggar's progress and keep an eye open for trouble. When whoever's behind this killing discovers we avoided the Garda, they might come back to finish the job. People that vicious don't leave loose ends. They'll want to stop your pilot from providing clues about who questioned him."

"That sounds good," said Phoenix, "as for myself, I've

been wondering how I'll get home. I can't go into detail, but if I can avoid leaving Ireland by an official route, that would be best. Any ideas?"

"Once we've dropped Brendan off, we'll head back to my place in Wexford. I've got someone I can call who owes me a favour. It will cost Olympus a tidy sum, but you're the man. They need you at Larcombe. The sooner Olympus track who was behind Krishnan's murder and why, the better."

"Terrific," said Phoenix, "yeah, you're right. This message is gang-related. Killing the doctor might have been personal. But I trod on someone's toes when I picked Gavin McTierney out of the hundreds of small-time hoods I could have targeted. The poor devil who got run over by a transit van driven by McTierney tugged at my heartstrings. That will teach me to let my emotions get in the way of business."

They approached the entrance to the accident and emergency hospital. Brendan tapped Phoenix on the shoulder as Fintan pulled into the side of the road.

"Safe home, my friend. Next time you drop in to see us, I hope we'll have time for a Guinness or three, yes?"

"OK, Brendan, be seeing you."

Fintan joined the busy line of Saturday afternoon traffic and made his way to the M50.

"We'll be in Wexford in two hours, even with this traffic," he said, "what do you make of that note, Phoenix?"

"I've read it a dozen times, Fintan. There aren't that many clues."

"He's better educated than most villains. Many couldn't write a complete sentence, let alone go to the trouble of breaking the note into paragraphs. He's not a young man either because if he were young and thick, he'd have littered the message with text speak. So, my dear Watson, our man is middle-aged, intelligent, and linked with a paramilitary organisation."

"No shit, Sherlock." said Phoenix, "that's an impressive profile. Do you wish to check the text message I sent Giles while you found out what happened to Les Biggar at the airport?"

Fintan had slowed as the lane he was in became congested. He glanced at the screen on the Phoenix's mobile phone.

"Ah, you were one step ahead of me, Phoenix," he laughed as the traffic ahead began to move again. "The ice-house agents are looking for links between McTierney and the IRA. They'll search for accomplices within the London gang structure who may have served with him. His use of the term 'comrade' sparked your interest. Just as it did mine, that's most likely how they could act with such speed this morning. These guys have a long reach, don't they?"

"Olympus is aware of the growth of the super gang. It's among our major concerns. This 'H' could be one of the big movers seeking to establish a national organised crime network, rather than thousands of small gangs controlling their postcode areas."

"A worthy opponent, then?" said Fintan.

They arrived in Wexford just before five o'clock in the evening. Fintan's single-storey building reminded Phoenix of the crofter's cottages he had seen pictures of in books as a kid. It was clear he lived a simple life. He imagined dozens of other Olympus agents did the same. Less clutter to be removed by your colleagues if you didn't make it home from a mission.

"Make yourself at home, Phoenix," said his host. "You'll

find glasses in the cabinet and a bottle of Jameson's that might suit you. It's a long time since that breakfast. Shall I cook us something?"

"You cook as well?" said Phoenix.

"We Irish enjoy simple food, my friend, and strong liquor. So, while we wait for the microwave to heat us something with which to line our stomachs, I'll make those phone calls."

The two colleagues settled in for the evening with food inside them and a full glass. Fintan waited for replies from his calls to his contacts. Phoenix waited for Larcombe to come up with answers on who they faced.

"I kept a weather eye open as we travelled south, Phoenix. Force of habit. Nobody followed us. We're safe here, at least for tonight. I'll check in with Brendan later."

Phoenix was eager to be getting on with things. He hated sitting around, waiting.

A phone rang; it was Fintan's.

"Brendan, what's the latest?"

Fintan listened to his colleague's report.

"Cheers, Brendan; find yourself a place to rest your weary head. We'll talk tomorrow."

"How's Biggar?" asked Phoenix when Fintan ended the call.

"He's holding his own. No visitors or suspicious characters are hanging around the hospital."

"What's your plan for getting me away from here?" asked Phoenix.

"Originally, I imagined you jumping on the ferry at Rosslare and sailing to Fishguard. Larcombe could have sent a car to fetch you and delivered you home in three and a half hours. The last ferry leaves at nine. You would have been home before breakfast. I can get you on a boat from

Kilmore Quay if that choice is off the cards. The skipper will take you roughly halfway; I'm just waiting for confirmation that someone I know from Tenby can transfer you to their vessel and set you ashore near St Brides."

"I know that part of the country," said Phoenix, "the roads are lousy; it will take longer to get to the M4 than drive the rest of the trip home."

"Beggars can't be choosers, Phoenix. We'll get moving if you've finished your drink; we have a thirty-minute drive to the Quay. Your deep-sea fishing boat skipper will cast off at ten o'clock. Not the best time to set off, but this kind of voyage needs to be under cover of darkness."

Minutes later, the two colleagues sat in the car heading for Kilmore Quay. Phoenix rang Larcombe Manor and talked to Athena. He asked her to sort out transport. A car would be ready to collect him as soon as he set foot on dry land, whenever that might be. Athena wished him a 'bon voyage' and to get home safe.

As Fintan pulled up on the quayside, his phone rang.

"Where are you now? Good; when you reach your destination, contact Padraig with the coordinates. How are the seas tonight? How do you propose transferring your cargo from Padraig's craft? Billy Pugh? Isn't that risky at night? Yeah, I'll tell him. Cheers, for now, Gareth."

"Do I want to know what that was about?" asked Phoenix.

"Gareth has left Tenby and is heading out into St George's Channel. It's not flat calm out there tonight, and the winds are strengthening. It will be several hours before the two boats meet. Any transfer of people between boats is risky. At night, it's bordering on stupidity. Gareth's isn't the most modern craft around, and a Billy Pugh basket is what they have available.

A New Dawn

Despite the risks of being seen, Gareth wants to wait until dawn to get you transferred. It will be another two to three hours in broad daylight until you reach St Brides. That may be an unacceptable risk. Maybe Padraig can persuade him to find another method. I'll talk to him in a minute or two."

Fintan led Phoenix along the Quay to a fishing boat at the far end. The skipper appeared from the hatchway.

"Padraig, how are you doing?" cried Fintan, wrapping the old man in a bear hug.

"Did you bring the money, Fintan?" Padraig replied.

"Is it just you and your Dermot on board?" asked Fintan, handing over an envelope.

"Aye," replied Padraig, checking all the money was there. "Is this your man?"

Phoenix stepped forward and extended a hand.

"Thanks for the lift," he said.

The old skipper shook his hand. Phoenix turned to Fintan.

"Well, it's goodbye then, Fintan. Good working with you. I'm sure we'll meet up again sometime. Maybe I can return the hospitality if you come to Larcombe."

"You're welcome, Phoenix. Good to meet the man with such a fine reputation. We'll keep in touch with Les Biggar; tell you how he's progressing. When he feels up to talking, I'll find out what I can about who put him in the hospital. Safe journey."

With a wave, Fintan left. Phoenix watched his car's rear lights disappear into the distance.

"Get yourself below and fast," barked Padraig. "I don't want anyone to see you coming on board."

Phoenix hurried below decks. He nearly collided with Dermot. Twice the size of his father, he looked around thirty. Dermot grunted a greeting and climbed up on deck. A few minutes later, they set out to sea.

Phoenix could count the number of hours he had spent on a boat in the open water on the fingers of one hand. As the hours ticked by, he wondered what Sir William Hunt would make of him. The man who had been a second father to him had served his country in the Royal Navy for decades. His protégé could do nothing but throw up and curl in a ball, praying the nightmare would soon end.

Phoenix had to rely on the seamanship of Padraig and Gareth to deliver him safely to dry land. But how easy would it be for two tiny boats to miss one another in a barren landscape of vast grey seas? Thinking of the water sent him to the ship's side yet again. Dermot watched him impassively.

"Almost halfway," shouted Padraig.

Phoenix groaned.

"Lights on the starboard bow," Dermot shouted.

The larger Welsh craft closed on Padraig's fishing boat; Phoenix heard voices. There were three people aboard the new arrival. Their accents were similar, but he could differentiate between two older men and a woman. He wondered how he would cope with the transfer when it came.

Padraig steered his boat with great care to the leeward side of the larger vessel. Getting in close enough to get his passenger on board would need every bit of the skill he had learned from fifty years at sea. There were few clouds now, and the moon was bright. Both he and Gareth had what lights they possessed to illuminate their dangerous dance.

The two boats drew closer; the sea decided to toy with them. It wasn't going to be as easy as that. Padraig and Gareth tried again. Padraig made another attempt in the relative calm of the shelter provided by the bigger boat.

Phoenix stood on deck with his bag strapped to his back. A contraption lowered over the side of the Welsh boat. Phoenix swallowed hard. What the hell was that?

"Grab onto the ropes and hang on," shouted a male voice. Phoenix made a grab, caught hold, and a strong arm swung him up off the deck and onto the transfer basket. He and his companion rose and were soon on board. He looked back to Padraig's boat. It was already a fair distance away. He shouted his thanks, but he didn't think they heard him, as his voice was whipped away by the wind. Dermot and Padraig headed home, their work done.

Phoenix was shown below by the man on the transfer basket. As he reached the bottom step, the woman whose voice he had heard earlier greeted him.

"Welcome aboard," she said, "can I make you a hot drink? I'm Bronwen, by the way."

Phoenix asked for a coffee, then wondered how long he would keep it in his stomach.

"Gareth's at the wheel, and my husband Mervyn fetched you on board. We'll get you back to St Brides in three hours. Are you hungry?"

"No, thanks," replied Phoenix.

Bronwen went off to get the coffee. Phoenix checked his watch. Two o'clock. They would still enjoy the cover of darkness if he got ashore before six. So he settled down to endure the next leg of his homeward trip.

There was a lack of conversation over the next three hours. Phoenix had heard few words from Padraig and Dermot between leaving Kilmore and climbing aboard Gareth's boat. These three were just as tight-lipped. They were smuggling someone out of one country and into another. It was business, not a social event. It was a risky business at that. He wondered how much Fintan had agreed to pay them.

Phoenix was finding his sea legs at last. He felt less fragile than before and even relaxed enough to take a nap. At ten past five, Mervyn tapped him on the shoulder.

"This is it," he said, "we're as close to shore as we can take her. I'll take you onto Haven Beach in our dinghy. Get your gear, and let's go."

Phoenix followed him on deck; Gareth nodded to him from the wheelhouse. Bronwen was still somewhere aft. Minutes later, he stood alone on the sand, watching Mervyn on his return journey. He jogged off the beach and into the shadows. The narrow road petered out as it reached the shore. There was only room for a few parking bays by the church gate. This morning there was only one car. Its set of headlights flashed once.

His Larcombe driver was waiting. He threw his bag in the back and sat in the passenger seat.

"Good morning, mate," said a friendly voice.

"Rusty, I never expected to see you."

"Athena thought it might give you three hours to fill me in on what happened."

Phoenix recounted his mission from start to finish. He left out the prolonged bout of seasickness; you can have too much detail.

As they approached the driveway to the manor house, Phoenix asked whether Rusty had heard any news on Biggles.

"Still making slow progress," Rusty replied.

"Have the ice-house staff discovered who carried out the attack and the hit on Arjun Krishnan?" asked Phoenix.

"Steady on, Phoenix. You've had a tough mission and a long journey. However, Athena wants you to get a few hours' sleep first. You're no good to Olympus if you're knackered."

Phoenix wanted to argue, but his heavy eyelids told him Rusty was right. He didn't complain. He would sleep for a few hours, and then he could lie awake for a while, sorting out his plans for dealing with the mysterious 'H'.

Planning makes perfect.

Chapter Twelve

Sunday, 6th April 2014

"Come on, sleepyhead," Athena whispered in his ear.

Phoenix had been awake for ages but would not give up without a fight.

"Rusty rang earlier to bring me up to speed," Athena continued. "We need to call an emergency meeting this afternoon to evaluate our response."

Phoenix turned over onto his back. Athena sat on the side of the bed with Hope in her arms. His daughter stared at him. She turned her head towards her mother and gave a big sigh.

"Exactly," said Athena, "it's two in the afternoon, and Daddy's still in bed."

"OK, I'll get up," growled Phoenix, "but I need something to eat and hot coffee before I get to work."

"Everything is ready for you. Shift yourself and come through to the lounge."

The shower started him feeling human again, and when

A New Dawn

he had eaten and finished his coffee, Phoenix was fit and ready. He carried Hope with him as he and Athena met with the others. What could be the most critical meeting at Larcombe in years was probably the most informal.

"Welcome back, Phoenix," said Henry Case as they entered the room. Rusty and Artemis sat together, deep in conversation. Giles leafed through intelligence notes he had gathered while Phoenix was in Ireland. Minos and Alastor were dressed in smart, casual clothes, alien to Phoenix. He struggled to recall ever having seen them in anything other than a suit and tie.

"The outcome and aftermath of that mission were a real shock," said Phoenix. "Rusty and I must have upset someone last month. It appears we disturbed a hornet's nest. Please tell me we can control it?"

Henry recapped the Irish situation.

"Biggles will survive, thank goodness, but he won't be flying for several months. Olympus will continue to support him financially until he gets back in the air. The agents in the Republic conducted themselves admirably, as I'm sure you agree, Phoenix. Giles will shed light on the people responsible for altering the planned mission you were sent on in due course."

Giles then assessed what Olympus faced on both sides of the Irish Sea. He told his colleagues that Gavin McTierney was born in 1980. His father, grandfather, various uncles and cousins were involved with the Provisionals in Dublin. As a teenager, McTierney ran with a gang of thugs against the peace process. They were responsible for several punishment attacks. During the hoax bombing campaign on the mainland, at least a dozen gang members lived in the UK. Unfortunately, the authorities never identified the persons responsible.

McTierney rose through the ranks of one of the Hackney street gangs and was controlling it by 2010. Under his leadership, the gang expanded its influence. Its drug dealing, extortion, and human trafficking trade thrived. The overriding factor in that success was the constant threat of violence. McTierney not only threatened violence; he used it frequently.

Only one name from the 'comrades' from his time in Dublin in the late Nineties fit H's profile, the man who claimed responsibility for Krishnan's murder. Ardal James Hannon, thirty-five years old, hailed from Dublin. Before studying Business at University College, he attended a private college in the city. He moved to England in 2005.

Hannon's last known address was in Cricklewood. His first-class degree had opened doors for him in the City. His previous employer was a merchant bank that Hannon had left in 2009 to set up a business independently. That's when he disappeared off the grid. Hannon's name was no longer in the 2011 census.

"We're still searching for him," said Henry Case. "Given what we know from their past, we believe Hannon joined forces with McTierney. Others from their teenage days in Dublin could have established similar links in this country. We have photographs of Hannon from a decade ago, and we're looking for a match, but it's needle and haystack territory, as you can imagine."

"Rest assured, we won't give up," said Giles. "Hannon represents the brains behind an operation of this stature. Over the past three or four years, the street gangs have moved out into the suburbs. The emphasis has shifted from small street corner deals and inter-gang squabbles to a well-structured business model. We were discussing this very thing only recently. Hannon is a perfect fit for the mastermind behind this change of tactics."

"Whatever he calls himself now, and wherever he is," continued Henry, "he's combining the different gangs into a large cohesive unit. That takes a special talent. The UK is multi-ethnic, and criminal enterprises come from various ethnic backgrounds. Outside the indigenous white British crime syndicates are the Russian mafia, Triads, Yardies, Pakistani and Indian mafia, and Sri Lankan, Tamil, Turkish Cypriot, and Vietnamese organised crime groups. A man who can get these criminals together is possibly the most dangerous criminal this country has ever faced."

"We know the London gangs have contacts across the UK," said Phoenix. "If these links strengthen, then the potential for the network they would create is horrific. We have to stop this man."

"We have to find him first," said Athena, "and that has to be a priority for the ice-house. However, the Olympus Project needs protection against any interference in its operations. We must discover where Hannon discovered the link between Phoenix and Rusty's direct action in the capital and Larcombe Manor. If they traced them back here and followed me to Rhoose when I took Phoenix to Les Biggar, we have an urgent security problem to remove. Henry, I was hoping you could set up extra surveillance surrounding our property. We must follow the trail to where it originates if they are watching us. The elimination of that threat will begin at the source and continue until eradicated."

"Understood, Athena," said Henry.

"You will be sending a strong message to Hannon," said Minos, "if it's proven he is the mastermind behind this. There may be repercussions. Are we ready to engage with these people head-to-head? We don't have the personnel to cope. Our recruitment drive will boost our numbers, but another fifty or one hundred agents are neither here nor there. If Government statistics are to be believed, up to six per cent of teenage boys are members of gangs. If that applied to the UK's two and a half million teenage boys, the figure would be astronomical. Nothing is simple, of course. The situation is fluid; boys stay in a gang for a while and then leave. Many come back; others never do. The core number is more likely between fifty and sixty thousand."

"There are two police officers for every gang member," said Alastor. "If this was the only matter they had to handle, they might stand a chance. It's not, and while their attention has been elsewhere, these gangs have grown unchecked."

"Their numbers may fall over the next few years," said Artemis. "If this network of super gangs ever becomes a reality, as with any legitimate company, opportunities for judicious pruning are available."

"What they euphemistically called 'downsizing' when it was at its peak in the late Eighties and early Nineties," said Rusty.

"The difference being legitimate companies got rid of people by making them redundant," said Phoenix. "If McTierney and Hannon typify the modern gang leader, the getting rid of will be permanent."

"I think we have given you enough to be getting on with," said Athena to Henry, Giles, and Artemis. "I apologise for disturbing everyone's weekend. We'll see you in the morning for an update. Good hunting."

She and Phoenix took Hope back to their apartments. Although the sinister shadow of Hannon filled their thoughts with menace for the rest of that Sunday, they turned their attention to family matters. The wedding was less than two weeks away.

"Thank goodness you weren't with Biggles when those thugs attacked him," said Athena after she had got Hope settled for a nap.

"I was never in danger while Fintan and Brendan were around. They performed extremely well. We'd be fine if the money Fintan paid the two fishing boat skippers were enough to buy their silence and that of their crews."

"I'm not so worried over that, Phoenix. Instead, the awful prospect of the enemy at the gate concerns me most."

"Henry will find them if they're there," said Phoenix. "Giles and Artemis will discover the weak link that triggered Hannon's interest in us too. It might take longer to uncover the new identity Hannon has assumed, but the ice-house has never failed us in the past. If Hannon has access to a high level of intelligence-gathering equipment, that should make it a simpler job for Giles to track him. One would hope GCHQ spots high levels of suspicious activity in their domain, but they've never breached our security, have they? It makes you wonder why we bother spending taxpayer's money on them."

Athena fired up her laptop and retrieved a file Alastor had sent her last year.

"This was last summer when they prepared draft legislation for the snooper's charter. Alastor provided me with background detail. GCHQ stores content for three days and metadata for thirty. That's expensive. Network bandwidth is a massive cost. They have three hundred analysts working full time on trawling through the data from wiretaps. Add in the support staff, and there's little change out of eighty million."

"Just for the flagship snooping programme," said Phoenix, "blimey; what's the overall figure then?"

"Around two billion comes from the Single Intelligence Account, and there's an additional slush fund of over half a billion set aside to fight cybercrime."

"It's just as well we keep an eye on threats at home and abroad to lighten their workload. No wonder Zeus is always searching for new people to fund Olympus. Security doesn't come cheap."

"I'll warn Zeus we might have a problem. Perhaps he can divert funds from another field of operations to finance extra agents. Although Minos was sceptical of the impact our proposed increase in numbers might make, fifty more on top of our original target would give us a significant edge."

"You know my opinion, Athena," said her partner, "one of us is worth ten criminals. Whatever the actual workforce the super gang achieves, we can bring them to book. Failure is not an option."

"Where have I heard that comment before?" Athena replied. "The Titans were a threat that Olympus had to eliminate. The battles are getting fiercer, and they're coming closer together with every succeeding year."

"It's our task to make inroads into the problem, Athena. First, the authorities need time to regroup following the budget cuts they suffer. Then, there must be a root and branch overhauling their role in our society. The criminals will have a field day until they focus on what truly matters."

Athena sighed.

"Even if that refocusing took place, and our armed forces, security services, and judiciary were overhauled and refocussed, things wouldn't change. That would only happen if our leaders accepted significant levels of collateral damage. Change is painful; nobody takes unpalatable decisions. When that happens, evil smiles and continues to flourish."

"Then we must show them the way forward; guide their hand. Our actions must highlight the benefits of change. We must never shrink from taking difficult decisions."

"Tomorrow will be with us before we know it," said Athena. "Let's call it a day; this has been the busiest weekend I can remember since you arrived."

Monday, 7th April 2014

In the morning, there were early signs of optimism in the air. The sun shone on Larcombe Manor. When the agents arrived at the morning meeting from the ice-house, there were smiles on faces around the room.

"Henry, you received your priorities yesterday, so let's get straight into those this morning. I can postpone other items on my agenda."

"Don't let the smiling faces and the spring in their step fool you, Athena," said Henry. "Giles, Artemis and several others have worked throughout the night. It's the adrenalin from the progress they achieved that's keeping them awake. They did the lion's share of the work. I'll let them do the honours."

"We didn't take long to identify the leak," said Giles Burke. "An operative at the car crushing facility we used for the Mercedes was responsible. He must have recognised the make and model as a familiar sight on the streets where he lived. This operative knew that the Mercedes belonged to a gang leader from a neighbouring borough. He questioned why they were destroying a vehicle in such good condition. Any answers were evasive. He probably noted the registration of the transport vehicle. Later that day, a message was passed to a gang member. We have now checked our operative's bank account details, and he received five hundred pounds for his information."

"Police had questioned the gang leader with the Merc over the incident in Hackney," Artemis continued. "He had three witnesses who confirmed he had been at the dentist. They were treating him to another gold tooth. He was home within an hour of being detained. The police have no further leads to follow."

Giles picked up the story. "It was that gang leader who followed up on the information provided by our leak. His street contacts found the safe house in Chiswick. The frequency of cars arriving out of the blue, then lorries collecting those same vehicles over the next forty-eight hours, suggested a car theft network. If anyone were going to steal cars to order and export them overseas, it would be them. So, when Phoenix and Rusty collected their belongings, after collecting Dwight Thacker, a car that had been watching the place followed them back here."

"How did Hannon get in on the act?" asked Phoenix.

"Every road leads to Hannon," replied Henry Case, "we're still trying to identify him, but he's the kingpin. His city links and business degree suggest he has laundered money for a collection of gangs over the years. With McTierney and other former colleagues from Dublin, he used the money connection as a conduit to bring groups closer together. No doubt, he convinced them that 'together we are stronger'. For this network to survive, information gathered on the streets must flow up the chain of command just as freely as the cash."

"The street gang wrongly assumed the Chiswick house was a base for collecting cars stolen to order," Artemis explained, "and followed the boys back to Larcombe. The flight to Dublin they identified following the short surveillance was probably thought to be part of the operation. That was the limit of what they could send up the line to Hannon. If he is as computer literate as we believe, it wasn't a great leap for Hannon to work out from CCTV images his comrade got killed by someone driving a copycat Mercedes."

"Which was later sent to the crusher," Phoenix nodded as the light dawned. "Without talking to the late Gavin McTierney, Hannon didn't know how his mate managed to piss off this gang to the extent they murdered him in broad daylight. This business has never been about Olympus; even the message left in Shanklin."

"What's the next step?" asked Athena.

"We need your permission to proceed with direct action against those involved. Agents will kill the Chiswick leak and the street gang member who passed on the message. They will eliminate the driver who followed our men back to Bath and the gang leader. We can remove any evidence linking these people to Larcombe. The safe house is compromised; it has been emptied and put on the market. As for any surveillance on Larcombe other than by that lone driver, there's nothing to suggest it still exists. As soon as he drove back to London from Rhoose, surveillance ended."

Athena looked at Phoenix. She recalled their conversation from last night regarding unpalatable decisions.

"Go ahead, Henry," she said grimly, "get it done. It will send a message to Hannon. We can expect reprisals, but we must use that to our advantage. For now, he is invisible. This move will force him out into the open. Please continue searching for his new identity. Meanwhile, well done, everyone. Get a few hours' sleep, and we'll see you again tomorrow."

Henry, Giles, and Artemis left the meeting room. Athena addressed the critical items on her agenda, and Minos and Alastor left to continue their checks into the potential new Olympians' backgrounds. Rusty and Phoenix remained with her after the two senior agents had left.

"That was a brave call, Athena," said Rusty. "I'm only sorry we didn't cover our tracks well enough on that London mission."

"Don't blame yourself, Rusty," Athena replied, "we have been fortunate over the past eight years. Hundreds of direct actions get carried out without alerting the authorities or the criminals we've targeted. We'll amend our operating procedures and keep moving forward."

"The flow of information Henry indicated makes sense of what happened at the weekend," said Phoenix. "Hannon had linked Chiswick and the hit on his mate McTierney. He heard someone following us, but nobody specified the exact location. He learned of the flight plan Biggles had logged and called his old comrades in Dublin. They battered the reason for my trip out of Biggles and killed Krishnan on Hannon's orders. Hannon had nothing to gain for that murder except to use it to convey a message to me. The note said it was personal. Fintan and I assumed he meant the doctor had killed or mutilated a woman he knew. However, it was McTierney that made it personal. Their friendship must have mattered a great deal."

"If we tidy up the loose ends in London," said Rusty, "then we may not have the threat to our security we feared."

"We can only hope," said Athena, "let's wait to see what tomorrow brings."

With the meeting at an end, Rusty went back to his apartment. Artemis would sleep for a while yet. He went for a swim. Phoenix and Athena took advantage of a sunny afternoon and walked around the grounds with Hope. Every moment of ordinary life was precious. In the stable block, Giles Burke was fast asleep. Beside him lay Maria Elena, wide awake and watching her lover's chest rise and fall.

Tuesday, 8th April 2014

Everyone was wide awake and ready to start the new day. The agents gathered in the meeting room for nine o'clock.

"Your update, please, Henry?" asked Athena.

"Mission complete, Athena. We interrogated each man, searched their properties, and destroyed any incriminating evidence. Nobody will find their bodies. I'm confident no links to Larcombe remain outside anything gleaned by Hannon. We will eradicate every trace of that when we find him."

"Good work," said Phoenix. "It might have seemed extreme, but preserving the Olympus Project is vital."

"I didn't enjoy issuing the order yesterday," said Athena, "but it was for the greater good. Do we have news from Ireland yet?"

Henry smiled and nodded in Giles's direction.

"Over to you, Giles," he said.

"Fintan reported in at eight this morning," said Giles, "he and Brendan have been busy. They have uncovered the

Irish connection. When Gavin McTierney and Ardal Hannon ran together in the latter days of the last century, they were in a gang with one Seamus O'Connor. If Hannon was the one with the brains, McTierney and Connor provided the brawn. For the past fifteen years, Seamus has been a criminal. He was responsible for the deaths of at least a dozen men. Their bodies turned up in Dublin's inner city, Limerick, southern Spain, and various beauty spots around the Republic. O'Connor is an experienced, strategic and well-resourced gangster. He is Ireland's third-biggest drug dealer, up from number five last year. He is ambitious and has much younger, more volatile assassins ready to do his bidding. Two eighteen-year-old boys visited Shanklin on Saturday morning to murder Krishnan."

The room fell quiet. There was a pause of over a minute before Athena spoke.

"Issue the authority for direct action, Henry. Fintan, Brendan and any extra agents they need are to hunt for Seamus O'Connor. He must pay the price for his actions. It seems to be well overdue."

"What do we do with the men who attacked Biggles and the doctor's murderers?" asked Henry.

"O'Connor ordered his men to attack Les Biggar. That order was a direct act against Olympus. That's why he pays the full price. The thugs who beat up our pilot should receive punishment in kind. As for the teenage killers, I'm sure Fintan can direct the attention of the Garda towards them to help solve the murder. We can only pray a long spell in prison gives them a chance to mend their ways."

"Hang on," said Phoenix. "How did O'Connor know where to send these kids?

"Brendan talked to Les Biggar in the hospital," said Henry. "We knew he was a tough nut. Biggles took a heck of a beating. They believed that he'd told them everything he knew. But, he never gave up the reason for your mission. He only said you were meeting a guy called Krishnan."

"So, how did they get on to him?" asked Athena.

"O'Connor got his people to check where Krishnan was staying in Dublin," said Giles.

"The guy in reception at the hotel." shouted Phoenix, "the little snot took fifty euros from Fintan. We thought he'd helped us out."

"That's Gerard Collins," said Giles, "he's from the same housing estate as the killers. Someone came asking about Krishnan at the hotel before Fintan rang him. The doctor was followed to Shanklin by the two teenagers. They murdered him within minutes of his stepping inside his new premises. You and Fintan were one step behind them all day."

"What do we do with Collins?" asked Artemis.

"We'll leave that to Fintan," said Athena. "I'm sure he can come up with something suitable."

The rest of that morning's meeting continued with more routine matters. Henry Case contacted Fintan O'Sullivan after he returned to the ice-house and issued his orders. Over the next forty-eight hours, these were carried out.

Brendan had since visited Les Biggar in the hospital. He took grapes for the pilot to enjoy, asked how his recovery was going and showed him the latest photographs on his phone of the thugs who attacked him. That cheered the pilot up no end.

Brendan discovered that Gerard Collins liked to park run at weekends. Fintan suggested a kneecapping would give him time to consider the direction his life was taking.

The Garda in Terenure received an anonymous call

related to the murder in Shanklin. They had arrested two tearaways from Dublin.

Seamus O'Connor disappeared from outside his home. He had driven home late at night but never reached his front door. His family had no idea why or where he might have gone. His gang colleagues assumed a rival outfit had kidnapped him. A reward for information has received no response so far. Brendan knew where he'd gone. He scattered his ashes on the grounds of Shanganagh Park, near where Biggles had dropped off Phoenix.

Fintan thought it had been a nice touch.

Athena and Phoenix looked forward to the wedding as the week ended at Larcombe. Everything was going to plan.

"We're all set, darling," she said as they walked in the grounds, pushing Hope in her buggy.

"Only one dark cloud on the horizon," said Phoenix.

"What's that?" Athena asked.

"We still haven't found Hannon. He must be aware of the loose ends we tidied up in London. Even if he connects those to the car theft ring and hasn't uncovered the Olympus connection, we should still have expected a reaction. Instead, it's too quiet."

"Let's take Hope back indoors," said Athena, "although the sun is warm today, I suddenly felt a chill run down my spine."

Chapter Thirteen

Saturday, 12th April 2014

A newspaper report from *Bournemouth* described how twenty-eight-year-old Peter Laycock was gunned down last night inside Tesco Metro on Bourne Avenue.

Laycock, from Boscombe, stood by the hot deli counter on Friday evening when two men entered the store at seven. The store's CCTV showed they wore ski masks, black hooded tops, and denim jeans. Both carried handguns.

They shouted at Laycock, and he ran, chasing him around the store. He collided with a trolley pushed by an elderly female customer and fell to the floor. One man pointed his gun at terrified staff and shoppers and yelled at them to keep quiet. The other man calmly walked up to Laycock and shot him in the head.

Peter Laycock was known to the police. He had committed several offences from his early teens. He had convictions for handling stolen goods, possession with intent to supply, and grievous bodily harm. His attackers fled and were picked up outside by a car that drove off at speed.

Laycock's mother, Sylvia, commented: - "Our Pete was a rogue, but he never deserved this."

Mrs Phyllis Freegard of Ashley Road, Bournemouth, was treated for shock by paramedics who attended the store. Later, she had recovered to tell our reporter: -

"This doesn't happen in a nice town such as this. I only popped in to buy things for the weekend. This man came hurtling around the corner as I reached for a tin of cat food off the top shelf."

A spokesman for Dorset police said this was probably a gang-related issue, and anyone with information should ring the Crimestoppers number.

At Larcombe Manor, there were new arrivals. Hayden Vincent and Kelly Dexter moved into the stable block. They had handed the keys to their house in Shrivenham to a fresh pair of agents that morning.

While carrying out their missions, several vehicles remained at the house, either in the garage or driveway. The people carrier and Ford Kuga were part of the Olympus transport fleet. However, there was one car Kelly had no intention of losing; her Porsche 911. So there were plenty of admiring glances as she swung the car into the parking space outside the stable block.

Kelly was used to that. Her car was a classic, and she was a good-looking woman. The Porsche had been a present to herself after they invalided her out of the Logistics Corps. She left Helmand Province with shrapnel wounds to both her legs. It had been a dark time for her;

she was lightened by meeting Hayden Vincent while she served there.

Kelly's driving skills were legendary in her Porsche or any other vehicle Olympus needed her to handle.

Her partner was right behind her in an Olympus transit van. Agents travel light. Their Shrivenham home held few personal items of any sentimental value. Apart from their clothes, the van contained weaponry and technical gadgets.

As Kelly swung her handbag over her shoulder to walk back towards Hayden, she felt the comfortable weight of her Smith and Wesson MP Shield bump against her shoulder blade. What more could a girl want?

Henry Case was the first person to approach them.

"Good morning, you two. Welcome to Larcombe. Allow me to show you to your quarters."

Henry took them inside and opened the door to what had once been the two single rooms occupied by Phoenix and Rusty Scott.

"It's basic, as you can appreciate," said Henry. "But now it's been redesigned for use by a couple. I'm sure you'll make yourselves at home."

"It certainly seems to have received a female touch," said Hayden, looking around their new quarters.

"After Phoenix moved into the main house with Athena, his room lay empty for a while. We refurbished it when Artemis joined us to be with Rusty Scott."

"I can't wait to meet up with everyone," said Kelly. "We've been out in the field for so long. So much has changed here since we joined."

"I'll leave you to get your things from the van," said Henry, "let you get settled. You know where the canteen is when you're hungry. If you have any energy left, the recreation area is still in the old workers' cottages. Athena and

Phoenix are busy with wedding preparations and looking after young Hope. There's nothing scheduled for you until Monday, so enjoy the rest of your weekend."

"Thanks, Henry," said Hayden, "we might drive into Bath later to look at the sights. It's a beautiful city. We might find something to brighten up these quarters."

Henry laughed. With that, he left them alone. Henry heard a giggle as he walked back up the corridor to leave the stable block. He stopped. He was outside of Giles Burke's room. Henry walked out into the sunshine; his suspicions had been correct. He had lost out in the race for Maria Elena's affection.

Henry was upset, of course, but as the gravel crunched under his feet and he headed for the ice-house, he congratulated himself. His training had allowed him to identify the half-heard, brief giggle as indisputably Spanish. He didn't imagine many intelligence officers could match that claim.

Sunday, 13th April 2014

'Police wanted a man gunned down in a gangland-style execution outside a nightclub in Watford for attacking two men in a bar last month; it emerged today. The fugitive, forty-five-year-old Kent Briscoe, from Bushey, died when ambushed in the queue waiting to enter Blazes nightclub at midnight last night. He staggered into the road and hailed a taxi, ordering the driver to get him to the hospital. There are reports Briscoe got shot a second and third time as he slumped in the cab's back seat. The taxi driver called the police and paramedics. The two hooded gunmen sped off in a black van. Paramedics and a doctor from the air ambulance team treated Briscoe, but he died at the scene.'

The DCI leading the murder inquiry said, "This appears to be a targeted attack; given Mr Briscoe's history, it could be drug-related. The recent assault we needed to interview him over was also drug-related."

Armed police and helicopter searches were in progress as the hunt for the gunman and the getaway car continued. Police say despite a large crowd being outside the nightclub at the time of the shooting, no witnesses provided detectives with information regarding the suspects' description.'

Monday, 14th April 2014

'Police are searching for suspects in a violent shooting in *Nottingham* that occurred early on Monday morning. Delroy Williams, thirty-nine, was killed inside his red Audi. The suspects fired several shots into his car before fleeing the scene. Nottingham police received reports of gunshots near Albert Grove and Derby Road at 1:40 a.m. Minutes later, the victim's father said he went outside to check on his son because he heard him arguing with someone before the gunshots. The victim was found unresponsive. Paramedics transported Williams to the hospital, where he died a short time later. Family members said Williams had been sitting in his car listening to music, as he often did.'

"Nobody saw a thing, as usual," said the victim's mother, Molly Williams. "My husband was woken by gunshots. He went out to see what had happened. We knew Delroy hadn't arrived home yet. My husband found him in his car."

'The investigation was ongoing, police said. Officers blocked off residential streets and combed the neighbourhood for evidence on Monday morning. They found the car parked near a row of small businesses. Owners said they were not around when the shooting occurred. Delroy Williams had many friends on social media. Hundreds of posts appeared in the first two hours after the reports of his death. The tone of the comments varied. Some said what goes around comes around, as Williams had run with street gangs since he was eleven. Others remembered him as a sweet man who loved his children. His ex-wife and current partner were both 'heartbroken'. When asked what the motive for the killing might have been, police declined to speculate, merely stating it was too early in their investigations to comment.'

The morning meeting at Larcombe featured the standard agenda items. In addition, there were updates on surveillance targets around the UK and overseas. The search for the new identity assumed by Ardal James Hannon continued but with few significant leads.

Hayden Vincent and Kelly Dexter were now the senior training officers. But, first, they had to update the Olympus manuals. Then, when the recruitment drive Zeus had ordered showed fruition, any recruits would receive the most up-to-date relevant training.

Athena had received notification of another visit from the Charity Commission, which would happen on Thursday.

"Typical," she said, "forty-eight hours before the big day. The letter suggests a routine visit as opposed to a wholesale inspection. We appear to be off the hook over the issue with Garry Burns's photograph."

"I don't think you'll hear anything further on that, Athena," said Artemis, "well, not from the police, at least. Any record disappeared once I left the force, and my DCI left not long behind me; long forgotten at Portishead by now."

"It might be as well if you are underground while they're here, Artemis," said Henry Case.

"I agree," said Athena, "we need to issue a lockdown order for Thursday, Henry, for the duration of their stay. Minos, Alastor, and I will entertain them in the main house. We'll escort them if they wish to look around the grounds."

"Perhaps you could give our nanny the day off?" said Phoenix. "I'll keep out of their way in our apartment looking after Hope."

"Giles can hide her in his quarters," said Henry, "unless you wish to explain why we have a young Spanish girl here. What would her role be in the charity if the inspectors stumbled across her and questioned her?"

It wasn't only Giles who was taken by surprise. Minos and Alastor didn't have a clue, but the others knew of the relationship. They hadn't realised until now, though, that Henry had discovered the truth.

"Maria Elena can look after Hope on Thursday," said Athena, "there's no need to alter her routine. If our visitors learn I have a daughter, what of it? As for you, Phoenix, you and Rusty can either go to the ice-house for target practice or visit the recreation area. It's doubtful they'll wish to walk far once we've answered their questions.

"We'll make the necessary preparations," said Minos, "we know the drill. The paperwork for the charity will be in order, don't worry."

"In that case, Thursday won't be a problem," said Athena. "Although, the sooner I can get rid of them, the better. I need to go to Bath to finalise things for Saturday. Then, I can pick up the dresses and suits from the cleaners, check on the flowers and get my hair and nails done. Artemis and I are pampering ourselves on Friday; we're going to the Spa."

"Aren't you the lucky one," said Rusty to his partner.

"I'll be thinking of you as I bathe in the naturally warm, mineral-rich waters just as the Romans did over two thousand years ago," Artemis said. "The open-air rooftop pool has spectacular views, and the aroma steam rooms offer various treatments. It will be heavenly."

Phoenix gave a hollow laugh.

"While you two are lying around until your skin puckers up like an old prune, Rusty and I will have a few cans in the orangery. I've ordered bacon rolls to keep us going. I've never had a stag do before any of my other weddings. Going out on the town in Bath isn't an option."

"That's enough," said Athena, "stop feeling sorry for yourself. You're only jealous. Let's get on with the rest of our day. Saturday will be here before we know it."

Tuesday, 15th April 2014

'The hanging death of Sean Painter has puzzled authorities. Officers continue to pound the pavements in *York*, hoping to find answers to the questions surrounding it. Painter, forty-four, was found hanging from a tree by a bedsheet not far from his home on Monday at 9:23 a.m. Searchers scoured nearby woods for him. Sean Painter had been missing since

Saturday. He was last seen by a friend who dropped him off at the George and Dragon pub in the city centre.'

"Eight of his friends went looking for Sean," said Janey Digby, a barmaid from the pub. "Half an hour later, they discovered the body a few hundred yards from his house. At that point, they notified the police."

'Police continue investigating whether Painter's death was a suicide or a homicide. They are working on the streets. Talking to people who knew Painter. To discover what was going on in his life in his last weeks, days, and hours.'

Last night, a police spokeswoman said, "The body is undergoing an autopsy on Thursday. But, unfortunately, results won't be available until Tuesday because of the Bank Holiday weekend. So while we've reached no conclusions in this matter, it is important for law enforcement to handle these investigations with the utmost care and considers every possibility."

'Blake Wilson, seventy-two, a George and Dragon regular, said, "I searched for Sean while walking my dog, Mitzi, and I saw the body. All signs of life had gone. His cold, vacant eyes stared out at me accusingly. What a shocking waste of life. What drove him to it?" This reporter has questions for the police.'

'There was no ladder or a convenient point from which to climb. So how did Painter get to where they found him hanging? That wood has dozens of access and exit points. Like Blake Wilson, people often walk their dogs there; courting couples park nearby, and joggers use the surrounding footpaths. It may be difficult to pinpoint relevant evidence, but surely there must be doubt over this being a suicide?'

'The autopsy will yield more clues; scrapings under the

nails suggest Painter tried to fight off an attacker. They would assess bruises and ligature marks to see if they were consistent with Painter taking his own life. Painter spent ten years in HMP Full Sutton for possessing a firearm with intent to cause fear or violence. He was a violent criminal with strong links with the criminal underworld. It might be easier to find a motive and opportunity for murder than to find a reason for Sean Painter to take his own life. We await the autopsy results with great interest. More from this reporter on Tuesday.'

At the HSS offices in Bath, Phil Hounsell was checking the accounts. He had been right. The sizeable deposit he had received from Annabelle Fox at Larcombe had eased their financial pressures. Security work for the lads was still coming through; enough to keep them ticking over, at least. He had two missing-person jobs for him to pursue. Happy Easter.

Wayne returned to the office with two doughnuts and two coffees.

"Still sticking to the diet, I see then, Wayne," he said.

"Yes, boss, I've cut down to only one doughnut. How are things looking?"

"Good, for the time being," said Phil, closing his laptop.

The sight of the ten thousand pounds deposit had reminded Phil of something he had overheard at the weekend.

"Oh, by the way, Wayne, I was walking by the Roman Baths late on Saturday afternoon with Erica and the kids. A couple walked past, and I heard them chatting."

"Earwigging, boss? Once a copper, always a copper, eh?"

"Unless my hearing has gone haywire, his voice sounded like that bloke who rang me a month back; do you remember me saying there might be a new line of work coming our way?"

"I remember you were evasive about the nature of the work, boss, but that's it,"

"I can't say much more, but if he's a local now, we might bump into him more often."

As they polished off the doughnuts and drank the coffee, Phil thought of the two people he had seen. They had just left the Baths and walked before him and his family. They turned right and headed through the pillars past the Pump Rooms towards the Abbey. Newcomers to the city, he'd thought, as he had continued up to Milsom Street, but not tourists. The woman was beautiful, and the man was dressed in casual clothes that masked his physique. Phil knew if they stood toe to toe, he'd be looking at the guy's chin. God forbid, they stripped to the waist; he'd be unfit and overweight, while his Olympus contact would be well-muscled, with a washboard stomach.

"I think I'd better cut out the doughnuts from now on, Wayne," he said.

"You're the boss," said Wayne.

Wednesday, 16th April 2014

There was a surprise visitor at Larcombe late on Wednesday afternoon. The Reverend Sarah Gough arrived in her somewhat battered VW camper van. She spluttered her way over the cattle grid and up the driveway. When she pulled up in front of the main building, there was an audible sigh from the radiator.

"Ah well," said Sarah, "you've got me here, Maggie. That's the main thing. I'm sure Annabelle will put me up for a few nights, and you can have a good rest. Then, if you need someone to tinker with you, perhaps there will be a friendly mechanic in the congregation."

Conversations with her car, her bicycle and her cats were a common occurrence. However, Sarah often tried out her sermons on them, and there had never been a critical review, so she ploughed on regardless.

Sarah had climbed out of the van and struggled to lift her suitcase from the back. A loud voice interrupted her labours.

"Excuse me, madam, but you can't park here; this is private property. Perhaps you would like to turn around and leave?"

Sarah emerged, red-faced with her exertions, from behind the door. Her suitcase had fallen open, and various items of clothing and accessories dropped to the floor. Stood over her was a rather imposing gentleman.

Henry Case tried not to look at the female undergarments that now littered the front steps of the manor house. Instead, he raised his eyes to look at the unexpected guest's face. He stopped when he saw the white clerical collar.

"Ah, I may have been mistaken. You are not trespassing. Well, that may not be the best choice of word in the circumstances. I don't suppose you ever do; trespass, that is. You must be Miss Gough. We understood you were due to arrive on Friday. Do you need a hand with your things? Well, perhaps I'm not the right chap...."

Sarah Gough let this pompous oaf squirm a while longer. Did he know how deliciously long his eyelashes were? She could sense that her face stubbornly refused to reduce in colour from scarlet to pink. Why did that have to happen? Oh heavens, she thought, I haven't felt like this for such a long time.

Henry tried again. He stuck out a hand.

"Welcome, Miss Gough. I'm Henry Case, head of security here at Larcombe Manor. If you rescue your things, I'll look after the suitcase. We'll find the bride-to-be, and no doubt she will sort out your quarters. Do you want to give me the keys to your van? It sounded 'dicky' when I heard you coming up the driveway. I'll get our garage people to check her over for you."

"She's called Maggie," said Sarah, "thank you, Henry, that would be marvellous."

"Would you let me show you around tomorrow, padre? Some places are off-limits, but the grounds are lovely in the springtime. You can inspect the church, too; get your bearings ready for Saturday."

"That sounds splendid," said Sarah, and she meant it.

Henry beamed at her, picked up her suitcase like a feather, and strode inside the house. Sarah gathered up her bits and pieces, mortified that Henry knew she wore red underwear beneath her cassock. Until now, it had been her little secret.

'In Telford on Wednesday evening, Pavel Kowalski was bludgeoned to death with a claw hammer. A dog walker found twenty-four-year-old Kowalski's body in an alley fifty yards from the town centre. Police are appealing for witnesses.'

That news item came not long after Sarah Gough had stored her clothes away in her super bedroom, overlooking the front lawns. Before joining Annabelle Fox and her partner for an evening meal, she looked at herself in the mirror.

Sarah was not a natural beauty, unlike her university chum, Annabelle. If she was brutally honest, she could afford to lose a few pounds; but her flock had the image of the Vicar of Dibley in their heads from the TV series. Sarah shrugged her shoulders and talked to the mirror: -

"You probably won't see him again after the weekend, so why raise your hopes?"

She joined her hosts in their apartment. The meal was excellent, the company warm and friendly, just as she had expected. Little Hope was in bed for the night, so Sarah didn't get a chance for a cuddle as she had hoped.

"I have a meeting tomorrow with the Charity Commission," said Athena, "their inspectors are paying us one of their regular visits. So I hope you won't be too bored, Sarah."

"Your head of security, Henry, has offered to take me on a tour of the estate," replied Sarah. "Not to worry, he seems capable of taking care of people."

"He's prone to do that alright," said Phoenix, "we wouldn't be without him."

He wasn't surprised when he received a kick on the ankle from Athena.

Sarah tried to suppress a yawn.

"Oh dear, the long journey and two glasses of wine are taking their toll. I'm not the girl I was at university, Annabelle."

"Time for bed, then, Sarah," said her friend, not wishing for tales of drunken nights as an undergraduate to be the subject of conversation tonight. Sarah Gough was asleep by eleven o'clock. Phoenix and Athena were not long behind her.

Just before midnight, twenty-eight-year-old Liam Rush, from Croxteth, *Liverpool*, died from injuries from a fall from the Waterfront multi-storey car park. Police enquiries are concentrating on his connections to organised crime in the city.

Thursday, 17th April 2014

The inspectors arrived at Larcombe at ten o'clock. Henry Case met them at the front door and then took them to the charity's main office. He introduced them to Annabelle Fox, the CEO, Sir Julian Langford, and Michael Purvis, her team leaders.

Athena, Minos, and Alastor then provided their carefully crafted answers to the questions the inspectors had for them on this occasion. Minos and Alastor had done well; the relevant documentation on safeguarding and treatment provided for the poor devils in their charge was at hand and up to date.

Meanwhile, Henry Case showed Sarah Gough around the orangery. She marvelled at the beauty of the building and the solitude it afforded.

"This would be a perfect place for me to write my sermons," she said.

"As it's a fine day, Miss Gough, we'll cut across the lawns to the church," said Henry.

"I wish you would call me Sarah, Henry," she said. "Miss Gough makes me sound like one of those old spinsters in an Agatha Christie murder story. Padre doesn't sound right, either. I imagine you've been out of the army for a while. I think they call them female chaplains these days."

"Consider me reprimanded," said Henry. "I'm sorry."

"Don't worry," said Sarah, slipping her arm through his as they walked across the lawn, "I'm having fun, aren't you?"

Henry had to admit to himself that he was having great fun.

In the office, the meeting still dragged on. Athena thought the inspectors had run out of questions, but they had heard from colleagues about the excellent food on offer at Larcombe Manor.

"Perhaps we should break for lunch?" she asked.

"That would be great," said the chief inspector, "after we've eaten, might we visit the walled garden? I understand you grow many of your vegetables and fruit here?"

"Of course," said Minos, "I'll show you. It will be my pleasure."

When Minos emerged from the building with his three inspectors trotting along behind him, he spotted Henry and a woman wearing a clerical collar walking towards them. So that must be the vicar Athena mentioned, he thought; she's already here for the wedding.

Henry guided his companion along the path to the front of the house to avoid bumping into Minos. Sarah waved a greeting to be friendly, which was her nature.

The former High Court judge escorted his guests to the garden. Men were working there, as he expected. It was part of the elaborate cover Olympus provided every time inquisitive outsiders visited.

After a visit to the flower beds and shrubbery, Minos returned to the office thirty minutes later. The inspectors were entirely satisfied. As Annabelle Fox walked with them to the front door, the chief inspector stopped and shook her hand.

"We were impressed by everything we saw today, Ms Fox. I recommend we reduce our inspection visits; you now tick *all* the relevant boxes. As we walked onto the grounds, we saw your female chaplain. What a marvellous addition she is to what your charity offers these soldiers. Pastoral care is so important, isn't it?"

As the car drove off, Athena smiled. Sometimes, it helps to be lucky, too, she thought.

Epilogue

Good Friday, 18th April 2014

Everything was quiet at Larcombe Manor. Staff enjoyed the extra hours in bed; only a skeleton crew manned the icehouse. Athena and Artemis were due in the city for their few hours of relaxation at the Spa. Phoenix and Rusty planned how best to spend their free time. Should they go for a swim first? Work out in the gym? Or challenge one another to target practice in the shooting range? They knew where they had to finish; there were cans of lager and food later in the orangery. Life was simple.

Around the country, Friday was neither Good nor straightforward for several people.

At around two in the morning, Mick Fry, twenty-seven, died in a house fire in Gloucester. The victim had been drinking in The New Inn until midnight.

The Chief Fire Officer for the Gloucestershire Fire

Service who attended the scene said: - "I've got an open mind on this one. We need to conduct an intensive investigation to see whether this was an accident, caused by a carelessly dropped cigarette, or a deliberate act."

Over one hundred and seventy miles away on the northwest coast, in *Blackpool*, Ali Broughton, just twenty, drowned in the seas off Cleveleys Beach. His family and friends said Ali was a strong swimmer. He went out for a drink with mates early last evening but never returned home. The police appealed for witnesses.

Athena and Artemis returned from the city centre by five o'clock. Phoenix and Rusty had spent the afternoon putting the world to rights in the orangery over a few drinks. Maria Elena looked after Hope; Giles was at a loose end. He went swimming alone.

After lunch, Henry Case had walked over to the garage to discover that Maggie would be out of action until Tuesday lunchtime. He told Sarah the news about her beloved VW camper van. She was crestfallen; to make amends, he drove them both to Burrington Combe. Henry parked the car. He led her to the spot where legend said the Anglican cleric Augustus Toplady sheltered from the rain when walking from his parish in nearby Blagdon. The place under the rock in the steep, narrow valley inspired him to write the hymn 'Rock of Ages, cleft for me.'

Henry felt similarly inspired as they stood close together beneath the overhanging rock. He kissed Sarah Gough on the lips.

"Sarah," he said, "I hope we can keep seeing one another after the wedding."

"I should jolly well hope so, Henry," she replied, "but I assume you're referring to Annabelle's wedding tomorrow?"

Henry blushed at his mistake.

"I'm not very good at this," he said.

"Perhaps we should have more practice," said Sarah.

As Good Friday drew to a pleasant close for everyone concerned at Larcombe, around the country, there were more deaths to add to the statistics.

Over thirteen hundred people die every day in the UK. The media reports infrequent violent death or a series of deaths; on a fog-bound motorway, an overturned coach, or a light plane crashing in a field in bad weather. These stand out from the rest and receive more attention. But, sadly, for many men and women, their deaths are mundane, unspectacular, and almost predictable.

A newspaper editor would gloss over another knifing in a street fight between rival gangs favouring the death of a pedestrian hit by a drunk driver. But, unfortunately, it's the way of the world; the first doesn't get much sympathy, while the second tugs at the heartstrings.

Easter Saturday, 19th April 2014

On Saturday morning, there were three newspaper reports, which might have appeared unremarkable on their own, but one man was more vigilant than the rest of the country. Phil Hounsell was having breakfast at his home on the outskirts of Bath. Erica and the kids had gone shopping.

Phil was having a lazy day. He and Wayne went out for

drinks last night; he was paying for it now. The hangover made him concentrate harder to get the letters on the page to stay focused.

Police discovered a teenager named Danny Simpkins's body in the Whitehawk area of *Brighton*. He had been strangled. Phil thought that odd; so many youngsters carried knives today. But, on the other hand, there was no suggestion of his murder being personal. He buttered another slice of toast and turned over the page.

Chris Vince, of *Lichfield,* had died at the garage where he worked as a mechanic. Vince, thirty-one, was killed in an explosion late last evening when alone in the workshop. The blast destroyed several cars, and fire investigators cordoned off the building to determine whether the structure was safe. Vince was a hardened criminal who appeared to have tried to put his past life behind him. Police appealed for anyone with information to come forward.

Phil stood up and walked over to boil the kettle. Another cup of black coffee was required. Something here didn't smell right.

The third item received more prominence on the inside page. Greg Pitt, a farmer's son, twenty-four, was working in a trench yesterday evening when a wall collapsed. Pitt had been buried alive. Nobody heard a thing. His father looked for him with a torch at eleven o'clock when Greg didn't come back to the house. He had made the gruesome discovery and called the emergency services.

Police found drugs in Greg Pitt's Land Rover and several hundred pounds in cash. The Pitt's farm lay on the outskirts of **Leicester**. Phil sipped his coffee. Those years as a DCI solving cases from scraps of evidence came in useful. Events like this were TV drama territory. Ordinary criminals stuck to traditional methods. What were the odds against deaths by strangulation, explosion, and being buried under tons of dirt on the same day?

"Astronomical," thought Phil, "and if you throw in a bloke called Pitt dying in a trench, then this copper's nose smells something rotten."

At Larcombe Manor, the guests gathered for the noon wedding.

Geoffrey and Grace Fox had arrived from the station.

Phoenix spent the night in a vacant room in the stable block. He showered and dressed in his suit, ready to walk to the tiny church by eleven. Rusty arrived to accompany him at just before half-past eleven.

Athena sat with Hope on her lap.

Maria Elena was taking her to church. Giles and the nanny were due at half-past to collect her. Unfortunately, they were a few minutes late.

Artemis put the finishing touches on her hair, make-up and dress in her room. Then, it was time to help the bride finish her preparations. When she reached Athena's room, she could hear Grace Fox fussing over her daughter. She knocked and entered. Grace held Hope, and Athena stood in her gold wedding dress in the middle of the room.

"How do I look?" asked Athena.

"Stunning," replied Artemis.

"You both look wonderful," Grace gushed. She was brimming with happiness.

Athena and Artemis complimented Grace on her outfit. There had been no expense spared. She only had one daughter, so Geoffrey was forced to dig deep.

Her husband sat in the lounge, reading the newspaper.

He looked up as the three women walked through from Athena's dressing room.

"My word, you look splendid," he said to them.

Maria Elena, and Giles finally arrived at the door. The small party could make its way across the grounds to the church. Hope was with her nanny. Geoffrey took his daughter by the arm, and Artemis walked with Grace. As they came outside into the warm sunshine, it was easy to believe everything was right with the world.

At the gateway to St Michael's, Grace and Geoffrey could see Minos and Alastor standing with Henry Case.

Phoenix and Rusty waited by the door with the Reverend Sarah Gough. Everyone invited to attend the wedding of Annabelle Grace Fox to Colin Bailey was present. All thirteen of them.

In his penthouse office in the City, Hugo Hanigan was an angry man. The newspapers scattered across his desk suggested it was these that incensed him. He had engineered his response to the busybodies threatening to disrupt his plans for The Grid so carefully. First, a steady succession of killings across the country to eliminate inconsequential fools who disagreed with his ideas for a super gang to cover the entire country.

The press didn't see the connection; they were fools. Hanigan's unknown enemy hadn't roused from their slumber. Instead, after eliminating a few soldiers in Chiswick and Hackney, they were resting like a lion after a kill.

How dare they ignore him? He was Hugo Hanigan, the owner of the merchant bank that carried his name. An organisation that existed to facilitate the expansion of organised crime had many billions at its disposal to help him achieve his aims.

As Ardal James Hannon, he had been just one of the hundreds of entrepreneurs who scraped and scrapped their way out of the gutter. His transformation into a financial superstar was now complete. The City knew who he was; in time, the country would know his name and fear it.

He had acted in haste last night. He ordered a series of killings, each designed to provoke a reaction. But instead, the press pushed them from the front pages into obscurity. Why was no one intelligent enough to see his hold over the country already? The Grid was growing in size and strength.

Inside St Michael's church at Larcombe Manor, Colin Bailey and Annabelle Fox joined in holy matrimony. Sarah Gough performed her duties without question. It was the first wedding she officiated where the bride and groom's names were absent from every part but the required documentation. Sarah wondered whether Henry knew the reasons. Perhaps she could ask him in the future.

Annabelle was a friend, and Sarah could think of no valid reason she should object to whispering their first names when going through those parts of the service. As Sarah looked over the heads of the happy couple knelt in front of her, nobody else seemed to find it strange, so why be concerned?

The wedding party was soon outside the tiny church. Alastor took a minimum of the required photographs. There was no need for anyone outside the small congregation to receive a copy.

A short walk to the main house and they were inside the

dining room. Then, finally, the wedding reception could begin. An afternoon and evening of celebration stretched before them. The troubles that remained beyond the estate's boundaries were on hold for now.

Phoenix and Athena could relax at last. They were now Mr and Mrs Fox-Bailey. As they mingled with their guests, they discussed plans for Hope's baptism. Rusty and Artemis danced together as Phoenix watched, and he wondered whether his friend would soon follow him into marriage.

Phoenix spotted Giles and Maria Elena sitting together. Surely, they realised by now everyone knew they were an item? He was pleased to see Henry with Sarah Gough. They made an attractive couple and seemed to get along like a house on fire. Would it last, though? The closer they became, the higher the chance she would discover his dark secret. Could love ever survive between a minister of the cloth and the man they knew at Larcombe as a tough interrogator and executioner?

His in-laws enjoyed themselves; Geoffrey and Grace weren't returning to Belgravia until Monday; they were making the most of tonight. Hope slept upstairs; she wasn't alone. Kelly Dexter had volunteered to babysit. Hayden Vincent stayed in the stable block watching TV.

As Phoenix's gaze continued around the room, he noticed Minos and Alastor hovering on the sidelines, together as always. They would be the first to make their excuses and leave. Phoenix walked across to talk to them. He made fun of them too often. It was time to thank them for their sacrifices for the cause. Olympus couldn't do without them.

The party continued until past midnight. Not excessive, perhaps, but the majority understood that work was to be done in the morning.

Easter Sunday, 20th April 2014

As the revellers surfaced mid-morning to join Phoenix and Athena for brunch on the patio, Phil risked the wrath of his wife and made a phone call.

"Wayne, sorry to disturb you on a Sunday, mate, but could you spare me an hour?"

Wayne Sangster looked at the clock. He didn't know why he bothered. He had nothing planned.

"Sure thing, boss. Shall I come to your house?"

"No, we'll go into the office; there's a puzzle I need your help with."

After promising Erica he'd be back in time to take her and the kids out for the afternoon, Phil drove into the city.

"What's the problem, boss?" asked Wayne when he strolled through the door of HSS thirty minutes later.

Phil explained his suspicions concerning yesterday's deaths in Brighton, Lichfield, and Leicester.

"I've been doing some digging," he continued. "It meant fishing out old papers from the recycling box, but I found several more over the past week."

Phil showed Wayne a list of over a dozen names.

"So, what?" said Wayne. "You'll get an unexplained death every day somewhere in the country, won't you? They'll solve a high percentage of these before long. That might make the news, and it might not. It depends on how long it takes for the case to come to court and whatever other news pushes to the top of the pile."

Phil knew Wayne was right, but he wanted to pursue this. Unfortunately, his nose didn't usually send him in the wrong direction.

"What if something links these together? Each of the

ones I've selected was a criminal. They were involved in drugs and violent crime. You name it."

"Are you suggesting these are connected? Well, no police force is going to come to that conclusion, are they?" said Wayne. "They've each got their little patch with their targets. They wouldn't look for similar deaths in Leicester if they worked in Brighton.

"Humour me," said Phil, "check out this Gloucester one again. A bloke called Fry dies in a house fire. Someone's extracting the urine."

"OK, you've convinced me," said Wayne. "Where did these deaths happen?"

He stood up and walked over to a filing cabinet.

"We've got a map here somewhere," he muttered, "ah, here we are. Let's hang this on the wall and stick pins in the locations. Shout the names out, boss."

Phil called out the names. A few appeared in random towns, but Phil thought he could see a pattern. Bournemouth, Gloucester, Telford, Liverpool, and Blackpool. Surely not? Brighton, Watford, Leicester, Nottingham, and York.

"Draw a line between Bournemouth and Blackpool; then York to Brighton. It's not dead straight but tell me what you see."

"Parallel lines, boss," said Wayne, "give or take."

"Look at Lichfield," said Phil. "Is that a straight line between Telford and Leicester?"

"I couldn't use a ruler to connect them, boss, but I suppose so, yes."

Phil picked up the phone and dialled the number his Olympus contact left.

Hayden Vincent answered.

"Hello. What have you got for us?" Vincent asked.

"I'm not certain," said Phil, "but does the letter 'H' mean something to you?"

Les Biggar discharged himself from the hospital in Dublin after the Easter weekend. He was still in pain but eager to fly back to Cardiff airport and get home.

Olympus ensured he received a decent financial reward for the trip that almost cost him his life. However, it wasn't the need to work or to earn extra cash that drove him. He missed the flying. He missed the danger. After a few days' rest, he would call Larcombe Manor to say he was fit again for active duty.

In Kilburn, the 'Wishing Well' café continued to offer Guinness cake and other artery-clogging delicacies in the afternoons. Bridie Carragher watched the shop door more and more; to see who was there. She hadn't forgotten the man-mountain who captured her heart.

Bridie spent her evenings dreaming up recipes for cakes that would entice him back to her. She picked up the HSS business card at least once daily, trying to pluck up the courage to call.

Josie Dymond had attended Carrie Ditchburn's funeral in Cheltenham. At the wake, afterwards, she met with friends from their school days. Nick Angell, who now worked as a tree surgeon, asked her for her phone number. She imagined there might be a future for them. A future tinged with regret that Carrie was no longer alive to witness it.

Wayne Sangster often thought of taking a trip to London; to renew old acquaintances. But, unfortunately, his boss kept him too busy to give him a chance. Phil Hounsell could see the sad look on his colleague's face; as he stared into space.

Phil understood where his mind wandered and knew he had to save him from himself. He had only just persuaded Wayne to cut down to one doughnut a day. HSS wasn't that flush with cash to afford a new uniform for a staff member with an expanding waistline.

Fintan O'Sullivan and Brendan Connery returned to their respective homes. The excitement had diminished for now.

Olympus would come calling again for their help; they would be ready.

Next in The Phoenix series

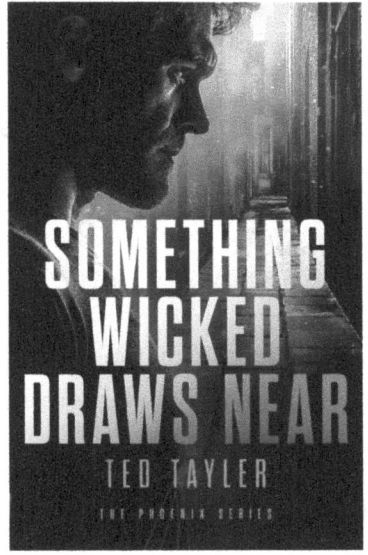

vinci-books.com/wicked-draws-near

When the law is threatened, a new justice rises

A sprawling crime syndicate launches a brutal campaign against Britain's legal system, executing jurors and hunting judges. Elite agent Phoenix and the covert Olympus Project strike back, shattering the syndicate's reign of terror. But as the violence spirals into a full-blown crisis, a ruthless powerbroker prepares to claim the underworld as his own.

Turn the page for a free preview…

Something Wicked Draws Near: Chapter One

It had been a typical Bank Holiday Monday following the wedding, with strong winds, thunderstorms and conditions better suited to staying indoors. Phoenix and Athena ventured outside for a walk with Hope to clear the cobwebs when a brief break appeared in the foul weather.

"Do you think someone is trying to tell us something?" asked Phoenix.

"We're happy," replied Athena, "that's what matters."

Hope was wrapped up warm in her buggy without a care in the world. She kicked her feet out and gave her parents a gummy grin.

The excitement of the celebrations was fading; the old manor house felt quiet and empty once her parents and Sarah Gough returned to their respective homes. That was why Athena insisted on getting outside. Phoenix would have lounged around in their rooms, feeling sorry for himself.

"I'm getting too old for a series of late nights in a row," he grumbled when Hope woke them up before seven that morning.

Athena had brought her from the nursery, plopped her next to her father, and headed for the shower.

"Talk sense into your father, Hope. Daddy's back to work in the morning. There's no rest from the wicked."

Phoenix smiled at that quip. He cuddled his daughter and wondered what he had done to be so lucky. He had a new wife, a beautiful daughter and a job he enjoyed, working with friends and colleagues he trusted and admired. Many never even had one of those things. He should be grateful.

A few hours later, he wheeled Hope's buggy into the house. He kicked off his muddy boots as he and Athena returned upstairs. Phoenix reminded himself that if he wanted to hold on to the things he cherished, they needed protection to his last breath.

Once they got dry and warm, Athena gazed over the lawns in front of the house. The subsequent passing storm battered the windows. Dark menacing clouds appeared to touch the rooftops of the stable block and the buildings on the edge of the estate. The tiny church where they had married on Saturday was just a shimmering haze in the distance.

"What a horrid day," she sighed.

"Erebus always thought of Larcombe Manor as his sanctuary," said Phoenix, as he joined her by the window, with Hope half-asleep on his shoulder.

"Those long years in the Royal Navy buffeted by mountainous seas, wondering whether he'd ever see dry land again. Larcombe offered a guaranteed haven; built to last by his ancestors."

The last days of April were due to deliver a mixture of sunshine and showers to the West Country. Larcombe Manor had seen it over the centuries, and its current guardians had plenty to occupy their minds. Everything would survive the battering of the winds and the heavy rainfall. It always did.

As May prepared to begin, the old manor house would shake itself dry and carry on as it had in the past. Phoenix and Athena needed to do the same.

Hayden Vincent had informed Athena of the telephone conversation he received from Orion on Easter Sunday morning. The tip-off suggested a possible cryptic connection between a series of gangland deaths around the country.

At the first meeting of the new week following the Bank Holiday, Athena gave Giles and Artemis the task of discovering any truth behind it.

Minos and Alastor had their vital research to carry out. They identified four potential candidates for the Olympus Project at the last Olympus meeting in London. Their backgrounds needed vetting with extreme care to ensure no possible rotten eggs slipped through the process. Zeus was cautious in the extreme, and with good reason, after the trials and tribulations caused by the Titans.

Athena decided she would leave her senior colleagues to do the groundwork alone. She felt confident she could trust them to leave no stone unturned. Phoenix could work with her on the finer details later. To be one hundred per cent sure that Zeus selected the right candidates.

The next item on the list concerned the training of the new agent intake. Finally, Kelly Dexter and Hayden Vincent were ready to start. The training manuals had been reviewed and revised. Rusty Scott checked them over, and when Athena asked if he was satisfied with the results, he nodded his approval.

"The sooner the first group of recruits arrive, the

better," he grunted, "I fear we'll need every pair of hands we can get this summer."

"We have enough to cope with," said Phoenix, "at home and abroad. We may have to prioritise our activities and channel our resources to areas with the most benefit. The one-off targets Zeus sends our way will have to wait. We need to concentrate on the bigger picture."

"I agree," said Athena, "perhaps our salvation lies on our doorstep? I suggest we check this data from Orion to see if it proves valuable. As well as a financial reward, it might be possible to offer Hounsell Security Services a role more aligned with that of Olympus. They could carry out the investigations on those singular names supplied to us by Zeus. A rogue policeman, a suspect politician; that type of thing. We wouldn't expect them to take direct action themselves. They report their findings, and an agent will do whatever we decide is necessary."

Henry Case's mind drifted while these matters were under discussion. The Reverend Sarah Gough left for home last evening. The transport team had patched together her battered VW camper van 'Maggie'. Despite a weary shake of the head from the mechanic that told a different tale to the words he uttered, "Maggie," he pronounced, "is good to go."

"I'll be in touch," Henry had said as the odd couple said their goodbyes.

"You'd better, Henry," Sarah had shouted. Her van spluttered and coughed along the winding drive towards the stone pillars marking the estate's boundary.

Henry glanced across the table at his colleague, Giles Burke. He looked weary this morning. Maria Elena must have worn him out, he thought. Lucky devil! Perhaps if he and the padre saw one another more often, their relationship might become more physical.

Henry had been content with their progress in their short time together, but it was unfamiliar territory. He hadn't wanted to force the pace and make a fool of himself, Sarah being an ordained minister. They probably had an unwritten set of rules somewhere. If Sarah had been a real padre, it would come under Queen's Regulations, and he would have known where he stood.

Civvy Street proved a minefield for Henry Case. The Army and the Security Services had surrounded him throughout his adult life. His lack of experience with the opposite sex had never been an issue. Henry always thought marriage was not an option for him, given his line of work.

Until happy couples popped up everywhere, he looked at Larcombe; he never wondered what he might have been missing. Even when Maria Elena arrived, although he had been as interested as Giles Burke, he knew the younger, more attractive man stood far more chance. But, with his looks and occupation, his options were limited.

"A penny for them, Henry?" Athena asked, sensing her security chief's distraction this morning.

"Beggars can't be choosers," blurted out Henry, startled by the question.

"My thoughts too, Henry," said Rusty. He assumed Henry commented on the HSS relationship. "Orion and his workforce can offer useful intelligence now and then, but Olympus mustn't form too close a partnership. It might lead to weaker security here at Larcombe."

Phoenix could see Henry was floundering. Their enforcer wondered whether he could extricate himself from the hole he dug with his outburst. Or to keep quiet in case he made matters worse and convinced everyone he hadn't been listening.

Athena's facial expression contained a mixture of amusement and confusion, which didn't help the poor devil much. Phoenix intervened to allow the security chief a breathing space to gather his wits and get himself back on track.

"With the tasks allocated so far this morning," he said, "we have reached a suitable point to finish matters for the day. We enjoyed a busy and exciting weekend. That might have caught up with us; we need a break. I suggest we take the rest of the day off and recharge our batteries. Then, we can pick up where we left off in the morning."

Nobody was in the mood to argue. Henry was grateful, and as the room emptied, the friendly atmosphere suggested Phoenix gauged things to perfection. Everyone present needed to catch up on a few hours of sleep.

Phoenix and Athena watched as the weary line of colleagues left. Then they headed upstairs to their apartment. Maria Elena returned with Hope from a quick turn around the grounds. But, unfortunately, the English weather didn't agree with the young nanny from Estepona. She missed her home country's three hundred days of sunshine each year.

"You are returning early?" she asked, "shall I take Hope to the nursery for the rest of the morning?"

"That won't be necessary," said Athena, "we'll look after her. You can put your feet up for an hour."

Phoenix spotted the puzzled expression on the young girl's face.

"Athena means for you to relax and have time to yourself. We'll look after Hope until after lunch. We'll see you again at two o'clock."

"Okay," With that, Maria Elena headed for the door.

As she turned the handle, Phoenix called out to her.

"Giles has time off now, too," he said, "perhaps you can relax together?"

Maria Elena turned her head, and her smile said everything. It was as if the sun had come out. Then she blushed and scurried outside onto the corridor.

"You're terrible," said Athena, "you embarrassed the poor girl."

"It's not as if it's a big secret anymore. Those two spent less than a second apart at the wedding reception."

"Somehow, I don't think Giles will get the rest he hoped for," said Athena. "Neither will we. A few extra hours with our daughter is no hardship."

"When we said our goodbyes before your parents travelled home, what did you and Grace discuss in your deep conversation?" asked Phoenix.

"Mummy's keen that Hope gets christened as soon as possible. However, I want to wait until she's older. Hope often sleeps through the night now at four months. She'll be more of a person towards the end of the summer. I want her to be more aware of what's happening around her. So we might get her christened here in late August. What do you think?"

Phoenix tried to remember how it had been for him, but he couldn't recall the occasion. He knew he went to church once or twice when growing up, but it never left a lasting impression on him, except that it was never warm.

"Sharron screamed right through the service when we had her christened," he recalled. "She was in good company. Three or four others lined up on the production line with her that Sunday. None of them seemed keen on the old bloke hanging on to them, nor on the icy water in the font. I was glad to get out. My ears rang for hours. Karen and her mother were happy enough. Her Dad and her brothers used it as an excuse to get drunk, as usual. My mother left as soon as she could. It's not a day that lived long in the memory."

"You poor thing," teased Athena. "What an impoverished upbringing you suffered.

They both fell silent. Hope played with one of her favourite toys and looked at her parents. She wondered why everything had gone so quiet.

Athena wished she hadn't made that last remark. She and Phoenix met four years ago, and their lives had altered dramatically ever since that day. Erebus made the Larcombe family aware of the new agent's history. But, as far as Olympus was concerned, the past stayed at the gates when he arrived that night.

Although specific incidents prompted the occasional remark directly linked to something he had done or resembled an occasion he attended, nothing that happened before his arrival was described in any detail. It was strange the mention of a christening prompted the revelation of a personal event from over a quarter of a century ago.

He hadn't talked much about his weddings either. Except that last Saturday was the first to involve a church service. Phoenix now possessed a registry office, a beach in The Gambia, and the Larcombe Manor church on his CV. Few men matched that, nor would they welcome it.

"I'm sorry, darling," she said at last, "that was unnecessary. The past is the past. You don't have to tell me more."

"There's nothing to apologise for, darling," he replied. "My childhood was impoverished in other ways. We weren't poor in financial terms. My parents clothed and fed me well enough. It was their love they denied me. I was a loner.

Even after I married and had a young daughter, I never felt the strength most people experience of having family surrounding them. I loved my daughter without reservation, but I had so many things I needed to deal with."

Athena picked up Hope and sat her on her lap, facing the two of them on the settee.

"How did life in The Gambia affect your feelings?"

"Sharron's murder devastated me. I lashed out and took revenge on as many of my tormentors as possible. Sue Owens got me out of harm's way, and our life in the sun was idyllic, but I couldn't let things rest. Every month I lived abroad. I spent hours checking the internet for news on what happened back in the UK. When doctors diagnosed Sue with breast cancer, she fought hard, but to no avail. One of the last conversations we shared was about what I would do when she died. I told her I would find a way to get home. I needed to complete that unfinished business."

"Sharron's killer?" Athena whispered.

"He was number one on my list. I didn't realise the others I identified as needing to be dealt with brought me to the attention of Erebus and the Olympus Project."

"You kept busy in those few months, I understand?" asked Athena.

"I prepared well, as usual. However, I didn't account for the tenacity of our neighbourhood copper and his fresh-faced companion. By June, I was no longer the hunter but the hunted. Strange how things work out. Orion is still on our doorstep, with no idea how close he lives to his nemesis, and as for Artemis, that fresh-faced young detective is now a valued colleague who lives with my best friend."

"So much has changed here in four years, haven't they?"

"The biggest change was that I found somewhere I wasn't alone. Erebus became the father I never had, Rusty became my first real friend, and even you and the Three Stooges made me feel as if I belonged. Finally, I found the family I had been seeking. Things have just grown from there."

"And now our family of three can look forward to the future,"

"With caution," sighed Phoenix, "this business that Giles and Artemis are investigating worries me somewhat. It could pose a significant threat. Evil is only just around the corner; you mark my words. As for this little one, let's plan the christening for the Late Summer Bank Holiday. Sarah Gough should have plenty of time to free herself up to officiate."

"That should bring a smile to Henry's face at least," said Athena. "I'm sure he's smitten by her, although where his head was at this morning, who knows?"

Silence fell in the room again. Phoenix was drifting off to sleep. He felt dog-tired and shook his head and stood.

"Let's take Hope for a walk. First, we'll need to get wrapped up against this wind and rain. Then, if we do it in stages, we can make it to the orangery and wait for the next shower to blow through. Then we can dart over to the swimming pool via the ice-house entrance. An hour playing with her in the shallow end, taking turns to swim lengths on our own, will serve us better than lazing around here."

"Translated, that means Daddy wants time alone to think, Hope," said Athena to their daughter, who knew when a smile was required and obliged.

"You know me so well, darling," said Phoenix.

"I'm learning," replied Athena. "Let's face whatever the weather or the future throws at us. Together we're a match for anything."

Something Wicked Draws Near: Chapter Two

Wednesday, 23rd April 2014

Hugo Hanigan breakfasted alone in his penthouse in London. A panoramic view of the capital's financial heart greeted him through his window every morning.

London replaced Amsterdam as the world's leading financial centre by the early nineteenth century. It had been a significant centre of lending and investment for two centuries. During the second half of the twentieth century, it played an essential role in developing new financial products such as Eurobonds in the Sixties.

English contract law was adopted in many markets for international finance, with legal services provided in London and financial institutions located there providing global services. Names such as Lloyd's of London for insurance and the Baltic Exchange for shipping were world-famous.

London held a leading position as a financial centre and maintained the largest trade surplus in financial services worldwide. Like New York, it faced new competitors, including fast-rising eastern financial centres like Hong Kong and Shanghai.

When Hugo arrived from Dublin in 2005, as Ardal James Hannon, changes were already underway. New products, such as derivatives launched in the Nineties, were ripe for exploitation. His first-class honours degree in Finance opened many doors. His innate instinct for choosing the right path served him well for a decade.

London continued to be the largest centre for derivatives markets, a minefield covering futures, contracts, or options. But, whether exchange-traded or over-the-counter derivatives he set his mind to, the Irishman excelled in turning a profit.

He had amassed a considerable fortune in the last four years since leaving his old haunts in Cricklewood to become Hugo Hanigan. He found success in foreign exchange markets and trading gold, silver and base metals.

London benefited from its position in Asian and American time zones and within the European Union. If an angle could turn an extra pound, Hugo found it and worked it until the well ran dry. He had few friends in the City; they thought him arrogant; he couldn't have agreed more. They believed him to be lucky, but they were wrong. Hugo Hanigan never relied on luck.

If others got their fingers burned by picking the wrong options to back or staying too long in a specialised market, that was their problem. Hugo never overstayed his welcome, nor did he support any worthless schemes. That wasn't luck. Hugo called it prudent management. He never mentioned the assistance he gained from the occasional well-placed bribe.

Hugo always identified the right person to contact and

paid well for his insider information. He never took the chance he might lose money on a product. Hugo had to cover every angle to ensure continued growth. The fortune he amassed was vital to support The Grid and his ambitions for what it might achieve.

Hugo never worried about anybody reporting him to the authorities with suspicions over how he conducted his business. But, of course, there might be a handful of fellow bankers who believed Hanigan's private bank was a cover for laundering proceeds from organised crime; none of them would ever be brave enough to express those opinions in public.

Everyone who ever met him told you the same thing. Hugo Hanigan - a thug in a Savile Row suit.

Hugo looked over the top of his copy of the day's Financial Times at the square mile of the capital that held his domain. He knew what others thought of him. He couldn't give a toss. They would be sensible to fear him. He would crush a few under the heel of his handmade shoes before long.

Hugo still read nothing in the media concerning the well-orchestrated campaign he ordered just before Easter. Just how thick were these people? He thought of advertising on national television; nothing pretentious, not what incomprehensible rubbish the marketing teams dreamed up these days that defied the viewer to realise which product the advert related to until the last few frames.

What they required was a basic map of Britain. A red bloodstain shows where a gang member's death had occurred over the previous weeks—a big arrow points out the connection.

Hugo buttered another slice of toast and poured a fresh cup of coffee. His watch told him it was ten-thirty. Hugo never visited his bank until noon. He could sit and seethe for a while longer.

One of his mobile phones rang. The 'Whisky in the Jar' ringtone told him which one to answer. A fellow countryman and one of his gangland colleagues.

"This had better not be bad news, Sean Walsh," he growled.

Hugo listened. Sean couldn't soften the blow. The jury reached a verdict at the Old Bailey in the case against Tommy O'Riordan.

"They found him guilty, boss," said Sean, "sentencing will take place next Monday."

"Right," screamed Hugo. "I want the names of every single fucking juror, get me the address of where that prosecution witness is hiding, and Sean, find out where that Judge and his family live. We need to send a message. One they can't ignore or sweep off the front page by a no-account celebrity with a sob story to sell. Tommy is one of our own."

Tommy O'Riordan was the head of a London crime family. In his mid-fifties with six brothers and three sisters, Tommy was the eldest son of Irish-Catholic parents who moved to Kilburn in North-West London after the Derry riots in August 1969.

Tommy's mother hoped the move to London would keep her children safe from the troubles. But, unfortunately, things went south soon after they moved onto the South Kilburn estate. Her feckless husband, Tommy Senior, soon found low-level criminals with whom to associate. He got caught every time he stepped out of line and spent most of the next two decades in prison.

The children finished school as soon as legal and found work helping keep the family together. Tommy took on his father's role as head of the family. However, life on the large council estate held too many temptations for him to follow an honest career for long.

The well-established Irish street gangs were eager for fresh blood to join them. So Tommy became the first in his family to join. As the years passed, his younger brothers followed his lead.

The female chicks didn't fall far from the nest either. One by one, as they entered their teens, his three sisters soon found themselves on the arm of one of the other gang members. The three girls married before they reached twenty years old. They now formed part of the Kelly, Walsh and O'Regan tribes that comprised a large part of the criminal fraternity lording it over the borough.

Tommy rose through the ranks until he made 'top dog'. He had his mother's stubborn streak, a reasonable degree of intelligence and determined nature. If only he hadn't inherited his father's weakness for petty theft, Tommy might have made something of his life. By sixteen, he was bigger and more robust than most of his peers. But, despite his mother scolding him for setting a bad example to his younger siblings, he started on the slippery slope towards a life of crime.

Tommy Senior made brief appearances at the family home. In between terms of imprisonment of various lengths. He did little more than drink when out of prison. Tommy wrote him off as a waste of space and kept asking his mother why she didn't throw him out. His mother shook her head.

"We married for life, Tommy. It may have always been a struggle for better or worse, but we had ten children to look after. If I threw him out, Social Services would soon be around here. They'd look to take the kids away from us. That was even more likely when the young ones still went to school. Only you and Colleen Walsh are in the house with me these days. They won't be bothering us anymore. Anyway, where else will he go when he comes out next time? Do you want to turn your father out onto the streets? Imagine what our neighbours would think then."

Ten years ago, his father died in prison. Nothing dramatic, aged sixty-six, he suffered a massive heart attack. Tommy's mother stood at her husband's graveside, surrounded by her family. Sons and daughters gathered with their various wives, husbands and partners. Dozens of grandchildren darted among the headstones to swell the congregation.

Members of other Irish families present, ingrained in the crime culture on the estates, stood shoulder to shoulder to see Tommy's father laid to rest. They didn't attend out of respect for the older man. They stood there because Tommy told them to be there for his mother's sake. Only people with a death wish refused a request from Tommy O'Riordan.

In the months that followed that bitter December morning, at St. Mary's Cemetery, in Kensal Green, Orla O'Riordan shrank in stature. Her daughters pleaded with her to eat, see a doctor, and ask for help, but Orla told them not to fuss over her and continued to decline.

Orla's old priest persuaded her she should look after her health for once.

"You've put your family first since I've known you, Mrs O'Riordan. It's your time now. I've made an appointment; you make sure you get along and see the doctor on Monday morning."

Orla did just that. It was pancreatic cancer.

Tommy came back with his family to St. Mary's a year after his father's burial to watch his mother lowered into the ground beside him.

At the wake in the biggest Irish social club in the borough, Tommy drowned his sorrows. Sean Walsh and his other lieutenants came to the top table to pay their respects. Others drifted around the hall, drinking, chatting in hushed tones, and polishing off the free food.

Sean Walsh returned from the bar with a bottle of Irish whiskey. The two men sat together and started on the hard stuff.

"Where's Devlin?" asked Tommy.

"Not seen him for a day or two, Tommy," replied Sean.

"I think it's time I had a word with Michael Devlin," muttered Tommy.

"Say the word. I'll have Devlin found and brought to you," said Sean.

Tommy nodded. Sean sent a text message.

The two colleagues continued to drink in silence. Tommy thought of Michael Devlin. He was a gang member he grew up with on the estate and only six months younger than himself. They had known one another for over forty years.

When Tommy joined the street gang in the early Seventies, he started with a series of petty thefts. As he matured, his talents graduated to extortion from market traders and armed robbery. The proceeds from his criminal enterprises were significant, and Tommy never drank his profits away or wasted them on fast cars and women.

He invested his cash wisely; the banks he used didn't ask too many questions. He married Sean's raven-haired sister, and their two children went to private schools and now lived and worked in Spain.

The O'Riordan gang were thought by the police to have committed over a dozen murders. Tommy reckoned they should think of a higher number. Drug dealing on a massive scale provided the most substantial contribution to the gang's war chest. The murders were necessary; but incidental. Although the police arrested dozens of soldiers that scuttled around the streets and alleyways across the South Kilburn estate like ants, they never found enough evidence to lay specific charges against the gang leaders. Eyewitnesses were thin on the ground.

Michael Devlin displayed many valuable talents within the gang's structure over the decades. Whenever they needed muscle on a job, he was one of the first two names they called. He was a follower, not a leader. Tommy needed men such as Devlin. Above all, though, he demanded their loyalty.

Rumours filtered through in recent weeks that Michael Devlin had done something unforgivable. So when the police swooped on the house in Kensal Rise, arresting five gang members in their early twenties, something didn't feel right. They seized a large amount of cash and several kilos of drugs.

The police declared it to be a significant event in the war against crime on the estates. A DCI with whom Tommy O'Riordan clashed dozens of times over the years appeared on TV. He declared the wall of silence destroyed, and it was only a matter of time before the police cleaned up the borough's estates.

Somebody had talked.

The wake continued until Tommy O'Riordan was ready to call it a day. Few men left the hall. They knew Tommy had an eye on them, even though he was well on the way to being drunk. Their wives and girlfriends drifted away, along with the children, and it was midnight before Tommy stumbled to the toilets. A few minutes later, Sean followed him. He helped him back off the floor and called for a hand to get their leader into a car.

It was early afternoon before Tommy surfaced. Colleen knew better than to disturb him. So when she heard him get up and head into the shower, she checked his coffee was available just as he liked it; black and hot.

Tommy was a man of few words when hungover. He flopped onto the settee and nodded when Colleen brought him his first cup. He picked up the daily paper, skimmed through it, and cast it aside. She left him alone, with the coffee jug on the side table, and made herself scarce. Tommy found a Racing channel on TV and waited for the coffee to ease the pain.

Colleen stuck her head around the door thirty minutes later.

"Do you want something to eat, Tommy?"

He shook his head.

Another hour passed, and Colleen heard him go back upstairs. Five minutes later, he came back. He had dressed in old clothes and was on his way out the door before she could ask where he was going.

Tommy decided to walk. The fresh air might benefit him, and he didn't want to risk getting pulled over by a snotty-nosed young copper. Tommy would still bust the breathalyser, even now. He called Sean Walsh.

"Have you found him yet, Sean?" he asked

"He's at the car recycling yard," replied his trusted lieutenant.

"I'll be there in ten minutes," said Tommy.

As he cut through the familiar side streets and alleyways, he recalled many occasions when he, Sean and Michael Devlin chased their rivals before beating the living daylights out of them. He remembered times, too, when these byways had seen them chased by the law. But, because they always held the upper hand with their local knowledge, they rarely got caught.

You thought you knew people, Tommy thought, as he turned the corner and saw the scrapyard on the far side of the street. When you grew up together and fought shoulder to shoulder, it was only natural that you believed it was for life. There was no excuse for what Devlin had done.

Tommy walked with his hands stuffed into his coat pockets. As he crossed the street, he withdrew his gloved right hand to feel the weight of the gun he carried under his old overcoat and inside his leather jacket. He hadn't brought the Smith and Wesson 45 Compact that had been his weapon of choice for a while. This one was a throwaway. A Glock with any identifying marks filed smooth. It would disappear as soon as this was over.

Tommy waited for a few seconds as he neared the gates, looking both ways along the street. Then, finally, he darted inside the yard, convinced nobody saw him. Tommy noticed Sean's car parked near the site office. That needed to move sharpish; links to him or his colleagues must be many miles away from what occurred here today.

He walked straight into the office without knocking. Maurice Kelly, the owner, sat behind the wooden desk. Sean Walsh stood beside him, facing the door. Kelly sat with the chair, rocking back on its legs, his back against the wall. When Tommy burst in, he almost fell off the chair.

"Tommy," he pleaded. "I want nothing to do with this, you understand?"

"I know, Maurice," Tommy growled, "where is the bastard?"

"In the workshop, Tommy," replied Sean. "I'll take you to him."

"I'll find him," said Tommy, turning on his heel and heading back out the door. "You keep an eye on this one and make sure he keeps his mouth shut. When he's got the message, we need to get rid of your motor. Get Maurice to drive it as far away from here on what's left in the tank. He can get a train back. You get off home and report it stolen in the morning."

"Maurice gave his men the afternoon off, Tommy, as we asked. It's empty. What are you going to do?" asked Sean, following Tommy as far as the office doorway.

"Deal with the problem; what else?" said Tommy in a whisper.

Michael Devlin sat on a metal chair in the middle of the workshop floor, his hands tied behind his back. His legs were strapped together. The chair stood in the middle of a large sheet of orange plastic sheeting. The smell suggested Devlin had messed himself. When he saw the big workshop doors slide open and Tommy O'Riordan entered, closing them behind him, he started to sob.

Tommy didn't speak. He didn't even turn his head towards Devlin. Instead, he skirted the plastic sheeting and headed for the tools lying on the long table at the side of the room. Tommy picked up a heavy spanner and felt the weight of it in his hand. He dropped it back on the table and sensed Devlin jump at the sound. He smiled to himself.

He continued walking around the floor covered by the sheeting. Devlin still sobbed quietly. Tommy had seen what he wanted as soon as he entered. The walk was just a charade. He wanted Devlin to sweat.

The four-foot-long metal bar would be perfect. Tommy picked it up by one end and trailed it along the floor behind him as he continued to circle his former friend. When he drew level with him, he stopped.

"Do you know the lowest form of a human being, Michael Devlin?" he whispered.

He crossed to the long table and turned the radio up full blast. Radio One music echoed around the workshop. Tommy took hold of the bar in both hands and, swinging from the hip, smashed it into Devlin's right knee.

The sounds from the tannoy muffled Devlin's screams. Tommy strolled around to the other side. Devlin's head dropped to his chest; Tommy aimed once more. The metal bar found its target. Devlin's left knee shattered, the same as the right.

Tommy dropped the bar and strolled back over to the table. He lowered the volume. For the first time, Tommy walked onto the plastic sheeting. He gagged at the smell coming from Devlin, but he needed to tell him the answer to his question.

"A grass, Michael. A grass."

He didn't know if Devlin heard him, but no matter.

Tommy made a final trip to the table to turn the music to the maximum. Then he walked around behind Devlin. Tommy removed the Glock from his jacket pocket. He placed the muzzle against the back of Devlin's head.

"I had so much more pain in mind for you, Michael. Because we were friends for so long, I've decided to be merciful."

Tommy fired once.

The loud music was superfluous; Tommy turned off the tannoy. It had been getting on his nerves. He removed the ties that bound Devlin and kicked away the metal chair so the lifeless body slithered onto the floor. Tommy wrapped the body in the sheeting, sealing it with tape. He winced at the crunching sounds from Devlin's knees when he tried to straighten his legs. He had a few tidying-up jobs, and then he could head home.

Grab your copy...
vinci-books.com/wicked-draws-near

About the Author

Ted Tayler is the international best-selling indie author of the Freeman Files and Phoenix series. Ted lives in the English West country, where his stories are based. He was born in 1945 and has been married to Lynne since 1971. They have three children and four grandchildren.

His thought-provoking mysteries appeal to readers of Sally Rigby, Joy Ellis, Pauline Rowson, and Faith Martin. His action-packed thrillers are a must for fans of Mark Dawson and J C Ryan.

Gus Freeman's cold case investigations are carried out with reasoned deduction rather than bursts of frantic action. In each of the 24 books, unsolved murders are accompanied by romance, humour, and country life. The core message in the 12 Phoenix novels is that criminals should pay for their crimes. Unfortunately, the current system fails to deliver the correct punishment, so Phoenix helps redress the balance.

Acknowledgments

The love and support of my family; without them, this would have been impossible.

www.ingramcontent.com/pod-product-compliance
Ingram Content Group UK Ltd.
Pitfield, Milton Keynes, MK11 3LW, UK
UKHW040119190326
469155UK00004B/1235